Skin
Game

Skin
Game

Lawrence Ross

Kensington Publishing Corp.
http://www.kensingtonbooks.com

DAFINA BOOKS are published by

Kensington Publishing Corp.
119 West 40th Street
New York, NY 10018

All Kensington Titles, Imprints, and Distributed Lines are
available at special quantity discounts for bulk purchases
for sales promotions, premiums, fund-raising, and educa-
tional or institutional use. Special book excerpts or cus-
tomized printings can also be created to fit specific needs.
For details, write or phone the office of the Kensington
special sales manager: Kensington Publishing Corp., 119
West 40th Street, New York, NY 10018, attn: Special Sales
Department, Phone: 1-800-221-2647.

Dafina and the Dafina logo Reg. U.S. Pat. & TM Off.

ISBN-13: 978-0-7582-1942-8
ISBN-10: 0-7582-1942-3

First trade paperback printing: September 2007
First mass market printing: October 2009

10 9 8 7 6 5 4 3 2 1

Printed in the United States of America

Skin
Game

Chapter 1

*Without leaps of imagination, or dreaming,
we lose the excitement of possibilities. Dreaming, after all, is a form of planning.*
                                —Gloria Steinem

As Ray made a left turn onto Crenshaw Boulevard, he knew that just like clockwork, Marty would start bitching. And he was right. Right as rain.

"I'm so fucking tired of working this stretch of L.A.," Marty said while puffing on his sixth Marlboro of the night. Marty was a tiny muthafucka who had a Napoleonic complex worthy of Jermaine Dupri.

Ray, on the other hand, was a little different. Tall and skinny, he was a bit more thoughtful and more self-assured, but knew both of them were floating through life. That's what happens when you take shortcuts.

"We need to find a new place, because this shit is getting tired, like quick," Marty continued. "Steven is fucking himself by limiting *Pimp* to this same old shit."

He looked out the window at the endless body shops and liquor store buildings, then turned back to Ray.

"You know, we could work some of the spots in the Valley or at the downtown clubs. All of the bitches down at the Chi Chi Room look the fucking same, and I think people are getting tired of watching them. Shit, *I'm* getting tired of watching them. I wouldn't mind seeing some white girls with big titties rather than all of these big black asses."

Ray tried to ignore him and kept driving. He'd heard Marty say the same thing each week for the past year, but they always found themselves going to the same clubs. It had to be that way.

"Look, if you want big asses, then you go where big asses are," Ray replied, pulling into the parking lot of the Chi Chi Room. "Steven wants big asses, our readers want big asses, and the Chi Chi Room has big asses. So quit complaining and come help me find some more big asses. Besides, what type of nigga are you when you talk about not liking a nice big black ass?"

"Muthafucka, all I'm trying to say is that we have other options," Marty said. He unbuckled himself and stepped out of the car. He took a long drag of his cigarette, then flicked it to the gravel.

"You see," he continued as they walked to the club entrance, "that's the problem with niggas. Just like way back in slavery, they only want to live on the plantation and then can't see anything else but that plantation. Never wanting to escape, they just stay fat and happy eating collard greens and pigs feet. I say that we could move off the big-ass plantation and you instantly tell me we need to stick with big asses. Narrow-minded muthafucka."

Ray stopped.

"One of the things I learned in college—"

"Ah, now you gotta pull out all of that college-boy bullshit!"

Ray had spent three semesters at Cal State Northridge before dropping out to get in the biz, and Marty hated it when he would start talking about something he'd read or been taught. It made him feel like he was dumb, and Marty didn't like feeling dumb.

"—is that you have to give the customer what they want. I read it in a book. I think the cat's name was Dale Carnegie."

"Dale who?"

"Carnegie, you simple muthafucka."

They got to the front door, where Blackie Whiteside, Chi Chi Room's doorman, met them. Blackie was named "Blackie" because he was as dark as a moonless night. And since he was damn near seven feet tall and three hundred pounds, the blackness seemed to encompass everything around him, like a black hole gobbling up galaxies. To say that Blackie was intimidating was an insult to him. Intimidating is what a local tough man is. Blackie was beyond intimidating. He had a stare that made tough men sober. Instantly.

"What up, you two?" Blackie said, pulling out the red stamp. He stamped Ray's and Marty's hands like he was squishing ants.

"Nothing much. Where's Sean?" Ray asked, sliding past Blackie's massive frame.

"He'll be out in about ten minutes," Blackie answered. "Go have a drink."

"Thanks, Blackie."

The two walked over to their usual bar stools as the music blared from the speakers. Destiny was on the pole, and the pervert pit around the stage was lightly filled. They were early.

"Okay, so who the fuck is Dale Carnegie?" Marty asked, sipping his Heineken. "You might as well tell me some of your college bullshit."

"I read his book in a business class. He wrote some shit called *How to Make Friends and Influence People* or some shit like that. I can't remember the exact title. Anyway, he talks about how he went fishing and how he liked strawberries and cream—"

"Who the fuck eats strawberries and cream while fishing?"

The woman on the stage began shaking her tits, so that they bounced up and down, almost hitting her in the face. Ray liked that. He had a glazed look on his face, the same as when a child gets a twenty-dollar bill in a candy store.

Ray was annoyed.

"I don't know, muthafucka, but Dale Carnegie says that he likes strawberries and cream. But that's beside the point. He went fishing and said that he likes strawberries and cream, while the fish liked worms."

Ray pulled a handful of dollar bills from his pocket and threw them in the air. The dollar bills hovered, and then fell all around the stripper. She dropped and started putting bills into her g-string.

"That's right, bitch, I made it rain," Ray said, with a silly smirk on his face. He turned back to Marty, his face pinched, as though thinking really hard.

"Okay, maybe I'm missing something, but what the fuck does strawberries, cream, fishing, and some goddamn worms have to do with big black asses?"

Ray drank a bit from his beer.

"The point of the story is that you don't feed the fish strawberries and cream because you like it. You'll never catch any fish. You give the fish what they want. So you fish with worms. And so we need to give our customers what they want. They don't want big-tittied white women. They want big-assed black women, so that's what we're going to give them. And that's why we'll stay here at Chi Chi's until the supply of big-bootied black women is exhausted."

Marty looked at Ray curiously and then sighed.

"I still don't understand why a muthafucka's eating strawberries and cream in the first place. I mean, who the fuck eats that shit?"

"Shut your dumb ass up," Ray said, finishing his beer. "Just shut your dumb ass up."

Ray turned back to the bar and waited for Sean to arrive.

Across town, it was a little after seven o'clock at 9537 Budlong Avenue, and things were in the "same shit, different day" mode for the Montez family.

"Keisha! Keisha! Bitch, I know you heard me!"

Keisha Montez kept putting on her makeup, ignoring the sound of the voice outside the door.

She can scream all she wants, Keisha thought as she took a pull from her joint, but she wasn't getting riled. Not today and not tonight. There was money to be made tonight, and Keisha was going to make sure she got her share.

Keisha, eighteen years old and full of life, was the beautiful star of Budlong Avenue. Her Mexican and black heritage combined to create a beauty that had tantalized men of all ages. And some, if given the chance, gladly would have tried to get at her before she was legal. About five foot five, with wavy hair and beautiful café au lait skin, Keisha was stunning. But she also lived in South Central Los Angeles, a place that spit out pretty girls left and right and ground them up for all to see.

As she looked around the dingy bathroom, all Keisha could see was the broken yellow tile, the faded bathtub, and the ever-dripping sink.

What a fucking mess, she thought while putting on her lipstick. *I've got to get out of here.*

Suddenly the bathroom door burst open, banging against the bathtub. Keisha didn't even flinch.

"Keisha! When I'm talking to you, you better fucking answer me!" Veronica Montez was the spitting image of her daughter, except her face was full of worry lines. That was for good reason. Veronica Montez stayed angry, 24/7. She'd been like that since Keisha's father, Felice Montez, had gone out to buy some beer. That was eighteen years ago and he hadn't come back with that beer. Actually, maybe *angry* wasn't the correct term. More accurately, Veronica Montez was pissed every minute in her life.

"This is my goddamn house and if I say jump, you better say 'how high?'. Do you hear what I'm saying, dammit?"

Her face was so tense that Keisha could see the veins in her forehead. Veronica walked even closer to Keisha, squeezing into the tiny bathroom.

"Getting out of high school was the worst shit that could have happened to you. Now you think you can do what the fuck you want," Veronica continued. "Uh-uh. Not today. Not as long as I'm paying for shit."

"What do you want?" Keisha asked, looking in the mirror and putting on her mascara. She tried not to let Veronica get to her.

"After you finish shakin' your ass at that nasty-ass club," Veronica began, fumbling through her purse looking for change, "bring me back a carton of Newports. Don't bring your ass back here without 'em."

She put about three dollars on the sink and left as quickly as she'd come in. Veronica knew, and Keisha knew too, that three dollars wasn't going to buy any box of cigarettes. But Veronica expected Keisha to make up the difference from the money she made at the club. Instead of supporting her children, the children supported Veronica.

Bitch, Keisha thought as she threw the money into her purse. *Fucking bitch.*

Makeup done, Keisha walked to the kitchen. Andre, her brother, sat at the table eating Cocoa Pebbles like it was early eight in the morning instead of being close to eight at night. For Keisha, a twenty-six-year-old black man eating a children's cereal while staying at his mother's house was symbolic of how fucked-up this house was.

"Hey, Keisha," he said, barely looking up from his cereal. "Let me ask you a question."

"What?"

Keisha just wanted to get her orange juice and get out of the house. She didn't feel like dealing with Andre's bullshit.

"Let me borrow some money?" he asked.

"Nigga, please. I ain't loaning you shit," she said, taking a swig of orange juice.

"I'm serious. Loan me fifty dollars."

"I don't give a fuck if you're serious or not. I didn't ask you if you were telling jokie jokes, or being dead serious. You still owe me for that hundred you spent on that stank-ass girlfriend of yours. So I repeat, nigga, please."

"Ah, see, why you gotta be like that?"

Andre leaned back in his chair and looked at Keisha as though he was searching for something. He was looking for an opening, some way to get what he wanted. Keisha knew that look and stood there, resolute. She wasn't going to give in to his con.

"Nah, see, I need that money because I need to get something for Veronica."

Keisha finished off her orange juice, looked at her

watch, and threw the empty orange juice bottle in the trash.

"Then this is what I suggest. Get off your narrow ass and find a goddamn job. Stop fucking asking me for money when all you do is sit around this goddamn house watching TV all day. Again, for the third and last time, nigga, please!"

Keisha walked out of the kitchen to the front door, and Andre followed her.

"Bitch!"

Keisha never turned around. She turned the deadbolt lock and opened the front door.

"I gots your bitch right here," she yelled, throwing up a middle finger at her brother. "Find some other fucking sucker."

Finally she was out of the house, and the cool night air surrounded her. It was as though she'd finally been allowed to breathe. And yet, she could still hear Veronica shouting from the living room.

"Don't forget my goddamn Newports!"

Back at the Chi Chi Room, the main lounge was starting to fill up. And sauntering in like a bad '70s pimp was the guy who owned the place. When he saw Ray and Marty sucking down Heinekens, he walked up to them and got right down to business.

"Don't waste my time, niggas, don't waste my time," he said. "My time is precious, valuable, and expensive."

Sean Edwards always had the same greeting for anyone who had the audacity to want to talk to him. But he saved his best for Ray and Marty. He tolerated them because they made him money. And money made Sean talk to anyone, even if he felt that they could be wasting his time.

"I liked it better when your daddy owned the club," Marty said. "He never rushed us."

"Yeah, well, that nigga's dead and he never made any money," Sean responded, taking a glass of Hennessy from the bartender. "I'm about money, while that nigga just wanted to get some pussy from time to time. I can get all the pussy I need. But money, nigga, that's what's hard to get. So as I said, nigga, my time is precious, so don't waste it. What do you two niggas want?"

Sean had owned the Chi Chi Room ever since his dad, Big Sean, died in 2000. Big Sean had opened the club back in the 1970s after his friend, the actor Rudy Ray Moore, was thrown out of a white nude club downtown. There hadn't been a place in Los Angeles for black men to go see naked black women shake their asses, so he decided to open one.

"I like ass just like the next man, and I wanna see black ass onstage every day. So I got up and did something about it," Big Sean would scream to anyone interested. "I'm the fucking Jackie Robinson of black ass!"

Maybe he wasn't the Jackie Robinson of black ass, but what he'd done was take that retirement money from the Hughes Aircraft factory, where he'd been an electrician since he'd gotten out of the army back in '51, and opened up a little black nudie bar in Gardena. It was an instant success. Gardena was and is an L.A. backwater, so no one messed with him or the club. He paid his taxes just like the bakery across the street from him did, and he made sure that the only reason police showed up was to get private dances on their breaks from eating donuts. Things were good when the old man was alive. A combination of big asses, a little spending money, and some friends meant that he was living the life he wanted.

But even when the old man was alive, it had been

apparent that there needed to be some changes at the Chi Chi Room. The club was getting old. The red velvet walls could tell you that. The women onstage were old. The men watching them were old. And now, unlike in the 1970s, there was competition.

So when Big Sean finally died of cancer, his son had a vision for something different. He dreamt of Chi Chi Rooms across the country, just like the white club Spearmint Rhino had done. Franchise black booty from coast to coast, Sean thought. But to do that as a black club, he had to shake things up.

He got rid of a lot of the fat women his father had on the stage and brought in some young talent. His father, like a lot of men in his generation, didn't care about a girl being fit. They just wanted a lot of body. But Sean knew that younger men, the hip-hop generation, wanted body, but not body fat. And that meant putting together a new roster.

"Yeah, I have a club over in Gardena, and I think you would be great onstage," Sean would tell a young woman at an L.A. nightclub. He could usually get five new girls per weekend this way, and one or two per month would stick. That formula had worked to the point where the Chi Chi Room was the top black club in Southern California. But Sean wanted more. That's why he was talking to Ray and Marty tonight.

"I heard you got some new dancers in," Ray said. He kept wondering why he had to do this same dance each and every week.

"Yeah, I got a few new bitches in," Sean said, shifting his weight from side to side. He was what the old black men at the barbershop called an itchy nigga. Always moving. Always twitching.

"What are you looking to do, and what are you niggas paying?"

"The usual. We're going to start them off with print first, and then move on. You'll get the same percentage."

"No doubt," Marty said.

Sean turned toward Marty and smiled.

"This dumb muthafucka," Sean said, pointing to Marty, "sayin' 'no doubt' like he's the one givin' the percentages! Nigga, let Ray talk, 'cause you don't know what the fuck you are talkin' about. See, that's why I hates an ignant nigga."

"Why I gots to be ignant?" Marty asked.

"If you can't figure it out, then that confirms it."

Sean looked around and then turned to Ray.

"Okay, I'm going to have Blackie take you up to the private room. Same shit as always, pick the ones you want and then let me know what they're going to do. And by the way, make sure to tell Steven that he's been late on his percentage payments and I don't appreciate muthafuckas messing with my money. It wastes my time . . ."

". . . and time is money," Marty and Ray both finished.

Sean paused and looked at the two.

"Nobody likes a couple of funny niggas," he said.

Out of nowhere, as though Sean had telepathically called him, Blackie showed up by Sean's side.

"Take these niggas up," Sean said. "I got some shit to take care of. I'll meet y'all in a second."

"Come with me," Blackie said, and all three began walking toward the stairs to the second-floor private room.

"I'll go get the bitches," Sean said. Sean started making his way to the dressing room.

The dressing room at the Chi Chi Room was a no-go place for anyone but the dancers and Sean, and he really shouldn't have been there either. The dancers were getting themselves ready for the night.

"How much did you make last night?" Keisha asked. She put on the purple thong and bikini top and began dusting her body with glitter. In the dim light of the stage, it made her skin sparkle, and the men in the pervert pit liked the trick of the trade.

"Bitch, why you all up in my business?" Debra said, more annoyed than angry. She had her good days and her bad days at the Chi Chi Room, and this was turning out to be one of her bad days.

Debra was what black men called a "big guh." She stood about six feet in her three-inch heels, and she always wore a black leather bikini that was two sizes too small but accentuated her size 38 yellow ass. The men at the Chi Chi Room went nuts every time she came out. She was a longtime feature dancer at the Chi Chi Room and was the dean of the strippers. But there were signs that her days were numbered.

All the women getting dressed were a little on edge, and the size of the dressing room certainly didn't help much. Even to call it a dressing room was giving the glorified broom closet too much dignity. Three women could just barely fit into it, but often there were four or five in there at one time.

"A couple of weeks working in the club and you all up in my business. Bitch, I don't know you like that. Wait until you have eighteen years in here before you come at me like that."

"Damn, why it gotta be all that?" Keisha asked. "I ain't in your business. I was just curious. Damn, can't I just get an answer instead of some fucked-up answer?"

Debra kept taking off her clothes as she decided whether to answer. "You look and sound just like an old friend of mine," she finally answered. "Two hundred dollars. That's what I've made so far."

"After Sean's cut?" Keisha asked.

"Yep."

"Shit."

For Debra to make only about two hundred dollars in tips meant that shit was going slow, Keisha thought.

"Well, if you only made two hundred," Keisha said, "then I'm looking at a one hundred-dollar night. I've got to figure out a way to make some real money from this shit."

"You've got to shake it hard so that Sean will move you from two nights a week to four," Debra said. She sat down at the makeup counter and began applying her makeup in heavy strokes. "If you aren't making more than one hundred, then he's not going to up your nights. It's not worth it to him."

"Why are things so bad out there?" Keisha asked. "I mean, I see a bunch of niggas out there, but none of them have money."

"All the big ballers are doing a bid. I can always tell when the LAPD is doing one of their goddamn sweeps," Debra said. "All of the gangsters and drug dealers get caught and then we pay the price. So we get left with all the muthafuckas that go to the ATM for a twenty and then get it changed into one-dollar bills."

"Yeah, then they wad up three of them to make it seem as though they're big ballers." Keisha laughed. "I hate picking up my tips and getting a bunch of ones smashed together."

The door to the dressing room opened and Patra walked in. She'd just done her first set and was panting and sweating like she'd run a marathon.

"Damn, bitch, take a fucking bath." Debra laughed. She reached over and threw Patra a clean towel.

"Thanks," Patra said, wiping herself off. Patra had

started about a year before Keisha had and was building a small fan base at the club. She'd gotten to the Chi Chi Room after Sean had seen her at the Upside Down Club as a go-go dancer. She was pretty, but not particularly stunning. Her features were slight, with beautiful dark skin and short twists. But she was flexible as hell, and that got the men going. Like Keisha, she was trying to become a featured dancer on the weekend.

Debra got up from the counter. It was nine o'clock and it was her turn to go back out onstage.

"How much did you make?" Keisha asked Patra.

"Not a fucking lot," Patra said, simultaneously toweling off and counting her money. "The muthafuckas haven't had enough to drink yet, so I get all of the one-dollar bills."

"Gotta work your way up, bitch," Debra said while at the door, "so you can be just like me."

"What? Thirty-eight and still shaking my ass?" Patra asked. "Hell, no. I'm getting out of this shit before I get to twenty-one."

"Same here," Keisha said. "This shit can get old fast."

"Yeah, well, I said the same thing back in 1985," Debra said. "But what the fuck am I gonna do that makes me five hundred a night? Work at Wal-Mart? Nah, you bitches will be right where I am in 2012. It's your destiny. Better to accept it now than to be disappointed later."

And with that, Debra left and went onstage. Keisha and Patra could hear the noise from the crowd as they glimpsed Debra. It was as though a pack of wolves had been given some fresh meat. And in some ways, they had.

Chapter 2

The dance is a poem in which every movement is a word.

—Mata Hari

Sean burst through the dressing room doors, unannounced as usual.

"Keisha, Patra, come with me. You're going to do a private dance," Sean said, pointing at them both.

"Can you knock, just once in your life?" Keisha asked as she sat in her chair, waiting to go onstage. "You have no manners at all."

"Why do I need manners when I own this shit?" Sean asked, switching his weight from side to side again.

"Who is it for?" Patra asked.

"Don't worry about it. Just get your ass up to the room and dance for them."

Sean left in as big a huff as he'd come in.

"I can't stand that nigga. I really can't," Keisha said, adjusting her bikini. "He always wants us to do a private dance for some fool so he can score some points. But how come we don't get any extra money? I ain't here to dance for free."

"I hear that, but ya gotta do what ya gotta do," Patra said. "We've got to make that money, girl."

"Yeah," Keisha said, getting up from her chair and checking her makeup for the last time. "But I'm tired of that bullshit. I fucking hate private dances. That's why I don't do them in the club. If this fool touches me wrong, I'm out of there."

Keisha and Patra left the dressing room and took a quick left up the stairs. Right next to Sean's office was a private room with blackened windows that overlooked the club. Sean normally rented it out to Lakers and Clippers players who wanted a little privacy with their titties and ass. This way, the players could get their grind on, without the hassle of dealing with the fans, and then slip right back out the back way.

"Come on, come on," Sean said impatiently. He was standing right next to the door, waving them in.

"Wait," Keisha said. "I was supposed to go onstage next, and that means I'm going to miss that money. What am I going to be paid for this private dance?"

Sean looked like he'd been sucking on a sour lemon.

"Why you always asking about money? You'll get taken care of."

"That ain't good enough, Sean," Keisha replied defiantly. "How much are we gonna get paid? I got bills and I'm not wasting my time dancing for free."

"Yeah," Patra agreed.

"Look, you'll get a hundred for the dance plus tips. That's more than you would get out on the stage tonight. Now stop jackin' your jaws and start shakin' your ass."

Keisha and Patra looked at each other and then adjusted their bikini tops.

"Deal," Keisha said. Time to go to work.

Sean opened the door, and Keisha and Patra walked in. Marty and Ray were sitting on the red velvet couch, sipping on apple martinis. The room was dim, except for some lava lamps in the corner. When Keisha and Patra walked in, Marty knew which one he wanted.

"All right, girls, show me what you got," Ray said, leaning back and sipping on his drink.

"Yeah, show me what you got," Marty said, giggling.

The two women looked at each other and Sean closed the door. Patra walked over to the stereo and turned on the music. R. Kelly began singing, and the two girls began straddling the men, Keisha over Ray and Patra over Marty.

"Lemme see that ass, girl," Ray said. Keisha turned around and slowly moved her ass in a wide circle, then suddenly started to shake it up and down, making it pop.

"Yeah, baby," Ray said. "Can I touch it?"

Keisha stopped and drew close to Ray's face.

"No, baby, it's all a fantasy."

As she said that, she let her ample breasts rub Ray's chin. He smiled awkwardly. In the three months she'd been stripping, she'd never gotten used to how embarrassed the men got when she touched them. It was like they didn't really know what to do.

"Now, now, baby," Patra said, removing Marty's hands from her breasts. "No touching the merchandise."

"Ah, baby," Marty said, pulling out a twenty. "Can I get a touch for this?"

Patra slowly swayed to the music like she was in a trance. She took the twenty-dollar bill out of his hands with her breasts.

"Just a little touch, and don't squeeze too hard," she answered, still swaying.

Marty cupped her breasts as though he was holding fine china. He giggled again.

While Ray tried to keep his hands to his side, Keisha danced to the music and began her simple routine. She put her ass in his lap to get his dick hard. Normally, that took about two minutes of grinding. Then she took off her bikini top and rubbed her breasts over his face.

"Come on, baby, shake that ass!" Ray said. "Show me what you got!"

Keisha's mind was elsewhere when she danced for men. When she was on the stage, she looked at the men in the pervert pit—the section surrounding the stage—with utter contempt. They all looked at her as a piece of meat, and she looked at them as human ATMs. After she danced for them, they could go outside and get run over by a car for all she cared. In her mind, they weren't that important, no matter how she led them along.

"Yeah, baby, yeah. That's how I like my bitches," Ray said.

Marty giggled yet again as Patra started beating his face with her breasts.

"I'm doing it all," Keisha said, rubbing her ass on Ray's leg, "just for you, baby."

But the private dances were the worst for her. The men were too close and they always wanted to talk to you. You could smell what they'd last eaten, and the bad cologne stayed with you all night, no matter how much you scrubbed in the shower. It was an unpleasant reminder of an unpleasant business.

"Hey, baby, I can take you out of this place permanently," they all said each night. The dancers called these men "Captain Saveahoes," as in "these men wanted to save a ho from the club." These were the men to be pimped. Sometimes you could get more cash, or maybe even a boob job from them. But you never allowed yourself to look at them as anything but customers. They didn't want you at home, not with the same issues as every other woman. No, the Saveahoes wanted their fantasy version of you, and no one was that good. So Keisha knew that it was best that she never get involved with them.

Oh yeah, Keisha thought, *then why are you here at this stank-ass club, playa, playa?*

"Do you date anyone you dance for?" another would ask.

"Yeah, but just not you," she would reply.

"How much for a night with you?" they'd ask, leering at her. Anyone who dances must have a price, they assumed. Sometimes they were right.

"You don't have the money, baby," she would coo.

So as she danced for Ray, she kept in her mind that she was going to make her hundred-dollar bill. That was the only thing that mattered. Still, she had to fake that she gave a damn about Ray. If not, the fantasy wasn't complete for him, and that meant a smaller tip. And a smaller tip meant that getting out of Veronica's house was just that much farther away.

"So what do you do?" Keisha whispered softly. She put her lips close to Ray's ear.

"I'm sort of an agent."

"Are you in music?"

"No," Ray said, taking a deep breath. He pulled out another twenty and placed it in her mouth. She nodded, and he cupped her breasts.

"No, I'm a different type of agent. I look for talent."

"Hmm, do I have the type of talent you're looking for?" Keisha asked. The song was almost over and

20 *Lawrence Ross*

she was glad this conversation, and this dance, was about to end.

"Actually, yeah, I think you do," Ray replied. "If you—"

All of a sudden, Keisha heard a slap.

"Uh-uh!" Patra exclaimed. "Uh-uh! Fuck that, nigga!"

Patra walked over to the stereo and turned off the music, her breasts swaying.

"What happened, girl?" Keisha asked, picking up her bikini.

"Yeah, what happened?" Ray said.

"That fool," Patra said, pointing her index finger at Marty, "decided that he wanted to slap my ass, even though I told his black ass not to do it. Nobody slaps my ass, and I told him that."

"Ah, girl, you know you liked it," Marty said, with a crooked smile on his face.

"If I liked it," Patra replied, "you would still be getting a dance with a hard-on. Now you just have a hard-on, muthafucka. Let's go, Keisha."

Patra opened the door and they walked out of the private room. They ran into Sean, who was coming up the hallway.

"Where's our money, Sean?" Keisha asked.

"What happened in there?" Sean asked.

"They got their dances, and then the dumb one decided to slap Patra's ass," Keisha said. "Dance over. Where's our money?"

Sean kept switching the weight on his feet again. Reluctantly, he reached into his pocket and pulled out a Kansas City wad of cash. He pulled off two fifty-dollar bills.

"Here's fifty for you," Sean said, giving Patra a bill, "and here's a fifty for you, Keisha. Now take your asses back down to the dressing room and get ready to go on the stage. You're on in five minutes."

"Wait, wait, wait," Keisha said, looking at her fifty-dollar bill. "You said we were getting one hundred, not fifty. Where's the rest of my money?"

"I said you were getting one hundred dollars," Sean said, smiling like he was the cat who'd just eaten a canary. "That meant you got a bill and she got a bill. Don't like it? Take it up with management. Now get down to the stage and shake your ass."

Keisha looked at Patra, and telepathically they both knew they wanted to strangle Sean, but they dared not do it.

"That's some bullshit, Sean, and you know that," Keisha said. "I'm going to remember that shit."

"Yeah, well, remember that shit on your way to the stage. If you don't like it, then I'll get somebody else to take your place. We clear?"

Keisha steamed as she looked at Sean, but Patra took her by the arm. "Yeah, we cool," Keisha said.

"Good," Sean said. "Now get down to the stage."

Keisha and Patra walked down the stairs to the dressing room.

Sean was pissed and stormed into the private room.

"Why do you always have to slap the asses of my dancers, Marty? I mean, how many times do I have to tell your dumb ass that we have a hands-off policy?"

Sean was really annoyed this time. Normally he just let things slide, but he couldn't afford to lose Patra or Keisha at this time of year. They were building a nice clientele at the club and he wanted to keep them happy.

"Don't listen to those bitches, man," Marty said, calmly sipping his drink. "They like to get their asses slapped. Keeps 'em motivated and alert. But they just don't want to tell anybody."

"Whatever," Ray said, annoyed as always with Marty. "Let's get down to business. I know the one that I want."

"Which one?" Sean said. He was looking out over the club through the smoke-glassed windows and noticed that it was packed. When Keisha walked onto the stage, the men went wild. *That girl has something special,* he thought to himself.

"I want Keisha," Ray said.

Sean turned around to look at Ray.

"Whoa, partner," he said. "I thought you were going after Patra. I just sent Keisha up because there were two of you."

"No, you didn't," Ray replied. "And stop bullshitting now that you know who I want. I want Keisha. Now get me her and then you'll get your percentage."

"Look, I'll ask her, but something about her tells me that she's not going to be interested."

Marty got up and with Ray walked over to Sean. He wasn't giggling anymore.

"It's your job to make her interested. We have confidence that you will get the job done."

Ray wasn't much with words, but he could be very persuasive when he wanted to be.

"I'll talk to her," Sean said,

Ray reached into his pocket and pulled out a card.

"Tell her that she'll get five hundred dollars for one hour if she calls," Ray said. "And I expect a call."

Chapter 3

*You have to recognize when the right place
and the right time fuse and take advantage of
that opportunity. There are plenty of opportunities out there. You can't sit back and wait.*
—Ellen Metcalf

It was three in the morning and the final ten men
were leaving the Chi Chi Room. Keisha, Patra, and
Debra were sitting in the dressing room, rubbing their
feet, having squeezed them into four-inch heels for
most of the night. For Keisha and Patra, it had been
a long night because they'd had to go onstage a few
extra times because of the private dance with Marty
and Ray.

"How much did you make tonight?" Keisha asked
Debra and Patra.

"Bitch, why you all up in my money again?" Debra
laughed.

"I'm just fucking with you," Keisha said, smiling.
"But how much did you make?"

"Well, I made about two hundred and fifty, so I'm
cool," Patra said. "What did you make?"

"About the same," Keisha said, counting her money.
"I made around one seventy-five. It started out bad,

but some niggas must have gotten paid or something tonight."

"I know, it seemed like it, didn't it?" Patra said. "I think I made about the same, plus that fifty we made from that private dance."

Debra looked up.

"Y'all had a private dance?"

"Yeah."

Debra looked slightly jealous. "Sean always trying to make the new girls work for his friends. Watch out for that muthafucka. He's a snake."

Patra got up to leave.

"Yep, we were supposed to get one hundred apiece for that private shit, but Sean lied and only gave us fifty. That was some bullshit."

"Well, darling," Debra said, picking up her purse and getting ready to go, "get ready for more bullshit working here. It's part of the job description."

Patra laughed and left. Debra opened the door to leave.

"You want a ride home?"

"Thanks, but I took Veronica's car. I'm good," Keisha replied. She still had to go to the store to get some Newports for her mother.

"All right," Debra said. "Make sure Blackie walks you out to your car. You never know what crazy fools could be out there waiting for you."

"I got ya."

Debra walked out and, like a snake, Sean slid into the dressing room.

"Keisha, I've got something for you," Sean said, holding a business card.

"Look," Keisha said, standing up, "I'm not interested in doing any private dances for your patrons. I don't do bachelor parties."

"Look, that ain't it."

Sean sat down on the makeup counter.

"Remember that guy you were dancing for? Well, he's a talent scout for *Pimp* magazine. He wanted me to give you his card because he'd like to see you in the magazine."

Keisha took the card and stared at it.

"What does he want me to do?"

"Pose. He comes here from time to time and looks for new girls to pose. Most times he leaves without anyone, but this time you impressed him. Take it as a compliment."

"What's he paying?" she asked. Keisha grabbed her bag and began to leave. Sean followed her. Blackie was sipping on a Coke at the bar, while Jojo was cleaning up the club. Keisha noticed that when the lights were up, the Chi Chi Room really looked cheap.

"I think he's paying $250 for a shoot. And if they like you, they'll book you for more."

Keisha stopped.

"Is he on the up and up? Or is he full of shit?"

"Up and up. But hey, if you don't want to do it . . ."

Keisha looked at the card again. Posing had been something she'd thought about, but she didn't know if she wanted to have her pictures floating out in the public forever. Being onstage was one thing. It was dark, and only a limited amount of regulars were watching. But putting it in print didn't help. But she needed the money, and this was a quick way to get it.

"I'll think about it."

"You think about if you want to be shaking your ass on this stage for the rest of your life, then get back to me," Sean said, smirking. "Blackie, take her to her car."

* * *

Keisha pulled into her driveway around four in the morning, turned off the engine, and sat still in the car. She was tired. The sun was about an hour from peeking above the horizon, but the crackheads in the neighborhood were still scurrying around in search of another hit. The neighborhood was semi-asleep, but it would be fully awake in an hour or so. Most of the residents on Budlong Avenue were churchgoing nine-to-fivers who didn't do any dirt except what was contained in their nicely mowed lawns. But it still was a dangerous place to grow up, a dangerous place to live day to day, and a dangerous place to stay. And that's why Keisha was desperate to get out.

She slowly got out of the car and made her way to the front door, carrying the carton of Newports for Veronica. When she walked into the house, she saw the same scene she always saw. Andre was passed out on the couch, getting his beauty rest for another day of sitting on his black ass. Veronica was half asleep, but the squeak of the door had awakened her.

"Where's my cigarettes?" she asked Keisha sleepily.

"No 'hi'? No, 'thank-you'?" Keisha asked sarcastically as she tossed the carton to her mother.

"Your thank-you is that you get a muthafuckin' place to put your head down," Veronica replied, opening the carton. She pulled out a pack, opened it, and pulled out a cigarette.

"You know, I should start charging your ass some rent," she continued, lighting the cigarette. "How much did you make at the club tonight?"

Keisha desperately wanted to get in bed, smoke a joint, and then go to sleep, but her mother wasn't going to let her go that easy.

"That's my money, and my business," Keisha replied.

Her mother stopped smoking for a second and looked at her long and hard, as though she was just meeting her daughter for the first time.

"Your business is my business," she said in a low, menacing voice. "If you don't like it, you can get the hell out right now. And I do mean right now. You're grown."

"I'm going to bed," Keisha said, ignoring her and walking to her room.

"Yeah, that's what you do best," her mother shouted, walking away. "Sleep and shake your ass. That's all you do!"

Keisha shut the door with a noisy bang. The crystal doorknob came off in her hands.

"Shit!" she muttered.

She was too tired to put it back on and could only fall down on the bed. It was then that her cell phone rang.

"Hello?"

"Hey, baby, how come you haven't called me this week?"

Donovan always had bad timing, and that was why Keisha had given him the boot last month. He'd done wrong, and now he was paying the price. He couldn't keep slinging crack on the block, Keisha thought, going in and out of jail and trying to be a player, and expect to keep her as a girlfriend. She'd seen what that lifestyle brought and she didn't want any part of it.

"Donovan, it's four-thirty in the morning. Why are you calling me now?"

" 'Cause I was up and I saw you get in," he said. "You know I don't like you dancing at that club."

Keisha bent down to look under her bed. There she found the cigar box with her weed. Andre had been stealing a little bit each day, but she still had enough for one joint. And one joint was all she needed. She took a Zig-Zag paper and licked it.

"You have absolutely no choice in the matter, son," she said, sprinkling weed in the Zig-Zag. "If you had done me right instead of chasing all those other hoes, you may have had a little bit of say—and I do mean only a little bit—but now you have nothing. So stop sweating me."

"But I still love you, Keisha. You know that," he said. "Why don't you give me another chance? I swear I can do better."

Keisha lit the joint and took a nice long hit. The smoke was just what she needed. Finally she let the smoke trickle out of her mouth in a stream.

"Yeah, but I can do better than you," Keisha said. "I know that now. You showed me that."

"Ah, baby, don't say that. You know that, like the moon and the Earth, we are meant to be together."

Keisha took the cell phone from her ear and looked at it. She didn't know if the weed had made her think she'd heard him say some corny shit, or if Donovan had actually thought that line would work. Either way, she wasn't buying what he was selling.

"Good night, Donovan," she said. "And don't call me at four-thirty in the morning ever again, or I'll come by and kick your ass like I used to. You understand?"

Donavan paused.

"You still love me, don't you?"

Keisha hung up on Donovan. *I hate him because he's right,* she thought as she took another drag of the joint. *I do love him, but I can't be with him.*

She turned over, reached under the bed, and pulled

out a shoebox. She lifted the lid of the box, put in her dollar bills, and then pulled out a white envelope. Inside was a single piece of rumpled paper.

Congratulations, Keisha Montez! You have been accepted into the 2007–08 freshman class of the University of California at Los Angeles. In the coming weeks, we will be sending you more information, including the academic schedule and orientation period. Please send us a confirmation that you will be enrolling at the university by September 1. Total tuition for the year is $7,700. Thank you, and we look forward to having you as a member of the UCLA community!

Keisha slowly put the paper back into the envelope, then put the box back under her bed. September 1 was weeks away and her mother hadn't been any help.

"Fuck that shit," she said, puffing on. She then took a final drag of her joint and lay down, wondering how she was going to make $7,700 for school and still get out of Veronica's house. "I ain't filling out no financial aid forms or taking out any loans. You want some money, then go back to that club and shake your ass some more," Veronica had said.

Chapter 4

The self is not something ready-made, but something in continuous formation through choice of action.

—John Dewey

The *Pimp* magazine headquarters was in a nondescript building in Inglewood, so Steven always had to rent out a place for photo shoots. When Steven thought about his hopes and dreams, he saw himself living in a Playboy mansion as the black Hugh Hefner. But that was his dream. Right now, he was conducting a photo shoot with a man holding a ten-inch dick and an uncooperative model with size 38F titties. His photographer Jeff straddled them both and clicked away with his camera.

"All right, Gabrielle, now I want you to lie on your stomach while Mr. Bigg is on top of you."

"Okay, but make sure that he doesn't mess with my hair," Gabrielle said, turning her naked body over.

"Mr. Bigg, please make sure to not mess with her hair," Steven said with a smirk.

"Right," said Mr. Bigg, yawning.

"She doesn't mind having a strange ten-inch dick

laying on her ass but is tripping off her fucking hair," Steven whispered to Marty.

"That's the business you're in." Marty laughed.

"Okay, Jeff, let's get the shots," Steven said, motioning to the photographer.

This photo shoot was taking place at the Studio. The Studio was in the San Fernando Valley, and almost every nude magazine used it from time to time. About ten years before, a porn director, tired of trying to find locations for his shoots, had built an all-purpose studio. The studio was divided into five sets. You could have your models use the kitchen set, the living room set, the office set, the pool room set, or the bedroom set. Steven liked to use it because his readers weren't that discerning when it came to what the background looked like. They just wanted to see the ass in the photo. And that's where Gabrielle came in.

This shoot was in the bedroom set, and Mr. Bigg and Gabrielle were on the bed. Jeff had to climb on top of the bed to get the shots for the magazine. Things had been rocky because Gabrielle didn't follow instructions well, and when a model didn't follow instructions, it made for long hours of shooting. They were now into hour four of a two-hour shoot.

"Goddammit, Gabrielle!" Steven shouted. "How many times do I have to tell you to keep your face to the camera? I mean, what the fuck is going on? You're fucking wasting my time when you can't follow even the simplest instructions."

Gabrielle was not moved by Steven's histrionics.

"If you think it's so damn easy, then why don't you put your ass in the air with a dick on it and then turn your head? I'll bet you that you'd find a way to keep your head down."

"But I'm putting the money in your pocket," he

reminded her. "And if you can't do what the fuck I say, then get up and I can keep my money. Just let me know."

"Well, if you just shut up, maybe we can get this damn shoot done and I can get the fuck out of here," she said sharply.

Jeff kept shooting, even through the conversation. He wasn't paid by the shot, but he did like to give *Pimp* a bit of an artistic touch, even if Steven always deleted it. Maybe the argument could be used as a theme. It would have helped if Mr. Bigg was a bit more animated in his facial expressions, but he always had the same dull look.

"All right, enough of that," Jeff said, climbing down from the bed. He changed the lens on the camera.

"Let's have you guys lie on your side," he said. "Gabrielle, raise your leg just so."

Jeff moved Gabrielle's leg so that it was high over her head. Mr. Bigg was behind her.

"Mr. Bigg, take your dick and put it on her leg so that it straddles it."

"Just like this?" Mr. Bigg asked. He picked up his dick like it wasn't even part of his body and tossed it on Gabrielle's leg. "Do you want it soft or hard?" Mr. Bigg was just trying to help.

"What do you think, Steven?" Jeff asked, leaning back and looking through his camera lens at the scene.

"Uh, let's go with hard."

"Okay," Jeff said, looking around. "Where's Kevin? Kevin!"

Kevin came running into the room.

"What?"

Jeff pointed at Mr. Bigg. "He needs some oil."

Kevin pulled a white bottle of oil out of his pocket

and handed it to Mr. Bigg. After sprinkling some oil on his dick, Mr. Bigg immediately began jacking off, like there was nothing wrong with masturbating in front of a crew of photographers and staff. And for him, there wasn't.

Suddenly the ten-incher turned hard, and he gently laid it down on Gabrielle.

"Damn, nigga, that dick is hot!" Gabrielle said. "And oily too."

She looked at his penis as though it was an alien.

"It can get hotter," he responded with a smirk.

"Yeah, in your wet dreams," she said. Gabrielle raised her head like Steven wanted and held the pose.

"Let's get this shit over with," she said.

Jeff took more shots, and in about five minutes, it was all over.

"That's a wrap, everybody," Jeff said. "Thank you, everyone."

Gabrielle and Mr. Bigg hopped up off the bed, and Kevin handed them a towel.

Steven and Marty walked off the set, not even bothering to thank Gabrielle and Mr. Bigg. For Steven, once a shoot was done, then the people in it didn't matter to him. They had worth to him only when they made him money.

The Studio had a room for viewing photographs, so Steven and Marty started looking at the day's shoot.

"Sit down, Marty, while I take a look at these photos," Steven said.

Steven Cox looked over Mr. Bigg and Gabrielle's photos in his office, and he was pleased. They gave him that simulated porn look that he wanted, and Gabrielle actually looked like she had been enjoying herself, even though he knew she hadn't been. And that was all he wanted—to give the reader what he wanted to see. Nothing more, and nothing less.

Steven had bought *Pimp* magazine after having lost his job as a lawyer. He'd gotten into a fistfight with another lawyer at the first law firm he worked for, and that didn't help his career track being subsequently blackballed from every other law firm. That was because he'd taken a kickback from Sean, and had manipulated some evidence to get him out from under some racketeering charges that had been the last straw. The agreement was that he'd leave quietly, and never practice law again, and the firm would keep the evidence under wraps. Steven negotiated a severance, and then signed on the dotted line. And Steven let Sean know that he still had the evidence, and if he wanted to stay out of prison, he would make sure the women of the Chi Chi Room were available to him.

Steven really didn't like law anyway, and with *Pimp* he'd taken a magazine that had previously had a weak regional circulation and turned it into the biggest-selling black magazine, next to *Essence* women's magazine. He was making money hand over fist and it all came from shooting titties and ass for horny men. Now he was going into another venture. He was going into porn, and Ray was his talent scout.

"Okay, so what do ya got?" Steven asked. Marty and Ray had been scouring the clubs for damn near a month now, looking for the right one. Steven wanted someone fresh, something that could capture the imagination of the black porn–buying public. He needed a star.

"I think I've found our girl," Ray said. "She's going to start off *Pimp* Video with a bang."

"Where are her pictures?"

Ray leaned back in his chair.

"I don't have any yet. I met her at the Chi Chi Room the other day. Believe me, she's a star."

"The Chi Chi Room? Goddamn it, that means Sean is going to want a cutback, isn't he?"

"Of course." Ray laughed. "But then again, this piece of ass is worth it. And I think she's a video virgin."

"Description, give me a description."

"She looks a bit like Vida Guerra, the girl on *FHM*. She's light skinned with perky, real breasts and a beautiful ass. She doesn't have a big ass like the regular bitches at Chi Chi's, but it's in proportion to her body. She's tight, man, she's really tight. I think she's mixed with something. Maybe Mexican or Puerto Rican."

"Measurements?"

"Probably about 36C-24-36. She's tight, I tell you."

"But tight doesn't mean that she can fuck. Okay, then bring her in. I want to see this star. And if she's as good as you say she is, then we may find ourselves making a lot of money."

"I'll get back to Sean about getting her in here," Ray said.

"Wait, I want to cut Sean out of this," Steven said, standing up. "If she's anything like you say she is, then I want to make her the black Jenna Jameson. We need to get her in some scenes and then test how she sells. But if I'm going to be investing my money, I don't want some Negro out there making money off of her. Pay him for the shoot, and then tell him that's it."

Ray got up to leave. "Not a problem. He's going to be pissed, but what the fuck can he do? The nigga's got no choice but to take the deal."

"And it's your job to make that happen," Steven said. "If she's as good as you say she is, then it'll be worth it."

Tonight, the Chi Chi Room was packed early because Keisha was going on early. She was rapidly building a loyal following.

She'd turned to stripping in the first place because it was the only place she knew where she could make a lot of money in a short time. South Central wasn't like the richer areas of Los Angeles. If you got a low paying job that didn't make you drive across town, you felt lucky. But no job was going to pay Keisha the money she needed for UCLA. So it was the Chi Chi Room for now.

For Keisha, getting onstage was power, both economic and sexual. The attention she got from the men made her feel like she could control them with each shake of her breast, every wiggle of her ass. She liked the fact that because of her body, she could pull money from the pockets of leering men. It turned her on, and yeah, it was sort of addicting.

"Now gentlemen, coming onstage is a girl who has been at the Chi Chi Room for only a few weeks, but we think she's going to be a star," the DJ said. "Please put your hands together for Keisha!"

Keisha walked up to the stage in clear high-heeled pumps, a silver thong, and a bikini top to the sound of Ice Cube's "Jackin' for Beats."

"Shake that ass, baby," one shouted. He was damn near frothing at the mouth, as he balanced his drink and cigarette in his hands.

"Show me those tits," said the other.

Normally, Wednesdays were slow at the Chi Chi Room, but it was important that new girls build their fan base on off nights so they could get prime nights like Friday and Saturday, otherwise known as Payday and Get Laid nights. So Keisha brought her ass to one, and showed her tits to the other.

Keisha gripped the pole in the center of the stage and began humping it. She wasn't a natural dancer, but she had a sensuality that the men seemed to like. She remembered how awkward she'd been only a month before, but now she was feeling like a natural. It was all about the tease.

She held her hands on the pole, stuck out her ass, and began making circles in the air with it. Dollar bills began raining down by her feet. A couple of deep knee bends, then a slap of her own ass, made the pervert pit go wild. It was now the middle of the song.

"Come on, guys," the DJ said, "make some noise for Keisha!"

Give every section a chance to see me, she thought, walking around the stage.

Keisha began playing with her bikini top and teasingly took off one string but kept her breasts covered. More bills began flying. She began to shake her breasts, giving the men a glimpse of her milkshake. With one hand on her breast, she then used her other hand to untie the other string. The bikini fell, and she stood there bare.

"Look at those beautiful, all-natural breasts, gentlemen," the DJ yelled over the song. "Keisha is tight, tight, tight!"

With "Jackin' for Beats" almost done, it was time for the thong to come off. But before that, she needed to make some contact with the pervert pit. So she slid along the floor on her belly, making eye contact with a thirty-something man. He had a wedding ring but tried to hide his hand.

When Keisha got to him, she used her breasts so that they just barely touched his face. Now on her knees, she began to slowly take off her thong. His eyes were as big as saucers.

As Keisha took off her thong, more dollar bills flew down on her, and she continued to concentrate on her married man. Finally the thong was off, and she put it on his head, stuck out her tongue, and then put her ass in his face.

"Damn, girl, that is a beautiful ass!" a voice yelled.

And suddenly the music was off.

"Gentlemen, please give Keisha a round of applause," the DJ said.

Keisha instantly stood up and picked her thong off the head of her married man.

"Thank you," she whispered into his ear. He was absolutely enthralled, as they all were.

Keisha walked around the stage, picking up as many bills as she could, and she tried to avoid the groping hands of the pervert pit. If given the chance, they would try to get a quick and cheap feel from one of the dancers.

Finally, Keisha walked offstage, and ran into Patra, who was about to go on.

"You make much?" Patra asked.

"At this cheap-ass club? Hell, no," Keisha said, trying not to drop the dollar bills she'd collected. She held them pressed to her left breast. "See you later."

"Later," Patra replied.

Keisha walked into the dressing room. No one was there except for Sean, who was sitting in a swivel chair.

"When are you going to let me work on Fridays?" Keisha asked, putting her money on the counter. "I bet I only made one hundred, and after the tip-out,

I'm probably only getting about fifty dollars tonight. That's some bullshit."

"Look, you've got to draw more people into the club before I can give you a Friday or Saturday," Sean said. "Bring niggas in, and you'll get paid. If not, then you won't."

Keisha kept counting her money, not looking at Sean.

"Have you called Ray yet?" Sean asked, twirling in his chair.

"Nah."

"Well, if you don't want the $250, then I'm sure they'll find somebody else to take it."

"That ain't it," she said, looking up. "I want to go to UCLA and I don't want a whole bunch of niggas knowing that I strip."

"You still talking that college shit?" Sean asked, waving his hand. "Fuck that shit. You could make way more than those college muthafuckas by dancing. What do you get after you leave college anyway? Getting some fucked-up job giving some white boy some coffee every day? Fuck that! It's all about the scrilla, baby, and the faster you learn that shit, the faster you'll make it."

Keisha kept counting her money.

"But if you do want to do that college shit, think about it. How many muthafuckas are going to see *Pimp* magazine anyway? Go get your money and then forget about that shit," Sean continued. "And besides, what do you think will happen—some college muthafuckas figure out that you're dancing at our club? Do you think they'll look on that better than if you're in some muthafuckin' magazine? Nigga, please. The genie's out the bottle, so don't worry about what you can't worry about."

"I'll think about it," Keisha whispered, putting the dollars into her purse.

"What? I couldn't hear you," Sean said as he stopped spinning.

"I said, I'll think about it."

"That ain't good enough. Ray is coming in here tonight, and he wants to know yes or no. So you better make a decision in about five minutes, or he's moving on to another bitch."

"Why the fuck are you so concerned about whether I do this shoot or not? What do you get out of it?" Keisha said, curious.

"I don't get shit out of it, but I do want to make sure that the Chi Chi Room is always providing the best women to magazines like *Pimp*. The men who buy *Pimp* want to know where they can see you. If you say you dance at the Chi Chi Room, then you make more money and we make more money. Again, I keep telling you bitches that it's all about the money. Y'all just never learn. So, again, what's it going to be?"

Keisha closed her purse and stared at Sean. She didn't trust his ass as far as she could throw him, but that was neither here nor there. She needed money, and he was right.

"Tell him that I'll do it," Keisha said, putting on her pants and blouse. "But this is a one-time thing. No more, no less."

"Tell him yourself," Sean said, pointing to the door, where Ray was standing. "Trying to catch a look, nigga?"

"I already paid for my looks," Ray said, walking into the dressing room. "So, Keisha, are you ready to shoot for *Pimp*?"

"Yeah," Keisha said, getting ready to leave. "I'm ready to shoot."

Ray smiled.

"Good," he said. "Look, meet us at the Vision Theater on Saturday at nine A.M. Don't be late, because Steven hates models who are late."

"Who's Steven?" Keisha asked.

"Steven is the man who can take you beyond this club," he responded with a laugh.

"Hey, nigga," Sean said, "don't try to take my bitches."

"Simmer down, baby. I'm just making a joke. Damn, a nigga can't even kid around anymore."

"Whatever, you two. I'll see you at nine," Keisha said, opening the door to leave. "Just have my money ready."

"Don't worry, we'll have your money."

Chapter 5

The sufferings that fate inflicts on us should be borne with patience, what enemies inflict with manly courage.

—Thucydides

Veronica was pissed, and Andre had no idea why.

"Andre! Andre!" she screamed. She was stomping up and down in the house. "Andre! Bring your black ass in here."

Andre slowly got off the couch and began making his way to the back of the house. Veronica was in Keisha's room.

"Where the hell does Keisha keep her money?" Veronica asked, rifling through Keisha's room. She went through drawers and was throwing clothes on the floor.

"Momma, what are you doing?" Andre asked, slightly appalled. He was high, but not that high. "Keisha is going to be pissed."

"You think I really give a shit? Where the fuck is her money?" Veronica asked again, turning toward Andre. "I know the bitch doesn't have a bank account, so it has to be in here somewhere."

Veronica walked into Keisha's closet, continuing to look for Keisha's money.

"What do you need her money for?"

"I just need it," Veronica said. "Robert's back in town and he needs it."

Robert was Veronica's sometime boyfriend who tended to be either on the run or in jail. He was always into a little bit of everything, but nothing good. Andre couldn't stand him being around, and Keisha refused to even acknowledge his presence. To her, he didn't deserve to be in her father's home, no matter if her father was not there.

Andre sat down on the bed. Veronica had taken the sheets and had thrown them against the wall.

"Momma, come on," Andre said. "Don't take her money, especially for Robert. Your boyfriend should get his own money."

"Muthafucka, you don't tell me what to do. Now get off your ass and find that money."

"Come on, Momma," Andre pleaded. "Robert hasn't been around for six months."

"Find that fucking money, Andre, or you're gonna find your ass out on the street."

Andre reluctantly began looking for the money. She kept looking in the closet, while Andre looked down and noticed a shoebox at the foot of the bed and pulled it out.

"I think I found it," he said, with a low whisper.

Veronica came rushing out of the closet and walked over to Andre. She took the shoebox away from Andre and opened it.

"Shit," she said, looking at Andre. She started pulling out dollar bills, and they began falling down on the bed. "That bitch must have over a thousand dollars in here. She's got a thousand goddamn dollars in here and she's bitchin' over buying me cigarettes? Nigga, please."

Veronica gathered the money and put it in her pockets.

"She didn't need it anyway."

"What does Robert need the money for?" Andre asked.

"Robert has to pay back a debt," she said, walking out of Keisha's room. Andre followed her into the living room, where Veronica now was putting on her coat. "And what does she need the money for anyway? She don't pay rent. She don't pay for groceries. And she sure as hell doesn't give any to you or me. So fuck it, she's just paying back rent."

Veronica opened the door to go.

"What should I say to Keisha when she gets home?" Andre asked. "She's gonna be pissed off."

Veronica looked back at Andre. "I don't give a fuck what you tell her. I took the money and I ain't givin' it back. So she'll just have to deal with it. I'll be back tomorrow. Here's fifty dollars. Go buy your girlfriend something."

Veronica threw a wad of money at Andre and then left. Andre sat down on the couch again and pulled out a joint. He lit the joint and looked at his watch.

Keisha should be home in thirty minutes, he thought. *That's enough time to get high.* He miscalculated, because as soon as Andre lit the joint, he heard Keisha's key hit the door. She was back from the Chi Chi Room.

"Before you do anything, let me tell you that I didn't have a damn thing to do with it," Andre said to Keisha, stopping her in her tracks.

"What the hell are you talking about?" Keisha said, throwing her keys on the coffee table. Andre took another drag from the joint.

"Here," Andre said, coughing. "Take the rest of this."

Keisha took a look at Andre holding the joint and started walking toward her room. Andre pulled the joint back and finished it off.

"What the fuck happened?" Keisha screamed. She came running back into the living room holding her empty shoebox.

"What the fuck did you do with my money, Andre? Where the fuck is my money, you son of a bitch?"

Keisha threw the box at Andre and sprang to hit him.

"I didn't have anything to do with it, I told you!" he said, cowering on the couch. "Momma took your money."

"Momma took it?" Keisha said, breathing deeply. "That bitch! What the fuck did she take my money for?"

"Because she had to get Robert out of debt."

"Robert? Robert?" Keisha asked incredulously. "She stole from her daughter to give money to her fucking drug-dealing boyfriend?"

"In a word, yes. Look, I tried to stop her."

"I can't believe this shit. I just can't believe this shit," Keisha kept repeating. It was surreal, as though she were in a dream.

She paced around the house thinking about what she should do next. She walked back into her room and surveyed the scene. The bed was overturned, the covers were thrown on the floor, and her clothes were out of her drawers. But there was one piece of paper on her bed. It was the UCLA letter.

"It was wrong, Keisha," Andre said, as he walked into the room. "I told her that, but she just said that you owed her that money."

"I didn't owe her a goddamn thing," Keisha said,

picking up the UCLA letter and crumpling it in her pocket. "I've never owed her a goddamn thing. But she blames me for every fucking bad thing that happens in her life."

"That's not true," Andre said. "She doesn't blame you for her life."

Keisha went into her closet and pulled out a suitcase. She began picking up her clothes and stuffing them into it.

"Like hell she doesn't," she said. "She blames me for Daddy leaving. She blames me for her not being this star she thinks she was destined to be. And she blames me for being me."

"Daddy was going to leave no matter what," Andre said. "He was trifling, and you had nothing to do with it."

Keisha stopped putting clothes in the case.

"Yeah, well, you tell her that. I can't tell you how many times she's said that she wished I'd never been born and that Daddy would have stayed if she hadn't been pregnant with me. So if she doesn't blame me, then she has a strange way of disguising it."

Keisha started packing again. The suitcase was overstuffed with clothes, and Keisha tried to close it.

"Where are you going?" Andre asked. He really looked sad.

"Why?" Keisha asked, finally closing the suitcase. "Do you want to tell her so that she can come by each night and take my money?"

"No, because even though I may be a fuck-up, I'm still your brother and I do care about you," he said.

Keisha stared at him. "If you really cared about me, you would have fought the shit out of her and got me my money. You and her are the same. You only care about yourselves."

Keisha took the suitcase and made her way to the front door.

"Wait," Andre said, walking toward her. He reached into his pocket and took out a wad of money. "This belongs to you. Momma gave it to me from your money, but I don't want it."

He held out the money and Keisha took it, putting it in her bra.

"Thanks," she said.

"Take care of yourself."

Keisha took a quick glance around and then opened the door.

"Yeah, you too."

And then she left Veronica's house for good.

As Keisha went down the street, she walked straight, and with her head up, dragged her suitcase. She got to the bus stop and sat on the bench, wondering where to go. She had few options, so for an hour, she watched as bus after bus stopped, opened its doors expectantly, and then drove off. She didn't know where to go. She wasn't particularly close to anyone from high school, and she definitely didn't want to stay with Donovan. With no family around, Keisha simply picked up her cell phone and tried her luck.

"Patra?" Keisha asked.

"Who is this?" Patra sounded like she had been asleep.

"It's Keisha."

"Hey, Keisha. What's up, girl?"

"Hey, I need a favor," Keisha said nervously. "I had to leave the house and I was wondering if I could crash at your house for a little while?"

"How long is a little while?"

"Let me make some money at the club so I can find a place of my own. I'll help pay the rent."

There was a pause on the phone.

"Okay, you can stay on the couch, but my place is tiny, so you're going to have to find a place of your own as soon as you can," Patra said. "But come on over."

"Thanks, girl."

Keisha hung up and waited for the bus. At least she'd accomplished one goal. She'd gotten out of Veronica's house.

The bus came and Keisha took a seat. She sat there, wondering why her life had been a struggle. It was like no one had her back, and she was constantly trying to figure out who was going to screw her next. Because in her life, there was always someone looking to get over.

She got off the bus and found Patra's apartment building. She buzzed the door.

"Hello?" Patra said through the intercom.

"It's me."

"Come on up." The door buzzed and Keisha dragged her bag up to Patra's apartment. Before she could knock, Patra had opened the door.

"Whoa," Keisha said. "You scared me." She walked in with her bag and Patra closed the door.

"I can hear when someone gets off the elevator. You want something to drink?" Patra asked, opening her refrigerator. "I've got soda, beer, and an old bottle of champagne from the club."

"I'll take a soda, thanks."

Keisha sat on Patra's couch and looked around. Her place was neat, with glass shelves holding a TV and some pictures, and a black leather sofa and chair. It wasn't a spectacular apartment, but Keisha was impressed. She didn't understand how Patra could afford an apartment like this based on what she got at the Chi Chi Room, but she didn't want to pry.

"So your mother kicked you out?" Patra asked, handing Keisha the soda.

"No, I left."

"Why did you leave?"

Keisha took a drink from her soda. "She went into my room and took all of the money I'd been saving up."

"Damn, your moms stealing from you? That's fucked-up. How much did she steal?"

"About a thousand."

"Fuck that," Patra said. "Excuse my French and I'm not, but I would have stayed at that house and beat down that bitch for doing that. You don't take my muthafuckin' money. How come you didn't just get the money back?"

Keisha took another sip of her soda. "Because she gave the money to her boyfriend, Robert, and it was too late. Plus, Robert's not a fool to fuck with."

"Why?"

"Because I think he takes pleasure in beating women, real pleasure. And if I were to confront him about taking my money, he'd go off."

"Did he live with y'all?"

"That nigga would come in and out the house as he pleased. I haven't seen him in about six months, but apparently he's back in town. He slings, so that nigga's never in the same city for any length of time. He's probably back here in L.A. because all of the big-time dealers are in County, and he thinks he can make some money—probably with my money. But my momma is so damn stupid, she doesn't even understand that this nigga don't give a damn about her."

"Sorry to talk about your momma like this, but dumb bitches are everywhere," Patra said. "So what are you gonna do next?"

"I don't know. Hustle and get as much money as I can as fast as I can, I guess."

Patra looked at Keisha. They weren't particularly close, but she did like her. And she kind of felt for her. But her space was her space.

"Look, you can stay here until the end of the month. But you're going to have to pay a bit of rent, and you need to buy your own food, so don't fuck with mine. At the end of the month, you've got to move out and get your own place. So do what you have to do with Sean, but make it happen."

"Cool. That's real cool."

Patra studied Keisha for a second.

"There's one other thing," she said. "What happens in this apartment stays in this apartment. You understand? What I do is my private business, and I don't want to hear about it. Don't ask any questions. We clear?"

"Clear."

Patra stood up and picked up both soda cans and walked to the kitchen. "You've lucked out because that couch is a sofa bed. So you can pull it out when you want to go to sleep. I'll get some keys made and you can come and go as you please. The television has cable, and you can watch it all night long for all I care. I can sleep through anything. Put your clothes in the front closet, and then you're all set."

"Thanks, Patra," Keisha said gratefully. "I won't be a bother."

"Sure, you will be," Patra said, smiling. "But don't worry about that. Bitches got to stick together, right?"

"Right," Keisha said, smiling.

Chapter 6

The crew was all ready to do Keisha's shoot, but
there was no sign of her. She was late, and Steven
hated people who were late.

"So where is the girl?" Steven asked. It was nine-
fifteen on Saturday, and they were supposed to have
started shooting Keisha at nine, but she was nowhere
to be found.

"Is she flaking out, or will she be here?" he asked
Ray, who was looking at his cell phone and dialing
Keisha's number.

"I'm finding out right now," he said. "Hello?"

"Who is this?"

"This is Ray. Keisha, where are you?"

Keisha was sitting on the bus, and a street poet
was in the back reciting poetry, to the consternation
of all the passengers.

"Shut the hell up," an old lady admonished the
poet. "I just want to ride this raggedy bus in peace."

"Peace, my sister," the poet riffed. "Peace is about being in peace with oneself, and one's universe, which is a piece of me—"

"I'm on the bus, about two blocks away from you," Keisha said into her phone, holding her hand over her other ear, trying to block out the poet. "I'll be there in about five minutes."

"Hurry up and get your ass here," he said, hanging up the phone. "She'll be here in about five minutes. She's on the bus."

Steven looked disgusted. "Dealing with this bus-riding hood rat gets on my nerves."

"You should let me pick up the hoes," Marty said. "I'll make sure they get here on time."

"I'd rather have her get here on the bus," Steven said, looking at Marty disdainfully.

He then turned to everyone assembled. This was going to be a shoot that featured Keisha, without any man in it. "Everybody get ready. She's on her way."

Keisha walked into the Vision Theater with her duffle bag in tow, and Steven smiled. Ray had been right. She was the exact type Steven wanted for his new video unit. Pretty, delicate, and she didn't look like she'd been abused or in a street fight. He couldn't wait to see her naked.

"You done good," Steven whispered to Ray. He walked over to her.

"Hello, Keisha, my name is Steven Cox, and I'm the publisher of *Pimp* magazine," Steven said, smiling. He wanted to put on the charm offensive as soon as possible. "Did you have any problem getting here?"

"No," Keisha said, looking around unsurely. She wasn't the nervous type, but she was a bit apprehensive.

"Good, can we get you something? Would you like some soda or water?"

Keisha put down the duffle bag she'd been carrying. "Water would be fine."

"Kevin," Steven screamed. Steven's assistant came running. "Get Keisha some water, and then set up her space so we can get started."

"No problem," Kevin said. "Do you mind if I take your bag?"

"Go for it," she said.

Steven took Keisha by the elbow and walked her toward Ray, who was sitting on the edge of the stage. On stage was a huge poster bed, and the crew was setting up lights all around it.

"Ray tells me that you dance at the Chi Chi Room. How do you like it there?" he asked, holding Keisha by the elbow.

"It's fine. It pays the bills."

"And that's what's important, isn't it? Everyone's got to pay the bills."

Ray got up from the stage. "Good to see you, Keisha."

"Cool," she said. Kevin ran up with a bottle of water, and Keisha sat on the edge of the stage looking at them all.

"So how long is this going to take?" she asked, opening the bottle of water.

"The shoot shouldn't take more than two hours," Steven said. "After that, you'll be out of here. I'll even make sure to get you a ride home so you don't have to take the bus. Not a bad way to make five hundred dollars, eh?"

Keisha stopped drinking her water and stared at Steven.

"Five hundred dollars?" she asked. "Sean told me that I was only making two hundred and fifty."

Steven looked at Ray and started laughing.

"Goddamn Sean," he laughed. "He'd cheat his mother if he could find a way. No, darling, you're getting five hundred for this deal, not two-fifty. I'll pay you personally. *Pimp* is a magazine of integrity, so we don't bullshit you. If I tell you we're going to pay you something, then we pay that to you."

"You can trust Steven," Ray interjected. "Sean—not so much."

Keisha drank a bit more water. Again, Sean had tried to screw her out of money.

"Let's get started," she said, decidedly pissed off. She put down the bottle of water. "What do you want me to do?"

Steven sidled up to her. "The first thing is that I want you to be as comfortable as possible. If you find something you don't like, then make sure to let me know, and we'll make a change. You got it?"

"Yeah."

"How old are you, Keisha?" Steven asked.

"I just turned eighteen."

"Good," he said, "because you can't do a shoot without being at least eighteen. Did you just graduate?"

"Yeah."

"From where?"

"I went to Crenshaw High."

"Cool. I went to Morningside," Steven said, laughing. "Way back in the day."

Keisha smiled.

"Kevin, go get the forms."

"I've got them right over there," Kevin said, walking to the first row of seats.

"We need you to fill out these forms before we get started," Steven said. He took the forms from Kevin and handed them to Keisha.

"They're what we call boilerplate contracts, in that every magazine uses them," he continued. "Just fill them out and let me know when you're done. After that, we can get started. Kevin, help her if she has any problems."

Steven and Ray walked onstage, and Kevin sat next to Keisha.

"Right here, you sign your name—"

Keisha shot Kevin a look. "I'm not one of your stupid hoes. I know how to fill out a form."

"Sorry about that," Kevin said sheepishly.

"No problem," Keisha said. She filled out the form and then handed it to Kevin. She walked onstage.

"Ready to go," she told Steven.

"Great. Kevin will take you over to the dressing room. Kevin is sort of our everything man. I need you to take off your clothes, and then Kevin will oil you down. You don't mind, do you?"

"Just as long as he's doing his job and not trying to get some sort of cheap thrill."

Steven smiled. "You wouldn't be getting a cheap thrill from rubbing oil on beautiful women, now would you, Kevin?"

"I try not to, sir," Kevin said, with a faint smile on his face.

"Okay, see you guys in about ten minutes. Normally we'd do your makeup, but I think it's perfect."

Kevin and Keisha walked toward the dressing room.

"So you do whatever Steven tells you?" Keisha asked.

"Pretty much," he said, opening the door. "It ain't the best job, but it pays the bills."

"That pretty much seems to be the modus operandi

around here. We're all just trying to pay some bills. So, what do we do?"

"It's pretty simple," Kevin said, reaching into a cabinet. He pulled out some clear oil. "Take off your clothes and then I'll oil you down."

Keisha took off her top, her bra, and then her pants and panties.

"Stand right here," he said. Kevin started oiling Keisha from the legs and thighs up. "Wow, no tattoos."

"Is that unusual?" she asked.

"Hell, yeah," he said, as he kept oiling her down. "Almost every girl that comes in here to shoot has a tattoo of her boyfriend who's doing a bid, or some knife mark from a fight gone wrong. They always have to touch them up after the shoots. If you want to make money, take my recommendation and don't ever get a tat. You lose value that way."

Keisha listened and felt Kevin's hands on her body. It was like getting a massage, because he was gentle, very gentle.

"Okay, now I'm going to rub oil on your ass," he said. "After that, I'll do your tits and we'll be done."

"Cool."

Kevin went slowly over Keisha's ass and then went over the rest of her body.

"Why do I have to be oiled up, anyway?" she asked.

"Makes for better photos," Kevin answered. "Steven thinks that too many black models are ashy in pictures. All right, we're done."

"Thanks."

Kevin smiled. "My pleasure."

"Look at our girl, everybody," Steven said, as Keisha made her way back to the stage. There were catcalls from some of the crew and some clapping.

Keisha always felt absolutely comfortable in her own skin and had no problem walking around naked.

"Okay, let me know what I've got to do," she said, walking onstage.

"Great. Keisha, I want you to meet Jeff, our photographer."

"Very nice to meet you," Jeff said, extending his hand. Keisha shook it and then sat on the bed.

"I'd like you to be as natural as possible," Jeff continued. "I'm going to be taking a lot of pictures, and all I need you to do is follow my directions. I know this is your first shoot, so I'll try to go slow. Have fun with it and we'll get really good photos. Plus, you're beautiful, so you should have no problem. Right, Steven?"

"Right," Steven said. "So let's get started."

"Okay, Keisha, I want you to get in the middle of the bed and just follow my directions," Jeff said. "Lights, let's get a reading on her."

Keisha crawled on top of the bed and Kevin held a light meter. "We're good," Kevin told Jeff as he hopped off the bed.

"That's it," Jeff said, as he looked through his camera at Keisha. "Okay, now lie on your back, open your legs, and spread your pussy apart so I can see the pink."

It was then that Keisha knew this was a lot different than dancing at the Chi Chi Room.

Jeff knelt at the foot of the bed and took snaps, as Keisha spread her pussy lips. Steven stood by silently, his hand on his cheek.

"Arch your back up a bit," Jeff said, taking shots. "That's it. Good girl! You're working well, Keisha. Now smile for the camera. You've got to make it seem as though this is the most fun you've ever had in your life."

Keisha felt as uncomfortable as she'd ever been, but she also felt strangely attracted to the camera. She was getting turned on and hadn't expected to.

"Can I move around?"

Jeff took the camera down from his eye. "There are some shots that I absolutely have to get, but then we can free-flow others. What do you think, Steven?"

Steven took his hand down from his chin. "I think we should let Keisha guide us for a bit. If she thinks she has a position that's sexy, then let's go with it. Let's see what she's got."

"Cool," Keisha said. She moved up to the headboard and placed a pillow right behind her head. She put her head on the pillow so that it barely reclined up. She then spread her legs slightly.

"Men like to feel that they can fuck the woman they're looking at, so you need to have me in a fucking position," she said. "Can't you see a man on top of me?"

Steven smiled a huge grin. "Uh, yes, I can see a man on top of you. Now give me a sexy look on your face and, Jeff, do your thing."

Keisha looked at the camera, and the look she gave was both innocent and sexy. It fed many demographics of *Pimp* readers, from the men who loved looking at a sexy woman, to the women who bought *Pimp* because they loved looking at women. Keisha nailed all of the looks, and Steven knew it. He had a winner.

Jeff took shot after shot of Keisha, and Keisha moved in any way she felt natural.

"Here's a doggie-style position," she said, getting on her knees. She was really getting into it.

"That's good," Jeff said. "Turn around and face the head of the bed, but look over your shoulder and directly at the camera."

Keisha followed his directions, and Jeff began taking shots, slowly walking around her. "Hold that pose, Keisha," he said. "You're doing great."

Keisha took directions well, and faster than she'd expected, it was all over.

"That was absolutely wonderful," Steven said. "Absolutely wonderful."

"I told you she was great," Ray said, bringing Keisha a white robe. "When I saw her at the Chi Chi Room, I just knew she'd be great."

"Did you have a good time?" Steven asked. "I mean, it's really important that you had a great time with us."

"Yeah, I did," she said. And she really meant it. It was much easier to pose than to shake her ass all night, and she made guaranteed money. "So when do I get to see the pictures?"

"We'll send them to you in about a week or so. I think you'll love them. So go get dressed and we'll get you your money."

Kevin joined Keisha back in the dressing room as she started wiping off the oil.

"So how do you think I did?" Keisha asked, putting her clothes back on.

"They are ecstatic," Kevin said. "But I want to caution you to keep your head up, even with them."

Keisha started putting on her clothes. "No need to tell me that, Kevin. I knew that when I decided to get into this game."

"And that's what I've been trying to figure out. Why did you get in the skin game? It's obvious that you're smart—smarter than most of the girls who come through here. So why this? Why dancing at the Chi Chi Room?"

"It's quite simple," she responded. "I like it because I'm very sexual. I like the attention, even from the leering men in the pervert pit. And if I can make some money at the same time, then that's a whole lot better than working at the Crenshaw Baldwin Hills mall for six dollars an hour, don't you think?"

She put on her shoes and was ready to go.

"Plus, it's just my body, nothing more or less."

Kevin opened the door for her to leave. "Just remember that it is always your body and not anyone else's," he whispered. "If you do that, you'll be fine. But if you ever feel uncomfortable, get out."

The crew had pretty much broken down everything, and Steven was talking to Ray and Jeff onstage when Keisha approached them.

"Keisha, I just want to say that I'm very excited about your work for *Pimp* magazine. You were a true professional, and I think the photos will come out great. I'd like to keep in touch with you"—he pulled out a business card—"so that we can use you for future projects. I have a new venture I'm working on, and I think you'd be perfect."

"Thank you," Keisha said, as she took the card. "I had fun. Let me know if you need me again."

"Will do. So I expect you would like to get paid that five hundred dollars you're owed," Steven said, reaching into his pocket. He pulled out a roll of bills and began pulling off notes. "One, two, three, four, five hundred dollars. Enjoy yourself."

Keisha took the money, and Kevin handed her the duffle bag. "What about Sean?" she asked.

Steven looked at Ray and smiled. "Don't worry about Sean. I'll talk to him. I don't like people cheating other people, so he'll get a good talking-to from me."

"Yeah, but then he'll fuck with me at the club."

"Don't worry about that. You'll be fine. I promise,"

he said, smiling. "Hey, I'm about to get out of here. Can I offer you a ride home?"

"Sure," Keisha replied. She was beginning to like Steven, and although she didn't know him well, she felt she could somehow trust him.

"Ray, make sure everything gets broken down, and then meet me back at the office. I'll drop Keisha off and then meet you there."

"It was cool seeing you again, Keisha," Ray said.

"Back at ya. See ya, Kevin, and thanks for your help."

"No problem."

"Let's go, Keisha," Steven said. "I think you'll enjoy the ride home."

Chapter 7

As Steven and Keisha walked out of the shoot, Keisha was ecstatic that she had five hundred dollars in her pocket and another couple hundred dollars sitting at home from Chi Chi Room dances. Things were starting to look up.

They left the theater and were out in the parking lot when Keisha saw Steven's ride.

"You expect me to get on the back of that?" Keisha asked incredulously.

"Sure," he said. Steven didn't have a car, he had a motorcycle. "This is a Suzuki Hayabusa, the fastest motorcycle on the planet. Did you see the *Biker Boyz*?"

"Yeah," she replied nervously.

"This is what Laurence Fishburne rode in the movie."

"Okay, but that doesn't mean that I'm going to ride it in my lifetime," she said. "Plus, I have a duffle bag."

"No problem," he said, handing her a helmet. "Just give me the bag and you put on the helmet."

Keisha had never ridden on the back of a bike, so she was nervous. But it was better than taking the bus.

Steven snapped the bag to the side of his bike and then climbed on. "Come on. Just hop on, and hold on."

"Yeah, that's what my first boyfriend told me," she smiled. She climbed onto the back of the bike and Steven started it up. The sound was deafening.

"So where are we going?" he asked over the exhaust noise.

"My apartment is on Centinela, in Inglewood," she yelled.

"Okay, hold on!"

Steven rolled forward quicker than Keisha had expected, and she found herself clinging to Steven with all her might. As he flew down Crenshaw Boulevard, the speed and excitement of being on the bike gave her a rush. Steven expertly flicked the bike in and out of traffic, and other bikers came up on the side of them from time to time. Steven would give them a wave or two, and then they'd fly off into the distance.

"Better than riding on the bus, eh?" Steven shouted back to Keisha at a stoplight.

"I'm loving it," she said. "As long as I don't fall off."

"You won't fall off." Steven laughed. "I won't let you."

Steven kept going and in less than five minutes, Keisha was at her door. Steven turned off the Hayabusa, and Keisha got off. She took off her helmet and handed it to him. Steven flipped the visor on his and took it.

"You're a very beautiful girl, Keisha, and I hope that we can work together again," he said.

"I'd like that," she said, and meant it. This had been a profitable and pleasurable afternoon.

"Take care."

And with that, Steven turned the bike back on and was off. Keisha stood on the sidewalk, watching him disappear.

Keisha walked into Patra's apartment building and took the elevator to the second floor. When she got off, she saw an older white man walking out of Patra's apartment, with Patra in a white silk robe. The white man walked past Keisha quickly, not looking up as he walked. Patra slipped something into her robe that Keisha couldn't see.

"Hey, girl," Patra greeted her. "How was the shoot?"

Keisha walked into the apartment and threw her duffle bag on the couch.

"It went great," she said. Patra closed the door. "Patra, who was that?"

"He's just a friend of mine. I see him from time to time." Patra looked at Keisha for a second, squinting. "Are we cool?"

Keisha looked back at Patra. "We cool."

Keisha put down her bag and sat down in the chair.

"So you're going to be a *Pimp*ed girl?" Patra said, sitting down in the chair.

"Supposedly. Did you know Sean was trying to screw me out of my money?" Keisha asked. "He told me that I was going to get two-fifty for the shoot."

"How much did you get?"

"Five hundred."

"Five hundred? Fuck, do they need anyone else? Tell Marty that he can slap me on my ass again if they'll give me five hundred for taking some fucking pictures."

"I'll be sure to do that." Keisha laughed. "But it went well. The owner of the magazine was there—Steven Cox. Ever heard of him?"

"Naw. Was he cool?"

"Very. Pretty handsome too. He gave me a ride on his bike. I thought I was going to die."

"You gonna fuck him?" Patra asked.

Keisha leaned back on the couch and threw her feet up. "I don't know yet. I've first got to figure out if it would be business or pleasure. I'd have to be clear on that before I made my move, and I'm not."

"Shit, why not mix them both? Fuck him and then get his money?"

"Nah, if I was going to do that, then I'd start fucking drug dealers, and I did that shit once with Donovan and I ain't going back to that type of drama. Plus, I see what it did to my mother. No, I'm going to figure out first if I want to fuck him. Then I'll figure out if it is business or pleasure."

"You are a smart bitch, I'll give you that," Patra said admiringly. "Okay, handle your business, or pleasure if you choose."

"Right now, I'm about to handle a nap," Keisha said, closing her eyes.

"I'll let you get some sleep," Patra said, getting up from the couch. "Have a good nap."

Steven rode into the parking lot of *Pimp* magazine. He parked his bike and nearly ran up to the office.

"So how does she look?" Steven yelled, throwing his helmet down on the floor.

Jeff had downloaded the photos into the computer while Steven was taking Keisha to her apartment. Now he had them on the computer screen.

"These look fucking great," Steven said, scanning Keisha's photos. "Jeff, you fucking outdid yourself with her shots."

"Hey, I wish I could take credit for them, but it was all her. You saw her. I mean, she did better direction than I could ever take credit for."

"No, I'll take credit for it," Ray said, walking into the room.

Steven kept clicking on photo after photo. "She just eats up the camera. Absolutely eats it up."

He stopped.

"This is what I want to do," he said. "Let's go all-out with her. I want Keisha on the Web site, and I want to put her on the cover. Ray, you done good, my man. Ya done good."

"She looks good on paper, but what about on tape?" Ray asked. "Isn't that going to be the ultimate test?"

Steven stroked his chin again, surveying the photos on the computer.

"I took her home for a reason, y'all," he said. "I know what I'm doing. I wanted to know where she lived and figure out if she wanted to get out of there. I'm betting that she does. And if so, I'm going to make it easy for her to move from Inglewood to Hollywood. Or at least our style of Hollywood."

They all laughed.

"Keisha's going to be a star, but even she doesn't know what I have in store for her," Steven said, leaning back in his chair. "Not one single clue."

He then turned to Marty. "Have you bought all the equipment for *Pimp* Video?"

"I've got the cameras, and I've even set up the locations. All I need is the talent."

"I'm depending on my USC film school grad to film me some great videos," Steven said, patting Jeff on the shoulder. "I want *Pimp* Video to be both classy and gonzo. I want tight pussy shots, cum faces, but I also want my girls to be able to speak well. This ain't some dumb-ass nigga shit you'd find over in South Central. Keisha fits that bill."

"So how do you want to use Keisha?" Jeff asked.

"I'm looking to bring her in slowly, tell her that she's going to be the black Jenna Jameson, and then have her fuck the right guys. She ain't gonna fuck just some Joe Blow niggas from around the way. I want names. And we're going get some big dicks— the biggest in the industry. That's going to be our specialty."

"When do you want to get started?" Marty asked.

"In two weeks. That means I need to convince Keisha soon. But I've got that handled. Just find me some male talent."

"What about Mr. Bigg? We can use him for her virgin filming," Jeff said.

"I was thinking about him, but I don't know. He's getting a bit tired, and plus, he's been in everybody's video. He's on my list, but he's not the first. I'll figure it out."

"Cool. Just let me know," Marty said. "I'll have niggas up the yin-yang wanting to fuck Keisha."

"Just make sure to get the right niggas. That's going to be the key," Steven said, pulling out a cigar. "Jeff, get these photos done, air-brushed—although I don't think she needs much air-brushing—and up to production. We need to get this magazine out and then post the photos on the *Pimp* Web site. Niggas are going to be wild about this shit, and we need to take advantage."

"Will do," Jeff said, getting back to the computer.

Steven looked at Marty. "We need to have a conversation with Sean. I want to make sure that we're clear that Keisha is ours now, and not his. And for that, I need you to contact Rosario de Silva and let her know that I may need her to come with us."

"For Blackie?" Marty asked.

"Yes, for Blackie."

"Done deal."

Chapter 8

*A liberal-arts education is supposed to pro-
vide you with a value system, a standard, a set
of ideas, not a job.*

—Caroline Bird

UCLA had a mandatory counseling meeting for all
incoming freshmen, and today was the day Keisha
had to come to campus. She sat down in the counselor's office and waited with her magazine.

"Keisha Montez? Is Keisha Montez here?"

Keisha got up from her chair and walked into the
counselor's office. The office was nice and neat, not
a paper out of place. Behind the desk was a young
blond girl who looked like she couldn't be that
much older than Keisha herself.

"Hello, Keisha. My name is Britney Kaplan, and
I've been assigned as your counselor before your
freshman orientation." Britney shook Keisha's hand,
and they both sat down.

"Hello," Keisha said.

"So, Keisha, I went over your file, and I am quite
impressed," Britney said, holding a manila folder.
"You ended up with a 3.8 GPA and had a very good

SAT score. We're lucky to have you here at UCLA. Where else did you apply?"

"Actually, I didn't apply anywhere else," Keisha answered. "I always wanted to go to UCLA and so I figured that if it was meant to be, then it was meant to be."

"Wow, that's some type of faith," Britney said, smiling. "Most of our students apply to over ten different schools just to hedge their bets. I rarely have a student—in fact, I can't think of even one student—who's ever just applied to UCLA. So you really knew what you wanted and went for it. Congratulations!"

"Thanks."

Britney put down the manila folder.

"Well, let me go over some of the things that you can expect here at UCLA," she started. "One, we'll be sending you an orientation packet in the mail, which will give you all of the information about campus. Murphy Hall is our administration building, and that's where you'll pick up your financial aid. By the way, I didn't see a completed financial aid packet. Did your parents fill it out?"

"I don't get along with my mother, and my father left years ago," Keisha said, looking Britney directly in the eye. She was not ashamed.

"Hmm, that could present a problem. For some reason, I've been seeing this happen more and more, and it's really a hole in the financial aid process that keeps the student hostage. Are you still living with your mother?"

"No, I moved out a week ago."

"Okay, then we might start trying to make you an independent student," Britney said. She opened a drawer and pulled out a form. "It takes about three years, so it's not going to help you this year, but we can at least get the clock rolling. Go to this Web site"—she handed Keisha a piece of paper—"and fill it out. It'll route you to the financial aid office, and they'll get in contact with you after that. How do you intend to pay for school if you don't have financial aid or help from your mother? Do you have a job?"

"I'll be fine," Keisha said. "I've been saving up money, and I do have a job that should take care of it."

"Are you going to move into the dorms?"

"I think so, but I'm not sure."

"Well, there's another deposit due in about two weeks to set your spot. Look inside the orientation package and you'll see all of the deadlines. Okay, understand that I have to go over the financials before even talking about academics."

"That's fine. I'd like to know if someone could pay for something before I wasted time on them," Keisha said. "But I'll make sure that I have the money when I need it."

"I'm sure you will. Now, let's get to the fun part. What do you want to major in at UCLA?"

"I want to major in women's studies," Keisha said. "I want to learn about myself as a woman, but also fight for women's issues."

"That is a great major!" Britney exclaimed. "Do you want to have a career working with women, such as a counselor? We need to have more women of color working in the field."

"I don't know yet," she responded. "When I was in the tenth grade, a woman came to my school and talked about getting her doctorate. I don't know, but I was thinking that I might want to get a Ph.D. and then teach, but I also would like to write, so I just don't know yet. I think I'll know better once I start taking classes."

"Great! It sounds like you're a young woman who knows what she wants to do in life, which is not typical of the students who walk in here as freshmen. You seem to have a good head on your shoulders."

"Thank you."

"Now, do you have any questions you'd like to ask me?"

"I do, actually," Keisha said. "How many blacks were admitted this year?"

"I think, and don't quote me on it," Britney said, "there are about one hundred blacks in this class. It's hard to know for sure because, under Proposition 209, you're not able to identify people by race unless they're sitting here in front of you. But even then, you're not really sure. Do you mind if I ask you a question?"

"My mother's black and my father was Mexican, to answer your question. I consider myself black."

"I didn't mean any offense," Britney stammered.

"Oh, no offense taken," Keisha said. "I just wanted to see if there was going to be anyone else that looked like me on campus. I'm guessing that I'm going to be swamped a little bit."

"But we try to make sure that all our minority students feel comfortable on campus," Britney said. "We have a community center and support staff, so if you ever feel like you're alone, you have someone to talk to. We do our best, but you know Ward Connerly messed it up for us."

"Yeah, he's not the most popular person for students at Crenshaw High," Keisha said. "You missed out on a lot of future doctors and lawyers because of that man, and unless the two basketball players you took with minimum SAT scores decide that shooting hoops is not their future and something serious is, then my community is going to have just that many fewer educated people."

"You're preaching to the choir, Keisha, you're preaching to the choir," Britney said. "I do my best with the resources I have. But with students like you, hopefully we can build up our minority student population and retention. And that's why I'm here. If you ever need anything, and I do mean anything, don't hesitate to come in."

Britney stood up and shook Keisha's hand.

"Thanks, I appreciate it."

"Again, I want to say welcome to UCLA. I think you are going to do very well here."

"I expect to," Keisha said, walking to the door. "It's my destiny."

As Keisha took a leisurely stroll through the UCLA campus after her meeting with Britney, she began thinking back to an earlier time. She'd come to the campus on a field trip when she was in the sixth grade, and her dream had begun then. As she walked, she remembered her conversation with her first mentor.

"I'm going to go to school here," she'd told her sixth-grade teacher, Mrs. Anderson. Mrs. Anderson had a light in her eye as she looked at young Keisha. Keisha had always been one of her favorite students, and she saw her potential. She'd knelt down to talk to her.

"Keisha, I'm going to hold you to that promise. I want you to go to UCLA because I went here, but in order to do that, you have to do something for me. Can you?"

Keisha nodded her head.

"To go to this school, you have to pay attention to your teachers every day. Can you do that?"

"Yes," she said.

"Then you need to do your homework every day," Mrs. Anderson continued. "Can you do that?"

Keisha nodded.

"After that, some people will tell you that going here is impossible, but I don't want you to believe them. I want you to keep thinking that it is not a privilege to go to UCLA, but your destiny. And that destiny can be fulfilled only if you sacrifice and do whatever it takes to get here. And if you do all of this, Keisha, Mrs. Anderson promises you that you'll be here as a UCLA student."

"Mrs. Anderson, what did you study at UCLA?" Keisha asked.

"Women's studies. I want to make the lives of women—and little girls like you too—better."

"Then that's what I'm going to study here," Keisha said.

Mrs. Anderson gave Keisha a hug, and from that moment, Keisha made it her goal to be a UCLA student, and now she was this close. All she needed was money. But she'd made a promise to Mrs. Anderson to do whatever it took, and that's what she was going to do.

Keisha got back to Patra's apartment and logged on to the Internet. She had to work later on but wanted to at least get started.

"Do you need a ride to the Room?" Patra asked. She was putting her bikinis into the bag and rushing around the apartment. Keisha continued to sit at Patra's computer.

"Yeah, thanks," Keisha said, not looking up. "I'm all ready to go."

"What are you looking at—porn?" Patra asked

jokingly. She walked over behind Keisha. "Why are you looking at the UCLA Web site?"

"Because I'm going to school there in the fall," Keisha said, filling out a form.

Patra's face changed. "You're fucking with me, right?"

"No, I'm not fucking with you. I got accepted into UCLA last month and I'm going to go in the fall. I'm trying to get some financial aid."

"You are going to college?" Patra asked incredulously.

"Yep."

"Then answer this question for me," Patra said, looking down at Keisha. "Why the fuck are you shaking your ass at the Chi Chi Room if you're going to college? Why are you fucking posing for *Pimp* if you're going to college? You don't need that shit."

"And where am I right now?" Keisha asked, looking up. "Where am I now? I'm basically kicked out of my momma's house and sleeping in your house. Do you think working at Wal-Mart is going to get me the money I need to get my own place, pay tuition at UCLA, and still have money for books and food? Stripping gets me cash, more cash than I can get anywhere else. And I actually don't mind doing it that much."

"I don't know about the last part, but that makes sense. Are you going to keep stripping at UCLA?" Patra asked. "I mean, you wouldn't be the first girl to strip through school, but it could get in the way if you ran into some UCLA students."

"Don't know. I'll figure it out later."

"Does Sean know about this?"

"Yeah, he knows a little bit. But he's not taking it seriously. I mean, does he really give a shit about any of us as long as we shake our asses? I ain't tripping off that nigga."

Keisha got her duffle bag and walked to the door.

"All I want are some weekend dates, and then I'll be cool with him. He can do whatever he wants after that. Let's head out."

"I got me a college girl living in my apartment!" Patra said, laughing. "Now let's go shake some ass and make some money off these niggas."

Chapter 9

Never work just for money or for power. They won't save your soul or help you sleep at night.

—Marian Wright Edelman

Steven was sitting on his Hayabusa in the Chi Chi Room parking lot when Rosario da Silva rode up on her black Ducati motorcycle. "Do you expect trouble?" she asked, taking off her helmet.

"Would I bring you here if I didn't?"

"No, I guess you wouldn't."

Rosario was from Brazil, and everything about her was small. She stood a little over five feet, with close-cropped hair and small, delicate features. No one would have guessed that she had killed five men as part of the Brazilian Secret Service. And that was exactly why Steven had her on retainer. She was his protection because no one expected her to be his protection.

"I expect to have a simple conversation about a dancer at the club I'm going to be using. Her name is Keisha, and we're going to discuss Keisha's future at the Chi Chi Room and with *Pimp*. It should go very well because Sean is going to make more money. But just in case, I decided to have you come with me. You know how Blackie can get."

"My friend Blackie." Rosario smiled. "Based on our last meeting, I don't think we'll have any problems with him."

"And that's why I brought you."

They began walking to the club. It was around eleven, and the club was packed. Blackie was at the door, as usual.

"What's up, Steven?" Blackie said, looking at Rosario. "I'm assuming that we're going to have a pleasant conversation, aren't we?" Blackie asked.

"All we want to do is talk to Sean," Steven said. "No more, no less. It's all up to Sean."

"Blackie and I are old friends," Rosario said, smiling. "Aren't we, Blackie?"

Blackie rubbed his nose. There was a black line running from the bridge to his cheek. "We're friends. But how about not breaking my nose again, friend?"

"As long as you listen to me when I tell you to do something, I think we'll be okay."

"Yeah," Blackie said skeptically. "Follow me. Sean's upstairs."

Blackie looked them up and down. "Watch the door," he told a colleague. "Come with me," he instructed Steven and Rosario.

He let them into the club and guided them to the stairs. Patra was dancing onstage, and the men were going wild. She had a look on her face as though she were three thousand miles away.

Blackie led them up the stairs, their feet muffled by the thick purple carpeting. When they walked into Sean's office, he was sitting behind his desk, working on his computer.

Sean finally noticed Blackie, Steven, and Rosario.

"My niggas," Sean said, grinning. Both Steven and Rosario sat down, while Blackie left.

"I'm here to discuss Keisha," Steven said, after giving Sean a handshake.

"Keisha, yeah, she's going to be good. How did the photo shoot go?" Sean said, sitting back in his chair. He rocked back and forth.

"It went well," Steven said. He took out a cigarette from his pocket and lit it. "Although after I talked to Keisha, we both realized that we had a certain difference of opinion. And funny that it involved you."

"Difference of opinion? What do you mean?" Even in his chair, Sean twitched nervously.

"Well, Keisha and I started talking, and she told me," Steven said, puffing on his cigarette, "that you told her she was only getting two hundred and fifty dollars for the shoot. Now I know I told Marty that she was getting five hundred, and he swore he told you that she was getting five hundred. So now I want to know whether or not it was a simple misunderstanding, or if you were trying to cheat Keisha. Because if you were trying to cheat Keisha, I consider that an attempt to cheat me. And if you were trying to cheat me, then that would make for bad business between us in the future. Do I make myself clear?"

Sean put a finger in his ear and began wringing it furiously.

"Look, I think I just must have forgotten the amount when I talked to Keisha. Marty is probably right. So did you already pay Keisha her money?"

"Of course I did. I always pay my girls immediately. And here's"—Steven put a hundred dollar bill on Sean's desk—"your referral fee."

Sean picked up the hundred dollar bill and put it into his wallet. "You didn't come here to give me this hundred dollars," he said. "And you certainly didn't bring Rosario here because you thought I might be cheating Keisha. What's this really all about?"

Steven smiled. "This is about Keisha, and her future."

Sean leaned back in his chair, wondering what Steven was up to. "Yeah, Keisha has a good future here. I think we're going to do some good things." Sean started looking at his computer and mindlessly typed something. He turned the computer toward Steven.

"See," Sean continued. "I'm about to add some more days for her."

"That's good. That's good," Steven said. "But that's not enough. I want Keisha headlining here. I want you to make sure she's working the Friday and Saturday shift, and I want her keeping all of her money, with no kickbacks to the club. She needs to be the Chi Chi Room's feature dancer."

"I don't understand," Sean said, shifting in his chair. "Why do I have to do any of that?"

"Because for all intents and purposes, Keisha is now *Pimp* property," Steven said. "Plain and simple, I want the men in here to want her. I want them to want to see more of her. Build a clientele. And then I'm going to do what I need to do to get them more of her. In the meantime, I'll consider it a personal favor that won't be forgotten."

Sean stared at Steven, trying to take the measure of him. It pissed him off that some former lawyer could walk in his club, a club he'd built from his father's work, and demand that his girls do this or that. But still, he wanted to keep a relationship with Steven, and he wasn't about to fuck that up because of one trick at his club. If Steven wanted Keisha for some shit, then Steven could have her. Plus, Sean knew that Steven still held some incriminating evidence that could find Sean spending five-to-ten as a guest of the California prison system. Better to give up a trick than to tempt fate. Plus, bringing Rosario meant that Steven wasn't going to take no for an answer anyway.

"Done. But I'll have to make some changes around here, and they might not go over well with some of the girls."

"That sounds like your problem, not mine."

"Right." Sean picked up his cell phone and pressed a button. "Blackie, send Debra up."

"She's about to go onstage," Blackie said. "Do you still want to see her?"

"Bring her ass up."

After about a minute, Debra, wearing her bikini for the stage, walked into Sean's office.

"What the fuck, Sean? I'm about to go onstage and I'm missing out on money," she yelled.

"Shut your ass up, and stop bitching," Sean said. "I'm making some changes. You're off weekends, and you'll be taking Keisha's schedule."

"Keisha's schedule?" Debra said incredulously. "What the fuck am I getting Keisha's schedule for? She just got here. I've been working here for years, even when your dad was running the club. I earned my spot here."

"I don't give a shit how long you've been working here, you're getting fucking old and now you're going to have your nights taken," Sean said belligerently.

"That's some bullshit, Sean, and you know it!" Debra shouted. "I earned my Fridays and Saturdays, and fuck it if I'm going to give them up. Fuck that shit, I'll go to another club!"

"Don't make checks you can't cash, Debra."

"Fuck you, Sean!"

"I see you're still running your business the same way," Steven said, smiling. "If you need to talk privately to Debra, we'll go out into the hall."

"No need to leave, because I'm out of here," Debra said, walking past Sean. Before she walked down the stairs, she turned. "Fuck you, Sean, and you're gonna pay for this shit. You fucked with the wrong bitch."

She stomped down the stairs, and Sean sat back in his chair.

"See," Sean said, "I control my hoes. They do what I want them to do, even if they don't like it. But that's bitches, you know. They need guiding and I'm the one to do it."

"Yeah, you control your bitches," Steven said ironically. "That you do." He and Rosario stood up to leave. They walked to the hallway, then Steven turned back. "One other thing, Sean—as I said earlier there will be no more kickbacks from Keisha. Make money with her at the bar and at the door for as long as you can, but don't look for kickbacks. For the other girls, we can talk. Understood?"

"Yeah, yeah, I understand," Sean said.

"Good doing business with you."

Steven and Rosario made their way down the stairs, where they almost bumped into Keisha, who was going into the dressing room.

"Hello, Keisha," Steven said.

"Hello, Steven," Keisha said, surprised. "What the hell are you doing down here?"

"Fixing a problem," Steven said, smiling. "By the way, I'm going to be calling you very soon. I have a proposition for you that could possibly make you a lot of money."

"If it's illegal, I'm not interested," she said.

"I'm a lawyer, Keisha. I may straddle, dance around, or hover around things illegal, but I never cross the line. It's legal. It's just whether or not you are willing to take a risk."

Keisha looked Steven directly in his eye as she tried to figure out what he was up to. And Steven never flinched.

"I'll wait for that call," she said, walking to the dressing room.

"You won't have long to wait. Check you later."

Keisha walked into the dressing room, where she saw Patra putting on her clothes. Patra had finished her sets early and now was going back home.

"Girl, Debra is pissed off at you," Patra said, putting on her top.

"She's pissed off all the time, so what's new? But what is it this time?"

"She said that you are taking her slots on the weekend."

Keisha's mouth opened wide. "I didn't take her spot. Who told her that shit?"

"I don't know, but Sean told her a few minutes ago that you were replacing her and that she was going to have to take your spot. You sure you didn't ask Sean for that weekend shit?"

Keisha put down her duffle bag. "Yeah, I asked him for the weekend, but I didn't tell him that—"

Right then, Debra came into the dressing room, sweating from dancing onstage. When she saw Keisha, everyone in the room froze.

"Well, if it isn't the bitch that stole my days," she said icily.

"Look, I don't know what you're talking about," Keisha said, settling in front of the mirror. She started taking off her clothes. "I told Sean that I wanted to work weekends, but I didn't say shit about taking you off weekends. So don't be going around saying that I took you off. That was his shit."

"That's why I hate working with bitches," Debra said, her eyes boring through both Patra and Keisha. "You can't trust 'em, and I don't trust your ass. I worked my ass off to get those weekend days, and now some new bitch is going to come in and take them away from me? Fuck that. I'll leave first."

"Debra, you can believe what the fuck you want to believe, but I don't give a fuck. I told you that I didn't have shit to do with it."

"Watch her," Debra said, looking at Patra. "She's in your apartment, and soon she'll have your man."

Keisha stood up and walked over to Debra. "Look, bitch, I ain't done shit to you. But when you start telling other people that I'm going to do something to them, then you've crossed the line. If you don't have something good to say about me, then I suggest you keep my name out of your damn mouth. Do I make myself clear?"

"We'll see, Keisha, we'll see. Once you stab someone in the back, you tend to like doing it over and over and over."

"Seems like you know that from personal experience."

They stared at each other, like hens fighting over a rooster.

"Break this shit up," Patra said, now fully dressed. "There's nothing I hate more than two women fighting over stupid shit. Keisha, you get ready to get onstage, and Debra, you get your ass out of here."

Keisha walked back over to the makeup table, and Debra walked over to the closet and grabbed her long coat. She slipped into it and tied it. She then grabbed her duffle bag and stormed out of the room.

"Do you want me to stay during your shift?" Patra said. "I can if you want."

"Nah, I'm cool. I'll see you at the apartment later."

"All right, have a good night."

"Thanks, Patra."

Patra left and Keisha sat by herself, trying to figure out what was happening. She was happy to get the weekends, but how had it happened? She didn't have to wait long to find out.

"Why aren't you out onstage?" Sean yelled, poking his head through the dressing room door. "You were supposed to be ready to go on two minutes ago."

"Why did you tell Debra that I took her days?" Keisha asked.

" 'Cause you did. You wanted them and now you've got them," Sean answered. "So what are you bitching for? Now get out there and shake your ass."

Keisha looked at Sean and made her way to the stage.

Chapter 10

The concept of romantic love affords a means of emotional manipulation, which the male is free to exploit, since love is the only circumstance in which the female is (ideologically) pardoned for sexual activity.

—Kate Millet

Weeks had passed since Debra and Keisha had had their confrontation, and at this point, Keisha didn't care. She was making money hand over fist working weekends as a feature dancer, and that was going to help her pay for UCLA and get out of Patra's apartment.

The month was now up, but Patra realized that she liked Keisha being around.

"Look, you can stay in the apartment as long as you want," Patra told her. "I don't know why, but I like having your ashy ass around."

And something else had happened. The pervert pit was starting to request her. Before, she'd simply been another dancer. Now she was a star attraction. And now that her issue of *Pimp* was out and she had made the cover, things were looking up.

"Girl, I didn't know you were going to be on the cover," Patra said, thumbing through the magazine. "And damn, you did show it all."

"Well, fuck, if I'm going to do it, I might as well go all the way," Keisha said, laughing.

"That you did," Patra said, still looking at the magazine. "Do you know how the issue is selling?"

"I got a message from Steven, asking me to call him today. Maybe I can find out then, but I'm not sweating it. I got paid, and that's all I care about."

"Well, let me know if they have five hundred for me, because I have no problem posing in the magazine. It beats shaking my ass."

Keisha looked at Patra for a second. She'd told her that she would not ask questions when she moved in, but one thing was bothering her, and she didn't know how to broach the subject without just being real with Patra.

"Patra, will you get mad if I ask you a question?" Keisha asked.

"Naw, I won't get mad," Patra said, putting down the magazine. "At least I don't think so. What's up?"

"Are you fucking for money?"

Patra sat down on the couch and stared at Keisha.

"Are you trying to judge me? I told you when you got here that I didn't want you to judge me."

"I'm not trying to judge you," Keisha responded. "I just wanted to know."

"Keisha, we all fuck for money," Patra said, looking out the window. "It's just that my fucking is a little bit more direct. I fuck, I get the money. It's pretty simple. Does that make you uncomfortable?"

"Not unless they try to get at me," Keisha said. "This is your life and we all do what we have to do."

"See, you've got to understand that you have something else you can do besides shakin' your ass, or taking naked pictures," Patra said, putting down the magazine. "You're going to move out of here, start at UCLA, and make a life for yourself. I think I did my homework twice in high school. I want the same thing you want, but now I'm paying the price. So yeah, I fuck these men and then take their money. Better fuck them than to have them fuck me."

"I'm sorry I asked," Keisha said. "I didn't mean anything by it."

"Don't be sorry, just be grateful you have options."

"You would be surprised at how much we're alike, Patra," Keisha said wistfully. "Opportunities are just figments of our imagination until they're realized. And both of ours aren't realized, so we do what we have to do."

"That's some deep shit, Keisha," Patra said, smiling. "What do you want to study at UCLA?"

"Women's studies. I want to get bitches like us out of this situation. Fuck depending on men."

"Good luck, girl, because right now, it seems like the men are the ones with the cash, and the women dance for them."

Keisha's cell phone rang. It was Steven.

"Keisha, how are you? Did you get the magazine I sent?" Steven asked.

"Yes, I got it. I didn't know that I'd be on the cover."

"Well, we always put the woman who we think is the most beautiful on the cover, and you are definitely the most beautiful."

The flattery, despite Keisha's intuition, was getting to her. She liked hearing Steven's compliments, and it felt like she was getting support from someone who cared for her.

"I know I'm not the most beautiful woman in *Pimp,* but thank you."

"You underestimate yourself," Steven said. "Your issue is selling so well that we'd like to have you come back in for another shoot. This time, we'd like to pay you one thousand dollars for the shoot."

"One thousand dollars?" Keisha repeated. "You want to pay me one thousand dollars to do another shoot?"

"You heard right. But there's one stipulation," Steven said.

"What's that?"

"You've got to go to dinner with me."

Keisha paused. She knew Steven was trying to make his move, and she hadn't decided if she was going to fuck him yet. But she could use a nice dinner.

"Are you talking about some Jack in the Box shit? 'Cause I can do that myself," Keisha said.

"Keisha, now do you think the publisher of a major magazine would take you to some shit like Jack in the Box? I mean, El Pollo Loco, I could see, but some Jack in the Box is out of the question."

Keisha giggled. "Okay, so we're not going to Jack in the Box. Where are we going?"

"Don't worry about it. Just wear something nice and I'll take care of everything."

"Cool. When are we going to dinner?"

"Tomorrow."

"But tomorrow is Saturday and I work tomorrow night. Sean's not going to—"

"Don't worry about it. I'll take care of Sean. Just be ready at eight."

"Okay, I'll be ready."

Keisha hung up the phone. "So he wants to take me out to dinner."

"Darling, that dinner ain't gonna be free," Patra said, walking toward her room. "Remember what I said about fucking? Just remember to fuck *him* and don't let him fuck *you*."

"You don't have to worry about that," Keisha said, plopping down on the couch. "If I wanted to let somebody fuck me, I wouldn't be living in your apartment. There's no one, and I mean no one, that I care about more than me. I make my own decisions, and when folks think they're playing me, I'm playing them."

"My girl," Patra said. She closed her door, and Keisha turned on the television.

For some reason, Keisha was nervous getting ready for Steven, and she didn't know why. Maybe it was because she hadn't been out on a real date since breaking up with her old boyfriend Donovan, and even then, his cheap ass had only taken her to Fatburger. But this was a real date, and she was nervous.

"What time is he supposed to get here?" Patra asked. She was taking Keisha's spot for the night and was getting dressed to go to the Chi Chi Room.

"Eight." Keisha had decided to wear a short black skirt with a black top. The skirt was short-short, and the top was small-small, but still presentable. She didn't know where they were going, but she knew she looked good. She just hoped that they weren't riding on his bike.

The apartment door buzzer startled them both. "Do you want me to leave before he comes up?" Patra asked.

"Nah, you can stay," Keisha said, walking to the intercom. "Who is it?"

"It's Steven."

"Okay, I'll buzz you up." Keisha pressed a button and the downstairs door released. Meanwhile, Patra walked into her room and then came back into the living room with a black bag.

"Here, take this," she said, handing the bag to Keisha. "It goes well with your outfit."

Keisha was touched. She'd grown close to Patra over the past few months, and this was one of those moments that told her they were going to be friends for a long time.

There was a knock on the door, and Keisha walked to it. She straightened herself first and then looked through the peephole. It was Steven, and he was carrying flowers.

"Hello, Steven," Keisha said as she opened the door.

Steven smiled.

"Hello, Keisha. You look beautiful. These are for you," he said, handing her the flowers and walking into the room.

"Thanks," Keisha said. She turned to Patra. "Steven, this is my roommate, Patra."

"Hello, Patra," Steven said. "You dance at the Chi Chi Room too, right?"

"Yeah, I do. And now I've got to get my ass down there," she said, grabbing her bag to leave.

"Oh, before you go," Keisha added, "I wanted to tell Steven that you were interested in posing for *Pimp*."

"You are?" Steven asked.

"Yeah, for five hundred dollars, I could definitely do it."

"All right, then come down to the photo shoot when Keisha comes in. We'll hook you up."

Patra smiled. "Cool. I'll be there. Thanks."

"No problem."

Patra left, giving Keisha a final sly grin.

"Just give me a second and I'll be ready to go," Keisha said, walking to the bathroom.

"Take your time," he said from the living room. He looked around the living room, trying to get a fix on who Keisha was. But all he saw was Patra's stuff. He wasn't getting anything about Keisha. She was still a blank slate. "We've got plenty of time."

"We're not going on your bike, are we?" Keisha called out.

"No, I brought my car, so you're good."

Keisha walked out of the bathroom and back into the living room. She was ready to go.

"Good, because I wasn't about to get on the back of that thing. Let's head out."

"After you," Steven said, opening the door.

As they stood in the elevator, Keisha began wondering what Steven was up to. Sure, he wanted to fuck her, but that was what every date was about. But what else? Why was he taking a stripper out to a nice dinner when he probably could have his fill of whomever he wanted?

"We're over to the left," he said as they entered the parking lot. "I have the yellow car." The yellow car was a yellow Ferrari.

Keisha was beginning to like hanging with Steven. *The brother's got style,* she thought. *I'll give him that.*

With a click from his keypad, the door automatically opened and Keisha slid in. Steven closed her door with a loud thump, walked around the back of the car, opened the door, and took his seat. The seats were made of soft, butternut-colored leather, and the smell was exquisite. Steven turned the key to the ignition, and the Ferrari roared to life. And when he pulled out of the parking lot, Keisha found herself plastered to the seat. The speed of the car was unimaginable. She'd never gone so fast in a car.

"How do you get a car like this?" Keisha shouted over the engine. Steven was roaring through traffic like a madman.

"By working hard and hustling, baby," he said, keeping his eyes on the road. "I'm a hustler like no one else. I expect to win in everything I do and I make sure I win by hustling. And when you do that, you get cars like this."

They turned on the Marina Freeway, and for some reason, the traffic was light. Steven looked at Keisha. "Hold on. I'm about to really go fast!" And with that, Steven pressed the accelerator to the floor.

"Do you feel that?" Steven yelled, as the speedometer approached one hundred miles per hour.

"Yes!"

"There's no substitute for speed, baby!"

The speedometer moved from one hundred miles per hour to 110 and then 120. Finally Steven started braking, and Keisha began to relax.

"I hope I didn't scare you," he said with a smile. "But I like going fast."

"You didn't scare me, not one bit," she said, pulling down the visor to check her makeup. "And if you like going fast, then I like going faster."

"I knew I liked you," Steven said, smiling. He pulled off the freeway and then pulled into a mall parking lot.

"Do you like Aunt Kizzy's?" he asked.

"I expect I will love it."

"Good, because that's where we're going."

Chapter 11

All men are tempted. There is no man that lives that can't be broken down, provided it is the right temptation, put in the right spot.
                    —Henry Ward Beecher

Aunt Kizzy's was the premier black restaurant in Los Angeles. As they sat down, Keisha licked her lips in anticipation of the meal.

"So tell me something about yourself, Keisha," Steven said as he put his napkin on his lap. "The only thing I know about you is that you dance at the Chi Chi Room, take great pictures for my magazine, and look stunning in a black skirt. But I can look in your eyes and tell that there's more to you than that."

Keisha leaned back in her seat and looked at Steven. "And if I had to analyze you, I'd say that you're a guy who likes fast money, fast cars, and fast women. As you said in the car, you're someone who likes to win, so you don't hang around losers. Am I right, or is there something more that I should know about?"

"Touché," Steven said, smiling. "I guess I haven't been as forthcoming as I could be. But isn't that what first dates are all about?"

"So that's what this is all about? We're on a date?" Keisha asked.

"What else would we call it? You're a woman, and I'm a man. We're about to eat dinner. I call that a date."

"Sounds good to me," she said. The waiter took their orders, and Keisha smiled.

"You start," Keisha said.

"Start what?"

"Start telling me about yourself. Then I'll go."

Steven took a sip from his drink. "Okay, here goes. I used to be a lawyer at a firm called Ketchings and Martin. Did a hella boring shit like litigate personal injury lawsuits against big corporations. I was making okay money, but I wanted something more. Then I got into a fight with this other lawyer at the firm, so they fired me. I found myself blackballed by law firms throughout L.A. when I tried to find another job. That was cool, but all of a sudden I needed some loot. So I'm looking at various investments and I found out that *Pimp* magazine was up for sale. I took a look at the books and decided to buy it. The rest is history."

"Are you stopping with *Pimp,* or are you going to do more?" Keisha asked.

"Oh, I've got plans. Lots of plans. And some of those plans may have you in mind."

"If you pay well, I may be down for it."

The waiter brought their dinner. "So now it's your turn," Steven said, picking up his fork.

"Okay," Keisha said. "I was born and raised here in Los Angeles. I have a brother and a mother I don't like and don't see, and a father that cut out without a word. I dance at the Chi Chi Room to make money. I like money and I need money. And I got into UCLA."

Steven stopped eating. "You got admitted into UCLA?"

"Surprised?"

"No, I wouldn't say surprised, but I guess I'm more surprised that you're dancing."

"You'd be surprised at how many girls dance at night and then go to Cal State Northridge or USC during the day. Where else can you make the money we make—working as a cashier at Wal-Mart?"

"You've got a point," Steven said, eating his chicken.

"So we've got the preliminaries done. Why did you decide to bring me here?" Keisha asked, looking directly at Steven.

"I just want to have a nice meal with a beautiful woman. Why do I have to have an ulter"—He stopped and put down his fork. "Okay, my grandfather always said that you can't bullshit a bullshitter, so I won't try."

"Good, because I was going to call you on it."

"I'm a businessman, and like I said, I have big things planned for *Pimp*. And you are in those plans," Steven said, wiping his mouth with his napkin.

"What do you mean?"

"I'm willing to make an investment in you. In fact, I already have."

"Pardon me?" Keisha asked.

"You've been working weekends lately, haven't you?"

"Yeah, so what?"

"How do you think you got those weekends?"

Keisha paused from chewing her food. "I thought Sean made the decision to do that? I mean, I'd asked him to—"

"Sean did what I told him," Steven said. "He couldn't give a shit about who works on weekends

and who doesn't. He looks at you girls as interchange-
able. I don't think he really even knows your names."

Steven went back to eating.

"So I'll bite. Why did you get me changed from
weekdays to weekends in the first place?" Keisha
asked. "And by the way, that caused a whole bunch
of shit with Debra because I took her days."

"Debra was getting old and she knew the writing
was on the wall anyway. The men who come to see
her don't give a shit if she's dancing on Tuesday or
Saturday. They ain't got shit to do anyway. But you,
you're a star. And as a star, you need to be profiled."

"But you still haven't told me why you give a shit,"
Keisha said, finishing her meal. "What does me
shaking my ass on a Saturday have to do with you?"

Steven scrunched his face, like he was trying to
figure out whether or not he should come clean right
at that moment.

"I told you that I'm expanding *Pimp,* right?"

"Yeah."

"Well, we are about to launch *Pimp* adult videos,
and I see you as being our star, our black Jenna
Jameson, so to speak. If you let me, I can make you
more money than you've ever thought about making. Fuck UCLA. You don't need that shit."

Keisha was truly taken aback. Of all of the things
he could have said, she wouldn't have guessed offer-
ing her porn.

"What makes you think that I want to be a porn
star in the first place?" Keisha asked, slightly angry. "I
dance, but that doesn't mean that I want to get fucked
by some muthafuckas I don't know."

"I don't know, but that's why I'm here to ask. If I
don't ask, then I won't know. Do you have anything
against it?"

"Hey, whatever floats people's boats. It's just not for me."

Steven took another sip of his drink.

"What if I paid you five thousand dollars per movie?" he asked.

Where Keisha had been taken aback before, she was simply stunned now.

"You would pay me five thousand dollars to fuck on tape?"

"DVD," Steven said. "We use DVD now. And yes, I would pay that much per movie."

Keisha stopped for a second. Five thousand dollars, she thought, was a lot of money. And it would basically change her life.

"Why me, and why are you going to pay me that much? What makes me so special?"

"It's because I think you have a look that other men will want."

"Do you want it?"

Steven smiled. "That's why I know other men will want you. I told Sean to put you on weekends because I wanted to get some feedback. Did the regulars want to see you, or did they not give a shit? Well, they give a shit. Sean says that sales are up 35 percent when you are onstage, and I know he wouldn't bullshit me. So if they are coming to see you on the dance floor, I figure that they'll buy a video."

"But what made you think I'd fuck somebody for money? I'm not a ho."

"I never said you were," Steven said, finishing his food. "But you are a businesswoman, and I could see that. So I present this simply as a business transaction. I'm pretty sure that you want to get out of Patra's apartment and have enough money to go to school.

"What I suggest," Steven continued, putting down

his napkin, "is that you realize that you'll fuck men in this life without getting paid, so you might as well get paid."

"It seems like I've heard that before," Keisha said. "Look, I'm going to think about it. As funny as it may seem, I don't particularly want to have people at UCLA thinking that I'm some ho. Right now, you have to walk into the Chi Chi Room to see me, and not that many folks are going to be able to point me out during the daytime. This issue of *Pimp*? It's one issue and then thrown away. But muthafuckas tend to keep their porn. And I don't know if I want to get my degree and then not get a job because of some fucking I did years before. So I'll think about it."

"You do that," Steven said. "But realize that I'm on a schedule. And if you don't want to do it, then I'm going to have to find someone else. But someone is going to get five thousand dollars. I just think that someone should be you."

"So this meal was all about me fucking someone for cash? What about you?" she asked.

"What do you mean, what about me?"

"Don't you want to fuck me?"

"Oh, that 'what,'" Steven chuckled. "Oh, yes, I want to fuck you. But in my world, business comes first. After that comes pleasure."

"Well, you're not going to fuck me tonight. I may strip, but I'm not like that."

"I figured as much, so I wasn't going to ask," Steven said, rising from the table. "But there's one thing that you'll soon learn about me. I'm a very patient man. So I don't mind waiting, especially for you."

Keisha smiled. "Good, because you may be waiting for quite a long time."

Chapter 12

The doors we open and close each day decide the lives we live.
                                    —Flora Whittemore

"How did you find me?" Keisha asked Donovan. It was Sunday morning and she'd gone to the Vons supermarket on Manchester Boulevard for some fruit, when she'd run right into Donovan. There he was, standing in the middle of the vegetable aisle, like he was waiting for her to show up. "I mean, what the hell are you doing here? You never come to this goddamn store."

"Whoa, slow your roll," Donovan said. Keisha's ex-boyfriend was a tall, light-skinned brother with wavy hair and green eyes. Her girlfriends used to rave over his eyes, but she always thought they looked sort of spooky. The hair was wavy because he constantly combed it, as he was doing right now. He never, ever tired of combing his hair. She'd been attracted to him because he was a smooth talker and he somehow always made her smile. Today he was dressed in a blue suit and tie, with light brown shoes. They'd first gotten together when she was a freshman in high school, and for four years, she'd put up with his shit. Now, she thought she'd made a clean break.

"I didn't come here because of you, and I think it would be damn dumb of me to stake out some random-ass supermarket in hopes of seeing you. That wasn't gonna happen. So let's just treat this as two old friends running into each other. How have you been?"

Keisha calmed down. She still liked Donovan, but she had no desire to get back with him, after what he'd done.

"I'm fine. How've you been?"

"You know, the same as always. I talked to your brother and he told me what happened. That was pretty fucked-up. He said that your mother goes around the house cursing."

"Well, I don't think about it or worry about it," she said, getting some grapes from the produce section. "I did what I had to do, and now I'm fine."

"Where you staying?"

"I like to keep that to myself," Keisha responded, continuing to walk through the store.

"What, you don't trust me?" Donovan asked, picking a bunch of grapes and eating them. Keisha stopped her shopping early because she didn't want to have a long discussion with Donovan. It was over, and she wanted to make sure it was over.

"It's not that at all," she said, walking to the check-out line. "It's just that I'm living with someone right now, and I don't need to bring all that drama to her house, because I know you can't keep a secret, and then my momma will be pounding on my door. I don't need that shit at all."

"I feel you. I feel you. Your momma has always been a loose cannon," Donovan said, picking from Keisha's grapes and putting another in his mouth. "So you're not going to tell me where you live, what you've been doing, or where you're going. So I'm just going to assume you're still shakin' your ass at the club."

The cashier looked up when Donovan talked about "shakin' ass" and in one of her rare times, it embarrassed Keisha. She quickly paid for her groceries and started walking out the supermarket door. Suddenly she stopped.

"Donovan, I don't want to get into it. I've moved on and for me to keep moving on, I need you to let go and do the same."

"Baby, I am over you," Donovan responded. "I'm about to head over to the Forum, and that's the only reason I'm in this store in the first place. The only reason I even stopped was to say hello."

Keisha looked into Donovan's face, and she noticed that there'd been a change somehow. She couldn't pinpoint it, but it wasn't the look of the in-and-out-of-jail drug-dealer boyfriend she used to have. He looked somehow serene.

"Can I offer you a ride?" he asked, as they stood in the parking lot. "Church doesn't begin for about an hour, and I think I can still get a seat—"

"Wait a second," Keisha said. "Church? You are going to church? When in the hell did you start going to church?"

"I started going about two months ago," he said. "I got tired of going back and forth to jail, and as you know, I was up to no good. So I found God."

Keisha rested her arms on the shopping cart and stared at Donovan. "Okay, what's your angle, Donovan? Who are you trying to scam now? What, you're going to church so you can sell dime bags to old ladies?"

"Naw, Keisha, I'm done with that. I've turned my

life over to the Lord. I'm not about that anymore. I've turned my back on evil."

"I know you, Donovan, and you've never turned your back on anything," Keisha said skeptically. "Sell that shit to someone else, and somewhere else, because I'm not buying it."

"That's your choice," he responded, straightening his tie. "But I know who I am and what I've done. But let me ask you a question. Do you know who you are, and what you've done?"

Keisha stood up straight and moved to go. "Good-bye, Donovan. Have a great time at church."

She began walking away from him, and he just stood there. "You still have time to come to the Lord," he yelled after her.

Keisha didn't look back as she walked out of the supermarket parking lot. *He's full of something,* Keisha thought skeptically, *but it isn't the Lord.*

As Keisha walked into Patra's apartment with her groceries, a small black man came walking out of Patra's bedroom. He was nervously fiddling with his shirt and appeared spooked when he saw Keisha. Patra, on the other hand, was as cool as could be.

"So, are we on the same time next month?" she asked the man as he made his way to the door. Keisha kept on going to the kitchen, trying to make herself as invisible as possible.

"Yeah, I'll be here. It's good to see you again, Patra," he said. Patra opened the door.

"See you, sweetheart."

The man walked out and Patra closed the door.

"What did you get from the grocery? I'm hungry," she exclaimed.

Keisha pulled out a bag of grapes and handed them to Patra, who then started picking them one by one and popping them in her mouth. She sat on a bar stool as Keisha kept putting groceries up.

"Do you mind if I ask you a question?" Keisha asked.

Patra leaned back and stared at Keisha. "Not another one of your damn questions again."

"I'm just curious," Keisha said, picking a grape and tossing it into her mouth.

"Shoot, then," Patra replied.

"Do you enjoy sex with them? I mean, does it feel like a job, or do you enjoy it?"

Patra kept munching on her grapes. "It all depends. I love sex, and if the guy is cute, then yeah, I can get into it more. If the guy's not cute, then I pretend that he is cute. But that's no different than meeting some guy at the club."

"But do you feel any pleasure?"

"Of course. If the guy has it going on, then of course your body reacts. That's just natural. I can definitely orgasm with these guys. But as far as emotion, there's not a chance. I don't want anything to do with my clients after they're done. They could fucking walk out of here and get run over by a truck for all I care."

Patra got up from her stool and slinked toward the living room. "But you know what's the trippy thing about escorting? After we're done, I can see in the eyes of the guys that they're really hoping for some type of connection. I think they actually come here because of that hope and not because of the sex. But that's not my problem. If they want a connection, they should get a shrink. Did you get some coffee?"

"Yeah," Keisha said, pulling the coffee out of the

cabinet. She opened it, scooped out a mound of coffee, and put it in a filter. She filled the glass pot with water, added it to the coffeemaker, and turned it on. She then walked back into the living room.

"I didn't get a chance to tell you about my date with Steven," Keisha said, sitting next to Patra. Patra took out a cigarette, handed one to Keisha, and then lit both. "So?" Patra asked. "What happened?"

Keisha took a drag from her cigarette. "The date wasn't about getting in my pants. No, check that. It was about getting into my pants, but not how I expected."

"What do you mean?"

"You know who set up my weekends?"

"Sean, right?"

"Nope, it was Steven."

Patra walked into the kitchen and poured two cups of coffee. "Why the hell did he care if you got weekends?"

"It was a setup," Keisha said, taking the coffee from Patra. "A setup for the dinner. Steven asked me if I wanted to do porn."

"Hmm," Patra said, sipping her coffee. "The natural progression for a stripper—or so people think. What did you tell him?"

"I told him that I'd think about it," Keisha said. "But do you know how much he offered?"

"What?"

"Five fucking thousand dollars."

Patra damn near spilled her coffee. "What the fuck do you mean, 'think about it'? He's going to give you five thousand dollars to fuck on film, and you're not going to take it?"

"It's deeper than that," Keisha said, putting down her coffee cup. "Look, I got into stripping to make some extra money, but I ain't a part of the whole fucking industry. I don't have a problem with someone else fucking on camera—hey, whatever floats your boat—but I don't know if I want DVDs of me distributed to fools for years and years. I have some dreams, and that shit could really derail those dreams."

"When you go to UCLA, what if some kid in your English class goes to the Chi Chi Room and sees you onstage? Wouldn't that derail your dreams?" Patra asked.

"That would be one kid on one night, and not thousands of videos for decades. I don't know if I want to go there. But the money is tempting."

"Look, this guy obviously thinks you can drive sales," Patra said. "He paid you five hundred bills to pose, and now he's willing to give you ten times that to fuck. Why not just do it once, get paid, and then roll out?"

Patra took the two coffee mugs to the kitchen. As she put them in the sink, she turned to the living room.

"Do you know how much I get to fuck these men?" she asked Keisha.

"No."

"Two hundred dollars. Two hundred muthafuckin' dollars per fuck. So when you come in here and say that you have an opportunity to make, in one day, money that would take me all month, then I say take it. And if you don't want it, I'll take it."

"Well, I did say that I'd think about it. Maybe I can wear a mask."

"Yeah, right," Patra said, smiling. "Those videos do well. Girl, if you do it, you're going to have to do it all the way. My suggestion is to get the money and then roll out. Plus, you need to get out of my house anyway."

Patra kept smiling as she said it, but Keisha knew there was a bit of truth in her words. It had been two months since she'd moved into Patra's apartment, and things were getting uncomfortable. Nothing had changed, but Keisha could tell that Patra was feeling squeezed, and her privacy was compromised. Keisha needed money for an apartment, and money to register at UCLA. School began next week, and she was still short. The five thousand could get her into the apartment, and pay some of her school fees.

"I'm going to start looking for an apartment tomorrow," Keisha responded. She wished she had a room to go to, but her room was the living room.

"Look, I love you, girl, and you know that. But I think it's time. I need my space again."

"No problem," Keisha said.

"I thought you'd understand," Patra said, walking toward her room.

Between the UCLA deadlines and Patra, Keisha knew that she was going to have to make a decision. Whether it was a good decision was up in the air.

Chapter 13

The whole purpose of education is to turn mirrors into windows.

—Sydney J. Harris

It was Saturday morning, and a group of about three hundred incoming freshmen and their parents stared wide-eyed at Belinda Enfield, a heavyset white woman with an easy laugh and a bright smile. The crowd was mostly white or Asian, and Keisha saw very few people who looked like her. She'd read in the *Los Angeles Times* that only two hundred black students had been admitted.

"Welcome to the UCLA orientation. My name is Belinda Enfield, and I will be conducting this session. I want you to have a great time, and feel free to ask any questions you may have. School begins on Monday, so we'd sort of like you to know where to go when you get here."

Keisha looked around, scanning the campus.

"I've been a counselor at UCLA for the past twenty years, so you can't stump me or ask me a dumb question," Belinda continued. "Well, you can ask a dumb question, but I won't laugh until your back is turned."

The group laughed. Keisha stood to the side, listening to Belinda talk about the deadlines that were approaching for the coming quarter, and she wished she had a parent to handle things for her.

"One of the most important things you must remember is that if you fail to pay your registration by next Monday, you will be dropped from your classes," Belinda said. "There are no exceptions. Now that you understand that, let's take our tour of the campus."

Like obedient little ants, the group followed Belinda as she walked around the campus and talked about the various buildings and their functions.

"This is Murphy Hall, and this is where all students have to go to pay for their registration, check financial aid, get academic counseling, pretty much everything. I would suggest that once you come on campus, you walk through Murphy and get used to where everything is. Signs are everywhere, and you should be able to find everything you want quite easily."

The UCLA campus was beautiful, with green hills and old brick buildings presenting an idyllic setting for learning. Summer school was still in session, so there were students walking around, but the main body of students wouldn't arrive until next week, when school officially started.

"Does anyone have any questions so far?" Belinda asked.

"I have one," Keisha said, raising her voice. Where all of the other students could rely on their parents to work things out, Keisha had to be aggressive. "I would like to get a mentor during my time at UCLA. Whom would I talk to about getting one?"

"That," Belinda said, "is a great question. Do you know what you want to major in?"

"Yes, I do. I want to major in women's studies."

"Talk to me after this, and I'll give you a name. She'll guide you through UCLA, and if you're smart and follow her advice, you'll find yourself graduating in four years."

Belinda turned back to the crowd. "Now, let's get back to the tour. Over to the left is the student union. In there, you'll find . . ."

Keisha followed along, barely listening. UCLA was about school, and not about socializing. She didn't care about the student union, the fraternities and sororities, or who was playing what game on what field. She wanted an education, and not the frills.

After about two hours of walking around the UCLA campus, it was time to go.

"I want to thank you all for coming, and I wish you nothing but success as you begin UCLA," Belinda said. Keisha started to walk away.

"Hey!" Belinda yelled, as the crowd began to disperse. It was noon, and the orientation was over. It felt like they'd walked ten miles around the campus. Now the crowd began walking to the parking lots. Belinda, however, had not forgotten about her promise to speak to Keisha. "Hey, you asked about getting a mentor," she said to Keisha, striding across the lawn. "I didn't get your name, so I'm sorry about yelling."

"No problem," Keisha said, smiling. "I'm just glad you have some information for me. My name is Keisha, by the way. Keisha Montez."

"Very nice to meet you, Keisha," Belinda said. "Did your parents leave already?"

"No," Keisha said. "My mother and I, well, we're what you would call estranged. And God knows where my father is. I haven't seen him in years."

Belinda looked at Keisha with compassion. "We're finding more and more students who are essentially independent students, coming to UCLA without the same support as the traditional student."

"I don't want any special treatment," Keisha said, carefully looking at Belinda for any signs of pity. "I've been able to get this far by myself, and I can get through UCLA by myself."

"Keisha, no one goes through UCLA, or any school, by themselves. We all need help, and that help is here to make sure you're ultimately successful, and not to make you feel dumb or incapable. You'll have to make a choice. You can remain independent and then understand that when you need help, you ask for it. Or you can let your ego guide you—like a lot of these kids with two parents, silver spoons in their mouths, and Daddy's credit card— and not ask for any help until it's too late. You tell me which option meets your goals."

"You don't have to tell me twice," Keisha said. "I'll take option number one."

"Good," Belinda said, taking Keisha by the hand. "Let's walk and talk about how we're going to get you through UCLA."

They started walking through the campus, with Belinda waving to various students.

"You said that you've been here for twenty years?" Keisha asked as they walked.

"Twenty long years," Belinda said, laughing. "But I live for this. I want all my students to succeed, because this is the chance of a lifetime. And that's why I'm taking you to see Mary in the women's studies department. By the way, why did you choose women's studies?"

"Circumstance."

"What do you mean, 'circumstance'?"

"Everything I've seen in my life has been about

women, especially black women, getting the short end of the stick in life," Keisha said. "My momma has moved from one bad relationship to another, always losing herself in men, and hoping that men will make her happy. The girls on my block, always getting screwed over by men, and then there's me."

They started up the steps of an ornate building. It was the Stephenson Building.

"What issues do you have?" Belinda asked, as they entered and then walked down the hall. "You're about to go to college. You have your future in your hands."

"Yeah," Keisha said as they stood before the women's studies department. "But what did I have to do to get here, and hopefully, stay here?"

They walked into the office, and a couple students were sitting quietly, reading books. On the wall throughout the office were posters honoring Betty Friedan, Angela Davis, Susan B. Anthony, and other heroines of the women's movement.

"Hi, I need to take a student in to see Mary Bronson," Belinda said to the student receptionist. "Tell her that Belinda Enfield is here."

"Just one second. I think she may have gone to lunch," the receptionist said, getting up from her desk. She walked to a room and knocked on a door. The door opened, and the receptionist walked to the front of the office.

"She's still here, and you can go right in."

"Thank you," Belinda said. Keisha followed Belinda into Mary's office.

"Hello, Belinda," Mary said. She had been eating a sandwich, and she'd gotten some mustard on her blouse. She quickly picked up a napkin and wiped her mouth and blouse. "And who is this?"

"Mary, this is Keisha Montez. She is an incoming

freshman, and she wants to major in women's stud-ies. I know that she has to take her general classes first, but she asked me a smart question about the de-partment and about getting a mentor, so I naturally thought of you."

"Well, take a seat, Keisha," she said, holding out her hand. Keisha shook it. "And welcome to UCLA."

Keisha looked around for a seat, but there were books everywhere. Mary's office was a complete mess.

"Sorry about the office, but this is what happens when you combine a pack rat, a counselor, and a professor in a small space. There's a chair right there."

Keisha moved some books and found a chair to sit on.

"Keisha is an independent student, and she tells me that she has a particular interest in women's studies because of what she's seen in life. Plus, she tells me that she has some particular circumstances, which she never told me about, that make this major interesting.

"I'm going to leave you two, but, Keisha," Be-linda said, pulling out a business card, "if you need some more advice, feel free to give me a call at any time. Remember what I told you about help. It's there if you need it, and everyone needs it."

"Thanks, Belinda."

"So, how can I help you?" Mary said as Belinda left.

"I think I want to major in women's studies."

"And how do you think women's studies can help you?"

"Actually, I don't know. I guess that's why I'm going to major in it," Keisha said. "I know that I want to work with women on self-esteem issues," Keisha said.

Mary cleared a space from her desk, looking for

something. Finally she picked up a brochure. "Here's a pamphlet that discusses what we do in the department. And here"—she reached down and picked up a syllabus—"is what classes you can take. Read the descriptions, and you can get a feel for who and what we are."

She handed everything to Keisha, who started looking at them.

"The reason I asked you about how you thought women's studies could help you was that I want you to understand that we simply provide the tools, but we need you to use them. We then create more tools, so that we can solve women's problems. But there's another thing I want to know. What are your circumstances?"

"I'm a stripper at the Chi Chi Room in Gardena," Keisha said, looking Mary directly in the eye, waiting for a reaction. There was none. "And I'm about to get into porn to help pay for UCLA."

Mary looked back at Keisha and then smiled. She stood up and walked to a corner of her office, then began shuffling through books. Finally, she picked up one and handed it to Keisha.

"Over the next four years, I want you to come to my office every two weeks and pick up a new book. In order to grow a plant, nice and healthy, you have to water it with nutrients. You have to start watering yourself with knowledge."

"*When and Where I Enter,*" Keisha read, "by Paula Giddings." She put the book in her lap and smiled.

"I thought that you'd fly off the handle when I told you that I stripped and was about to go into porn," Keisha said.

Mary smiled back at her. "Do you really think you're the first girl at UCLA to strip and do some porn? I'm not going to say that I approve of it—and

I don't—but the point of college is for you to come to your own conclusions and your own solutions. You make choices in life, and you think things through. Again, the women's studies department will give you the tools—"

"But I have to learn to use them," Keisha said, standing up to leave. "I'll be in your office every two weeks to learn how."

"That's what I want to hear," Mary said.

Chapter 14

*That you may retain your self-respect, it is
better to displease the people by doing what
you know is right, than to temporarily please
them by doing what you know is wrong.*
                                    —William J. H. Boetcker

Sean sat at the Chi Chi Room bar with Ray and Marty.
Ray and Marty were scouting for new women, as
usual, but Sean didn't care. He just sat there with a
silly grin on his face. It was Saturday, and the place
was packed. Moving Keisha to Saturday as featured
dancer had been a boon, because she was now the
most popular dancer in the club. He was seeing new
and younger men coming to the club, and that meant
higher sales. He couldn't have been happier.

"We told you that Keisha was a winner," Ray
said, sipping on a Heineken.

"I still want Patra," Marty said, picking up his
Heineken and then spilling it. The beer almost got
on Sean.

"Goddamn, nigga, can't you do anything right?"
Sean said, quickly moving out of the way of the spilled
beer.

"Yeah, where's Patra?" Ray asked. "Steven wanted
us to talk to her while we were here."

"You just missed her. I have her opening, and then Keisha closing. Keisha's out next."

Right as he said that, the DJ turned up the music and approached the microphone.

"Gentlemen, you've been waiting all week, but now give a big round of applause for the Chi Chi Room's star performer, and *Pimp* magazine's Girl of the Month, Keisha!"

The spotlight hit the far corner of the room, where Keisha stood, wearing a white thong bikini. Her body spilled out of it, showing off her toned curves. The crowd went nuts, but she didn't hear a thing. She was simply concentrating on giving a good performance. And that performance began with a damn good entrance.

On the cue of the music, Keisha began making her way to the stage, which was fifty feet away. She moved in an exaggerated way, crossing her feet as she walked, almost stomping, making her hips and ass sway side to side with metronome precision. A man tried to touch her, and she stopped, took his hand, and licked his fingers. He was a puddle in her hands.

"Shake that goddamn ass, baby," a voice in the pervert pit yelled. Keisha walked up the four small steps to the stage and stopped. She then bent at the knees and jiggled her ass so that it popped back and forth. The crowd went wild.

"That bitch is the bomb," Marty said. "Goddamn, but I never get tired of seeing her."

"Yeah, she's the goddamn bomb, and she's going to make me a lot of money."

Ray looked at Sean. "Yeah, she'll do that if you can keep her."

"What do you mean, if I can keep her?" Sean asked, taking his eyes off the stage for a second. "Nigga, she ain't goin' nowhere, and I don't give a shit what Steven says about it. I found her, and that means I own her."

"Nigga, this ain't slavery!" Ray exclaimed.

"Yeah, nigga, Jefferson freed the muthafuckin' slaves," Marty said.

"Nigga, shut up!" Sean said. "It was Lincoln, you dumb muthafucka."

"Lincoln what?" Marty asked.

"Abraham Lincoln, not Jefferson, freed the god-damn slaves, you fucking fool!"

"Whatever. Jefferson, Lincoln, who-the-fuck-ever. It doesn't matter. She ain't yours to keep. And if she follows Steven, he'll make sure of that shit," Marty said, dismissing Sean.

"This muthafucka may be dumb as a fucking doorknob," Ray said, "but he speaks the truth with that shit. Watch your step, Sean. Steven's not a mutha-fucka to be fucked with, and certainly not after some ho."

They all turned their eyes back to the stage, where Keisha was sliding upside-down on the golden pole in the middle of the stage. The men watched her as though she was a goddess, and the twenty-dollar bills flew in the air as though it was raining. Finally, her routine was done.

"Gentlemen, that was Keisha, the *Pimp* magazine Girl of the Month!"

Ray got off his stool and began walking toward the dressing room. The men in the crowd began cheering, as Keisha picked up her money, stuffing it into her thong and bikini top, so that she looked like a tree with leaves. As she left the stage, she never looked any of them in the eye. She walked to the dressing room, where Ray, who was standing right by the door, stopped her.

"Remember me?" he said.

"Ray, isn't it?" she asked, stopping as she was about to walk into the dressing room.

"That's right," Ray said. "Steven wants an answer."

"What do you mean Steven wants an answer?"

"I mean that he wants an answer tonight about whether you're going to take him up on his offer."

She slowly began taking bills out of her bikini, gathering them in a bunch. Why did she have to make a decision right now? Why was it so important?

Ray stared expectantly at her, waiting for an answer.

"If I decide to pass on this opportunity, what's going to happen?"

"Then Steven instructed me to tell you thank you, and good luck with your stripping career. He'd never offer you this opportunity again."

"Whatever," Keisha said disdainfully. "There are more people I could work for if I wanted to get into porn."

"Yeah, but do you know how much you'd be making for them?"

Keisha shook her head.

"About five hundred dollars a day, if you're lucky. And you might not be lucky. Most of these fools doing black videos are fly-by-night. No quality control, and no guarantee that you're going to get what they told you they were going to pay. So here's your opportunity. Take it if you want. Or keep shakin' your ass on that stage."

Sean walked over, followed by Marty.

"Hey, stop talking to my girls. Keisha's got to get ready for her next set. And as you know, time is money and money is time. And I don't like it when y'all mess with my money."

It was then that Debra walked out of the dressing room. Sean had thrown her a bone by giving her one weekend a month. But she still blamed Keisha for her issues.

"Oh, so it's the bitch and her admirers," Debra said, stopping for a second.

"Get your black ass onstage and stay out of grown-folk business," Sean said, scooting from side to side. "You wanted to get a Saturday—well, now you've got it."

Debra gave Sean a look, then shot Keisha a long look, when she started walking to the stage.

"Gentlemen, you've loved her as one of the Chi Chi Room's favorite dancers, and now she's back on Saturdays. Put your hands together for Debra!" the DJ said. The applause was decidedly less for Debra than it was for Keisha, and Keisha noticed it. Men were ordering drinks, talking among themselves, and basically ignoring Debra as she made it to the stage. It was like they'd seen the movie before, knew all the lines, and could recite them from memory. Debra tried to act sexy, but her moves were tired. All of a sudden, Keisha didn't want to be Debra, working at the Chi Chi Room for years. She wanted money, and not a career stripping. And to get that money, and get it fast, she was going to have to take that opportunity.

"Tell Steven that I'm in," Keisha said, moving toward the dressing room door. "But on my terms. I want to have a choice in this. Tell him to call me on Monday."

"Will do," Ray said. "Look for a call from him tomorrow morning. We shoot tomorrow. See you then."

Ray, Marty, and Sean turned and left. Keisha walked

into the dressing room, wondering if she'd done the right thing.

Keisha and Debra went back on the stage throughout the night, and both were making good money. But now it was three in the morning, and Blackie was throwing the last patrons out of the club. Sean was upstairs counting his money, and that left only Debra and Keisha in the dressing room. There was a stony silence between them.

"I want you to know that I didn't ask Sean to take you off of weekends," Keisha said, putting on her shoes. Debra didn't look up. She was putting on her makeup.

"Debra, dammit," Keisha said angrily. She was tired of this attitude between her and Debra, and she particularly didn't like how two women couldn't work out their differences. It was one of the reasons she was going to pursue women's studies at UCLA. "Listen to me. I didn't take your days. Steven from *Pimp* magazine told Sean to give me those days, and not me."

Debra slowly turned to Keisha. Her face belied the years of dancing at the club, and where Keisha had once seen a confident woman, she now saw a tired woman.

"I know," she said softly. "I know you didn't do anything. I just couldn't bring myself to think that my time was up. But it is, Keisha. It is. And I don't know what to do."

"You have a lot of things you can do," Keisha said, walking to Debra.

"Girl, the only thing I know how to do is shake my ass, and even that is getting tired. The only ones that are getting a thrill from my ass are the ones in the pervert pit that need to take a blue pill to get it up. Do you know what happens to old strippers?"

"What?"

"That's the point," she responded. "No one knows what happens to old strippers. They go back into society, having saved nothing out of this shit, and gained nothing from this shit. If I go, Sean will simply find another bitch to shake her ass, and he'll make money. There's no pension in stripping, baby, and if you're smart, and you are a smart girl, you'll get out as soon as you can. You can do better, but you don't want to be me."

Debra stared back at the mirror, dabbing away a tear that was streaking down her face. She tried nonchalantly to put on her makeup.

"But in the meantime, I'll shake my ass as long as Sean will let me. But just know that I don't blame you."

"Thanks, Debra," Keisha said, sitting in her chair. "So, how much did you make today?"

Debra stopped putting on her makeup and smiled. "Bitch, didn't I tell you to stay out of my money?"

Keisha laughed. "Why it gotta be all that?"

"Because that's how we bitches roll," Debra said, laughing. "My money is my money."

"Believe that!" Keisha said, picking up her duffle bag. "See ya next week, Debra."

Patra was in the parking lot, waiting for Keisha. She'd finished her night at the Chi Chi Room early and had gone to another club to dance. She was driving but had had a few drinks.

"See ya, Blackie," Keisha said, getting into Patra's car.

"Be safe, y'all," Blackie yelled.

"So how did it go tonight?" Patra asked, her breath definitely tinged with vodka. "When I was leaving, it seemed like a gang of men were coming in."

"It was a damn good night," Keisha said. "A damn good one. I made about seven hundred dollars."

"Damn," Patra exclaimed as she drove. She turned down their street and into their apartment parking structure. "I think I'm going to tell Sean that I need to take Debra's place on Saturdays. Ain't nobody feeling that bitch anyway."

"Ah, girl, I just patched shit up with her, and you're going to fuck it up."

"She finally forgave you?"

"Yeah, she knows the writing's on the wall."

"Hell, she was always big," Patra said. "But now she can barely get into her bikini. And I think she stopped working out, so shit's getting all jiggly, and not in a good way, if you know what I mean."

They walked into their apartment and Keisha instantly collapsed on the couch. "Good night," Patra said, going into her bedroom.

Keisha had gotten used to getting in early in the morning and then sleeping all day. There was a routine she kept. Close the blinds, turn off any alarms, and sleep away from the rising sun. And since Patra pretty much worked the same hours, no one disturbed her. But this morning, she had to keep her cell on for Steven. The money was too good to miss out on for a good sleep. And it rang exactly at nine.

"Hello," Keisha said sleepily.

"Wake up, darling!" Steven said on the other line. "I'm on my way to pick you up."

"Right now?"

"Yeah, right now. If you want to make five thousand, you've got to follow my schedule. So be ready in an hour."

"All right," Keisha said. Steven hung up and Keisha put her head back on her pillow. She was bone tired from working last night, but she tried to force herself to get more energy. After staring at the ceiling for about half an hour, she jumped into the shower and got dressed. As soon as she finished, she heard the doorbell ring.

"Just a second," she said, walking to the door. She looked through the peephole and saw Ray and Marty. She'd been expecting Steven.

"Are you ready?" Ray asked when Keisha opened the door.

"Give me a second."

"Cool, meet up downstairs in the parking lot."

Keisha closed the door and went into the kitchen. Patra came out of her room.

"Who the hell was that?" she asked sleepily.

"It was Ray and Marty," Keisha said, drinking a cup of coffee.

"From *Pimp*? What are they doing here?"

"I'm about to do my first porn shoot," Keisha said, finishing her coffee. "I gotta go."

"So you decided to do it?"

"Yep, and I better go now before I change my mind."

Keisha started toward the door, when Patra stopped her. "Always remember to fuck them and don't let them fuck you," she said. "Go get your money."

"I intend on doing just that," Keisha said, walking out of the apartment.

Chapter 15

Sex: the thing that takes up the least amount of time and causes the most amount of trouble.
                                    —John Barrymore

"You didn't think we'd come in a limo, did you?" Ray asked as Keisha walked into the parking lot. He and Marty were leaning against a black Hummer limo. The first thing that popped into Keisha's head was, why all of this for her?

"Steven only goes for first class," Ray said, as if to answer her question. "Get in—we have some places to go."

They all got into the limo, and the driver left the apartment complex.

"So how long is this shoot, and what am I going to be doing?" Keisha asked, a bit nervously.

"It can last all day, and you're going to be doing a lot of things," Marty said, smiling. Keisha found Ray okay, but Marty to be creepy.

"Who am I going to be working with?" she asked.

"That, we don't know," Ray said. "Since this is Steven's first shoot, he wanted to pick your partners so that you'd match up perfectly on film. You know, he really believes in you."

"Great."

"Do you want a drink?" Ray asked, pulling open the bar. "We've got some Crown Royal, Jack Daniels', Coca-Cola, 7-Up—"

"Let me have a 7-Up," she said, looking out the window. It looked like they were heading for the San Fernando Valley, which was pretty damn appropriate since it was known worldwide as Porn Valley. "It's too early for Crown Royal."

"If you don't mind," Keisha said, sipping on her soda, "I'm going to chill for a second. I didn't get a lot of sleep."

"Go ahead," Marty said, with his creepy grin plastered on his face. "You'll need your rest."

I still have a chance to pull out, Keisha thought as they rode. *I'll only do one video, take the money, and then be done. Even if this comes up later in my life, at least I can say that it was a one-time mistake and not some long-term career.*

After thirty minutes of driving, the limo turned into a strip-mall parking lot.

"Where are we?" Keisha asked.

"We are at the San Fernando HIV/AIDS testing center. Before you can work, you have to get tested. Are you okay with that?"

"Yeah, I'm okay with that," Keisha said. The driver parked and they all piled out of the limo. "Will my partners be tested too?"

"Of course. You can't work in the industry if you don't get tested. Too much money is at stake to have a positive performer on-set," Ray said.

They walked into the center, and instead of going to the waiting room, Ray led them straight into a back room.

"Steven set it up so that we could get you tested quickly," Ray said, handing her a clipboard. "Fill this out and I'll get that nurse. Come on, Marty."

Ray and Marty left the room, and Keisha filled out the form. It was pretty standard, asking her about her sex partners, and whether she had any diseases. Truth be told, she'd had only one sex partner, Donovan. She'd really thought she loved him until he started dealing drugs, and then she'd had to walk away. But after Donovan, she hadn't found anyone she'd wanted to sleep with.

How ironic, she thought, *that the second man I sleep with is going to be a stranger.*

There was a knock on the door. "Come in," Keisha said.

"Hello, Keisha," the nurse said. She was a slender white woman, and she wore a blue nurse's uniform.

"I'm Rebecca, and I'm going to be doing your test," she said. "Do you have any questions about the test? And have you ever been tested before?"

"No, I've never been tested. And no, I don't think I have any questions."

Rebecca looked over her chart. "So you've only been with one sex partner?"

"Yes."

"Did you use condoms while in that relationship?"

"Always."

"Have you ever taken drugs?"

"The only thing I do is weed from time to time."

"No heroin?"

"No."

"Good," Rebecca said, putting down the chart. "This should be fine then."

Keisha began unrolling her sleeve.

"Oh, we're not going to draw blood. We have a cotton swab that we use at this facility so we can get a result within twenty minutes. Plus, who wants to get stuck with a needle anyway?"

Keisha hated needles, and this cotton swab was a godsend. She opened her mouth and the nurse put the swab on her gums. After roughly scraping them, she was done.

"That's it," she said sunnily. "We'll have the results in about twenty minutes."

Keisha stood up to go, and the nurse opened the door for her. "Should I stay for them?" Keisha asked.

"No, we'll just fax the results to the Stage."

"What's the Stage?"

"That's where you're going to be working. Didn't they tell you?"

"No," Keisha said, "they didn't."

Ray and Marty were sitting in the lounge, where it seemed like every porn actor and actress was waiting. Keisha didn't know how she could tell they were in porn, but there was something about them that told her it was true. Before she walked toward Ray and Marty, Rebecca stopped her.

"Be careful, and take care of yourself," she advised.

Keisha was touched. She thought that Rebecca would be pretty jaded after dealing with so many sex workers, and she thought it was kind that she cared about her.

"I will," Keisha said softly.

"That was painless, wasn't it?" Ray said as they made their way back to the limo. "We want to keep you safe during the shoot."

"Yeah, I definitely want to do the same. Where's the Stage?"

"Who told you about that?" Marty asked.

"The nurse. That's where she said she was going to send my test results."

"Well, that's where we're going. Shouldn't be more than ten minutes away. The Stage is a studio set that the industry uses from time to time. We're going to use it because we couldn't get our location for the day. Plus, we'll have many chances to use our locations in the future."

"Who said that I'm doing this more than once?" Keisha said.

"Everyone always does it more than once," Marty said. "Everyone."

The limo pulled up into the parking lot of another strip mall. It seemed like the San Fernando Valley was nothing but a land of strip malls.

"Let's go," Ray said, opening the limo's door. It was now a little before noon, and the sun was out in its full glory. The San Fernando Valley was at least ten degrees hotter than Los Angeles, and Keisha began sweating the minute she got out of the car.

The limo pulled away and they began walking to a characterless building. When they entered, there was movement everywhere. An older woman was putting out cookies, apple Danishes, and coffee on a table. Two surfer-looking guys were moving heavy equipment. And a middle-aged Latina was animatedly talking to a short white guy with a camera, when she noticed Keisha, Ray, and Marty enter.

"Well, it's about time you guys got here," she scolded Ray and Marty. She had a slight limp as she walked. "We've been waiting for an hour, and now I'm behind and the shoot's behind."

"Look, don't give us any shit," Ray said. "This girl didn't have her papers in order, so we had to go by the clinic, or else we would have been here on time."

"Keisha, right?" she asked.

"Yes."

"My name is Marisa and I want you to come with me," she said, taking Keisha by the arm. "Marty, make your black ass useful and get this girl something to eat. Have you eaten?"

"No."

"Bring her some coffee and a Danish. Hurry up, because we don't have a lot of time to fuck around."

Keisha and Marisa entered the makeup room, where a small, almost delicate, young sister was getting her makeup done. Her hair was in rollers and she was reading a script.

"Trevi, this is Keisha. She's going to be working with you today," Marisa said. "And that's Allison, my assistant."

"Nice to meet you, Keisha," Trevi said, extending her hand. Keisha shook it.

Trevi couldn't have been taller than five feet. She was a Latina with curly, jet-black hair. She was tiny, with tiny features, except for the fact that she had fake breasts that pointed straight, rather than hanging naturally. They were larger than her body should have been able to support.

"Trevi is known in the industry as the orgasm queen," Marisa said cheerfully.

"Yep, that's right," Trevi said with a smile. "I can orgasm whenever I want."

"Now, that's a skill I'd like to have," Keisha said.

"I feel bad for those who can't," Trevi said. "Have you worked on any other films?"

Keisha sat down in an open chair. "No, this is my first film."

"So we've got a virgin, eh?" Trevi said.

"Yep, she's a virgin, and I wish I was the guy to take her cherry," Marty said, walking in with coffee and a Danish.

"You wouldn't be the one to get it, even if you were the last man on Earth," Keisha said.

"You don't know what you're missing," Marty said with a frown.

"And I'll die not knowing."

"Ha!" Trevi said, smiling. "I like you already. Get out of here, Marty. We've got lines to read."

Marisa opened up a case and began working on Keisha. "You've got beautiful skin," she said. "So often, I have to work on girls who have pretty features but absolutely fucked-up skin. But your skin is almost flawless."

Keisha leaned back in the chair and let Marisa work on her makeup.

"So are you nervous about doing your first scenes?" Trevi asked.

"A little," Keisha said. "I'm not really that nervous about having sex, but damn, I've never done any acting in my life. I just don't know if I'm cut out for this."

"Look, it's easy," Trevi said. "Do you remember what you used to do when you played with your dolls? Just go into a make-believe world and you should be fine. And if it feels good, go with it."

"And if it doesn't?"

"Fake it to make it, babe," Trevi said, laughing. "Fake it to make it. That's the motto of this industry."

Ray walked in with a piece of paper in his hand.

"Keisha, we got your test results and you're fine," he said. "Steven is on his way here, and he wants me to take care of you. I'm also going to be the director of the shoot. Our regular director, Jeff, is out of town. Here's the script. You're playing the part of—wait for it—Keisha. Read the lines and see if you can remember them. The faster you can memorize them, the faster the shoot will go. By the way, is there anything that you won't do?"

"I won't do anal," she said, looking at the script. "I don't want anything in my ass. Other than that, we're going to be straight."

"Cool. Since this is your first time, if there's anything that makes you feel uncomfortable, you make sure to let me know. We want to have a good time, and if you're not having a good time, then it's not going to be a good shoot."

"How many times do I have to have sex?"

"You're going to do four scenes. We'll introduce you to the guys you're going to be working with when they get here. And you have a scene with Trevi. Do you have a problem with women?"

Keisha stopped for a second. She'd never had sex with a woman, and never had a desire to do so. But this was a job, and it really wasn't like sex, but a job.

"No, I don't think I have a problem with it. I'll just feel it as I go."

"Cool," he said. "Read over the script and then we'll bring over your wardrobe for the shoot."

"All right."

Ray left.

"Finished," Allison exclaimed to Trevi. She handed her a mirror.

"You made me look beautiful, as always," she said, admiring her makeup and hair. "Too bad it's going to get fucked-up when the men begin pulling my hair."

"Occupational hazard," Allison said, laughing.

Trevi watched as Marisa worked on Keisha. She was applying makeup at a rapid pace, trying to make up for lost time.

"When did you get in the business?" Keisha asked.

"About two years ago," Trevi replied. "You'd never guess what I did before I started working in the business."

"What?"

"I was a kindergarten teacher," she said, laughing.

"No shit?"

"No shit. And I loved it, too. But you get paid shit wages and I wanted a car. I actually got into porn because I wanted a car. But after I made enough for a car, I found out that I wanted a nicer apartment, and then nice clothes, and so here I am two years later. I like the sex, and the folks are great, but I'm getting out in the next year."

"Ah, the exit strategy," Marisa said, laughing. "Everybody in porn has one, but they never seem to be able to implement it."

"You don't have to worry about me," Keisha said. "I'm doing this shoot, and then I'm out. I'm trying to make some cash so I can get out of my roommate's apartment and pay for school."

"So you're going to school? Where are you going?"

"UCLA."

"Wow! Well, go on, girl, get that money," Allison said.

Keisha kept reading the script, and the more she read, the more ridiculous it sounded.

"Okay, have you read this, Marisa? These are some of the dumbest lines I've ever read, and I've never read any other scripts."

"Honey, just keep your ass up high and moan loud and no one will care about the lines," Marisa said. "But here's the funny thing. The longer you're in this business, the more you will care for the lines, because the sex will be mundane. Sex is easy to get bored with, and when the lines in the porn are what you're looking forward to, then it's time to get out."

Marisa walked over to Allison and picked up the mirror. She handed it to Keisha.

"There," she said. "This is your first porn makeup job. I think we do it better than those high-paid bitches in Hollywood."

I do look beautiful, Keisha thought. *Heavily made-up, but beautiful.*

"When do we start shooting?" Keisha asked.

"In about fifteen minutes," Trevi said. "They'll bring you your clothes and then we'll get started."

Ray rolled a metal horse hanger filled with dresses and bikinis into the room.

"Speak of the devil," Allison said.

"I'm good, not evil," Ray laughed. "I need you guys to put on a bikini, and then pick out two dresses. Then meet me down on the office set in about ten minutes. We don't have a lot of time because we're already behind. So get going."

"What if there's nothing in my size?" Keisha said, looking through the clothes.

"Believe me, there's something there for you," Ray answered. "Trevi, do me a favor and bring the box of toys and lube down with you."

"I'll take it," Marisa said, opening a cabinet. She took down a box and opened it. The box was filled with dildos and different gadgets. "Have these things been sterilized?"

"I'm not sure, so why don't you boil them in some water. We have about fifteen minutes, so by the time you bring them down to the set, we should be ready."

Marisa left with the box. Ray and Allison followed her.

"I like my toys slightly warm anyway," Trevi said

to Marisa as she pulled off her top. Trevi displayed her tits. "How do you like them?" she asked Keisha.

"They look nice," Keisha said. "I never thought about getting bigger breasts."

"You will, if you stay long enough in the industry. Big breasts mean big money."

Keisha had to admit that even though Trevi's breasts were fake, they still looked good in clothes. Trevi slipped on a simple black dress, while Keisha found a red number that matched. They looked good.

"Pick some heels from here," Trevi said, pointing to a rack of shoes.

Keisha picked a pair of black high heels.

"Are you ready?" Trevi asked Keisha. She took her hand gently.

"As ready as I'm ever going to be."

"Don't worry. I've been there, and I'll help you through it."

"Thanks," Keisha said. And together they walked to the set.

Chapter 16

The Stage consisted of five sets: a kitchen, a bedroom, a bar, an office, and curiously, a home enter-
tainment den. Today's shoot would be set in all of
them. The crew had gathered in the office set. This
was *Pimp* Video's first shoot, and it was Ray's first
time directing. He wanted to make sure he set the
tone early.

"Okay, everybody," Ray started, as he addressed
the crew. "Most of you are veterans from the industry, but I want to remind you that this is *Pimp*
Video's first shoot."

Someone started clapping, and a "woo-hoo" was
yelled out from the crowd. There were about twenty
people holding cameras, boom mikes, and other
equipment. Steven was nowhere to be seen.

The set was cold, as though someone had turned
the air conditioning to eleven, instead of ten. And another thing struck Keisha. The set was large and im-
personal. Every porno she'd seen seemed to take

place in a house, or a bedroom, that was real, and not a set. But these sets were huge and fake-looking, right down to the fake phones on the desk.

Trevi and Keisha stood at the front of the crowd, and over to their left were three very muscular men. "See those guys over there," Trevi whispered to Keisha, as Ray kept talking. "They're who we're fucking today. The one on the left is Don Juan."

Don Juan was a short and slender dark-skinned man who had long dreadlocks. His shirt was off, and his chest was oiled so that his muscles glistened.

"Don Juan is pretty cool, but you have to let him know if you want him to pound you or take it easy on you, because he'll start jackhammering and you'll have a hell of a time getting him to stop once he starts."

"Who's the guy in the middle?" Keisha asked.

"That's Bruce Thumper," Trevi said. Bruce stood about six feet tall and, like Don Juan, had rippling muscles. He had long blond hair that was nicely cut at his shoulders, like he was a knight from King Arthur's court. "He has a ten-inch dick that's thick, and he likes to go deep," Trevi continued. "He's known for producing great loads of cum. Did you tell them that you wanted to swallow?"

"No, and I'm not going to," Keisha said. "I'll fuck them, but I'm not swallowing any muthafucka's cum, especially some fool I don't even know."

"Then you're going to have to take the money shot in the face," Trevi said. "They might let you take it on your ass, but I don't know how Steven and Ray work. But I know that the video is more marketable if he cums on your face. Just close your eyes, and you'll be fine."

"So who's the last guy?" Keisha asked.

"That is the legendary Long Island Dong," Trevi

said. Long Island Dong stood a little bit away from Don Juan and Bruce, not interacting with anyone. He was about six-four, wore blue Bermuda shorts, and had a bit of a paunch. He was older than the other two, with gray hair starting to sprout from his beard.

"Why does he keep rubbing his dick?" Keisha asked as she watched him.

"It's a habit," Trevi said. "He rubs it all of the damn time, mainly because it's so big, I think. But I think he's trying to maintain an erection. He's been in over one thousand movies, and I think he's on the blue pill 'cause he's having wood problems."

Ray was finishing his speech. ". . . at *Pimp* Video, we are going to use the raw techniques of gonzo, and the refined professionalism of features. Simply put, we're going to revolutionize black adult video. And the man who is going to make this all happen is Steven Cox. So let's have a warm round of applause for Steven."

Everyone, including Trevi and Keisha, turned around and saw Steven. He was dressed casually in all-white Sean John gear.

"I think Ray said it all," Steven said. "We're going to be here for a while, so let's have a good shoot."

"Positions, everybody," Ray said. "We're going to start off with pretty girls and then we'll start shooting. Don Juan, you're in the first scene, so make sure you're ready. Trevi and Keisha, come with me."

The three walked over to a blue screen, where a photographer was waiting.

"Trevi, you already know Phil, but Keisha, this is Phil, our photographer. He's going to take your pretty girls shots."

"You're going to have to school me on some of these terms. What is pretty girls?" Keisha asked.

"Trevi will show you," Ray said. "All through the shoot, we're going to be taking pictures of you. Pretty girls are the shots we take before we shoot. We'll use them for the cover and shit. All right, both of you strip to your bikinis."

Trevi and Keisha took off their dresses. The rest of the crew ignored them.

"Trevi, you know what to do, so why don't you go first?" Phil said. "Let's go ass, tits, high ass, leg, and then freestyle."

Trevi moved in front of the blue screen and started posing. She put her hands on her knees and stuck her ass out.

"Good shit, Trevi, keep going," Phil said, snapping photos. Trevi took straps from her thong and pulled them through the crack of her ass. With each shot, she smiled deliriously, as though she were having the time of her life.

"Give me some tit shots," Phil said, getting on the ground. He must have taken over one hundred shots. Finally, he was done.

"Your turn, Keisha," he said, switching memory cards in the camera. Keisha walked up to the blue screen.

"Just do the best that you can," Phil said, pointing the camera at her. Keisha smiled to herself. She was a fucking stripper, and if a stripper couldn't pose, then what the fuck was she doing on the stage? she thought.

"Yeah, that's it," Phil said. Keisha began moving as though she were onstage, except that she didn't have a pole.

Fake it to make it, she thought. Keisha moved to some invisible music, and like at the club, the crew stopped and looked. This was a jaded bunch, who swam in tits, ass, and pussy all the time. And yet, they knew when they had something special. And Keisha was special.

"More ass, baby," Phil said. "Keep moving, and give me more ass. Yeah, you are a fucking natural."

Keisha kept moving to an internal rhythm but was still tired from the night before. She didn't have the same energy that she naturally would have had. But everyone seemed to like what she was doing, so she kept going.

Steven had walked over to Ray, who was getting ready to shoot. "Ray, do I have an eye for talent, or do I have an eye for talent?" he said, proud of himself.

"Let's wait to see what happens when she has a dick inside of her before we start patting each other on the back," Ray said.

"All right, everybody, let's get going for scene one!" Ray shouted to the cast and crew. "Don Juan, Trevi, and Keisha, you're up. Let's go!"

Everyone broke and began getting in position. Keisha joined Trevi and the others in the office scene. Ray began taking control of the scene.

"Quiet, please!" Ray yelled. "Marty, get those people over in the corner to stop fucking talking, or throw them out." He turned to Keisha. "Keisha, I want you to walk into the room and read your lines. Don Juan and Trevi will read their lines, and then we'll get started."

In about ten seconds, Keisha was going to be a porn actress in a movie tentatively called, *Pimp presents Keisha,* and she was as nervous as she'd ever been. The plot centered on a woman named Keisha, played by Keisha, who's coming into Los Angeles without a job but needs a place to stay.

If Keisha had thought twice about it, she would

have used an alias instead of her own name. But nobody suggested it.

"Okay, everyone, quiet on the set!" Ray said. "Action!"

Keisha froze. She stood in front of a fake doorway that led into a faux office, where a real-life change was about to happen. All of a sudden, she couldn't move.

"Keisha!" Ray screamed. "Let's go! Walk into the office and read your lines!"

Ray's voice snapped Keisha out of her trance, and she instinctively walked through the door.

"Hello, welcome to Crenshaw Realty," Don Juan said. "My name is Chuck and this is my wife, Angie. How can we help you?" Don Juan was wearing black leather pants and a white shirt, and Trevi was wearing her black evening dress.

"Yes, my name is Keisha," Keisha said haltingly. "I'd like an apartment, please."

Don Juan reached into the drawer and pulled out some forms. "Fine, we have some vacancies right now in the Ladera area. Are you looking for a studio or a one-bedroom?"

"I'd like a one-bedroom," Keisha said.

Don Juan's cell phone went off. "Dammit!" he said overdramatically. "It looks like the pipes in one of our tenants' bathrooms has overflowed again. I've got to go right away."

"Don't worry, honey," Trevi said seductively. "I can take care of all this."

"Great. It was nice to meet you, Kimmie."

"Cut!" yelled Ray. He ran on the set and got right in the face of Don Juan. "It's not Kimmie, it's Keisha. Goddamn, how hard can that fucking be?"

"Who the fuck cares?" Don Juan replied, as Ray

walked back to the side. "Most muthafuckas are going to fast-forward this shit anyway."

"I fucking care, so if you want to do more *Pimp* videos, you'd better care too," Ray said. "Okay, everyone back at their spots. Action!"

"Great," Don Juan repeated. "It was nice to meet you, Keisha."

"I hope to see more of you later," Keisha said breathily.

"Call me and let me know what apartment you rent her," Don Juan said to Trevi. He then gave her a huge, wet kiss, full of tongue.

"Bye, baby," she said as he left the faux office.

"Keisha," Ray said from the side, "I want you to sexily climb on the desk, and then read your lines."

Keisha got out of her chair and then laid on the desk, sweeping the phone and the calendar to the floor.

"Nice," Steven whispered, as he watched from a corner.

"Angie, I have a small problem," Keisha said. "I just got to Los Angeles from Portland, and I don't have a dime to my name. So I don't know how I can pay for an apartment, but I need somewhere to live. Do you think you can help me?"

Keisha put her fingers on Trevi's arm. Trevi then put her hand on Keisha's thigh and began rubbing it.

"I think that we can work something out," Trevi cooed into Keisha's ear. "Just give me a second, and I think I can find some ways you can pay. Just don't tell my husband. He gets so jealous."

"Cut!" Ray yelled, walking into the set. Keisha got off the desk and Trevi sat down in the chair. "Marisa! Marisa!" he yelled.

"Yeah?"

"Where are those toys?"

"Coming!"

"That's a first." Ray laughed. "Toys coming. That's what you girls are paid to do."

Marisa came bounding through the set with a box full of toys. The other crew talked among themselves, and two were trying to catch a smoke with Don Juan.

"Here you go, all sterilized and ready to go," Marisa said. She handed Trevi a blown-glass dildo that was twisted at the end. "I made sure to bring you your favorite."

"Keisha, one of the fringe benefits you'll find in this industry is that you get to play with some expensive toys," she said, holding the glass dildo like a work of art. "This is the wrapped G-spot shaft. Seven inches of fun for you and me!"

Marisa began lining up the dildos on the desk as though they were little toy soldiers. "Do you have a favorite?"

Keisha picked up a tiny vibrator. "I want you to use this pocket rocket," she said. "My boyfriend used to use it on me and I came every time."

"You got it," Trevi said. "Are you cool yet with me going down on you?"

Keisha hesitated. "I think I'm more cool with you going down on me, than me going down on you."

"Honey, everybody's a little bit bi, so you'll get into it," Marisa said.

"Funny, but I don't see the men doing anything like that," Keisha said. Trevi and Marisa laughed.

"Darling, you don't see it, but it's happening. Just not on this set," Trevi said.

"Okay, enough talk. Let's get to the fucking!" Ray said. "Marisa, get all those toys out of here. Keisha and Trevi, get back to your places. Let's go, everybody. Time is money and money is time!"

Keisha and Trevi began walking back to the office set. "By the way, I like my dildos and dick deep, so don't be shy," Trevi said. "You can't hurt me."

"I'll remember that," Keisha said.

Chapter 17

*Most people are other people. Their thoughts
are someone else's opinions, their lives a mim-
icry, their passions a quotation.*

—Oscar Wilde

Keisha lay back on the desk, and Trevi tried to strike
the same pose she'd had before Ray had stopped the
scene. Continuity was not that important in porn—
in fact, most videos looped scenes during editing so
that they stretched out.

"Okay, are you girls ready?" Ray asked.

"Yeah," they both said.

"Okay, action!"

Trevi rubbed Keisha's leg up and down and then
ran her hand up her thigh.

"How about we have some fun and then call it
even for the apartment?" Trevi asked.

"That sounds good to me," Keisha said. Keisha
turned over so that she was on her back, and Trevi
slowly lifted her dress so that it gathered at Keisha's
waist. She then took off Keisha's panties and tossed
them to the side.

"You have a beautiful pussy," Trevi said, yanking
Keisha to the edge of the desk.

"I bet it tastes even better," Keisha said.

The man with the handheld camera was right behind Trevi, as she used her tongue to draw circles around Keisha's belly button.

For Keisha, this was extremely weird and uncomfortable.

What the hell am I doing? she thought, as Trevi kept flicking her tongue around her belly and thigh.

It didn't feel bad to her, but then again, this was not a fantasy of hers. Slowly, Trevi began kissing her closer and closer to her pussy, and Keisha began to tense up.

"Keisha, relax," Ray shouted from the side. "Just relax and let Trevi do the work. Both of you, take off your dresses."

Keisha sat up and lifted her dress, while Trevi simply let hers drop to the ground. Keisha then lay back on the desk. Ray had instructed a second camera to focus on Keisha's face, and one over Trevi's shoulder.

"Eat her good, Trevi," Ray said, looking through his monitor at the action. Over his shoulder, Steven was watching too.

"She's good, real good," Steven said. "And I think Trevi was the right pick for her first scene."

Trevi bent down and began licking Keisha's pussy, and the only reaction Keisha could give was to rapidly open and close her eyes. She began imagining that Trevi was Donovan, and she began to relax.

"Jesus," Keisha exclaimed.

"Oooh, that feels good," was the line Keisha was supposed to say, but she wasn't thinking about her lines. Where Donovan had been strong with his licking, Trevi was gentle, with a small tongue that flicked everywhere.

"Keep going, Angie, keep going," Keisha cooed.

Trevi had put her hands in Keisha's hands, and now they were clasping them and unclasping them in unison. This was a new experience, and Keisha wasn't sure if she ever wanted to do it again, but it was not unpleasant.

"Hold the positions, everybody," Ray yelled from the side. He walked back on the set, and no one moved. Phil came running out of the bathroom with his camera. Trevi was bent down, with her mouth still on Keisha's pussy, and Keisha had raised her head to watch Trevi's work.

"Phil, get me shots of this," Ray instructed.

Phil began taking shots of Trevi and Keisha's pussy.

"Keisha, give me a great fuck face, like you're really enjoying her eating you out," Phil said. Keisha did her best, and Phil clicked more pictures.

It reminded Keisha of something her grandfather used to say about pigs. When Keisha was little, she hated to eat chitterlings for New Year's, which was a family tradition. Her grandfather used to laugh and tell her that he liked to eat everything on the pig, from the rooter to the tooter. Keisha felt Ray was going to exploit every last thing he could from this shoot.

"Let's bring out the toys for this scene," Ray said. "After that, we're going to transition to Keisha eating out Trevi. Okay, we're behind schedule. Let's get going."

The crew moved back into position, and Trevi picked up the pocket rocket.

"Action," Ray yelled.

"How do you like that, Keisha?" Trevi asked, as she dived back between Keisha's legs. She began making exaggerated movements with her mouth and tongue, sucking on Keisha's clit. Keisha bit her lower lip and then put her hand on Trevi's head to guide her. Trevi turned on the pocket rocket and began rubbing Keisha's clit with it. That felt real good to Keisha, and it didn't matter to her that a woman was doing it.

"Right there, oooh, yes, right there," she said. She still had Donovan in her mind, but Trevi wasn't doing a bad job at making her forget him.

"Cut," Ray yelled. "Let's go to the couch. Keisha, read your line."

"That felt good, but let me give you something," Keisha said. Trevi lifted up and walked over to the black couch. Keisha climbed down from the desk and got between Trevi's legs. The two cameramen followed them as they walked, then returned to their positions, over Keisha's shoulder and on Trevi's face.

"Make it look good, Keisha," Ray said. "Give me a lot of tongue and a lot of facial expression as you eat her out."

Keisha stared at Trevi's pussy, as though it were an alien thing. It *was* an alien thing. She'd never been so close to another woman's pussy and it was going to take some extreme imagination to get her going.

"Come on, Keisha, we don't have all day," Ray said.

"Just close your eyes and take your time," Trevi said gently. "I'll help you through."

Keisha closed her eyes, said a little prayer to herself, and started kissing Trevi on the thigh. She kept kissing and licking her thigh until she finally decided that she had to go for it and get it over with. Trevi was shaved, except for a small bit of pubic hair. She decided to circle that hair, and then move on to Trevi's pussy.

"That's it, baby, that's it," Trevi said, moaning as Keisha's kiss got closer and closer to her clit. "Ooh, are you sure you've never done this before?"

"Never," Keisha said, lifting her head and smiling at Trevi. "But I'll do anything to get an apartment."

"Oh, you'll get an apartment all right," Trevi said. "And you'll get a luxury one if you can make me cum."

"I'll do my best," Keisha said. And then Keisha put her mouth on Trevi's pussy and began licking and sucking. She felt nauseated, and for her, it was the most unnatural thing she'd ever done. She ignored Trevi's moans and just tried to finish as fast as she could.

"Hold it," Ray yelled. "Everybody freeze. Phil, get in there and take the pictures."

Phil took his time getting on the set. He was fiddling with his camera and didn't appear to be in a hurry.

Keisha had to hold her position, in the same way that Trevi had held hers. But having her lips on Trevi's pussy was almost overwhelming to her. She lifted her head.

"Goddamn it, Keisha, hold your damn position. We need these action shots," Ray said.

"Then hurry up and take them," she shouted back. "You told me that if I felt uncomfortable, then I was to tell you. Well, I feel uncomfortable."

"I don't give a shit right now. Get your fucking head back in her pussy and suck it up," Ray said angrily.

"Come on, baby, it'll be over in a sec," Trevi whispered to Keisha. "If you don't do this, they'll start saying that you're uncooperative and then stop giving you work."

"I don't care about the work," Keisha said.

"Then you shouldn't have chosen to get in this business. This is just scene one. We've got two more left."

"Let's go!" Ray yelled.

Keisha got back in position, and Phil took what seemed like thousands of pictures. Finally, he was done.

"Phil, get Trevi's dildo out and hand it to Keisha. Keisha, I want some real action, and not that gentle bullshit. Okay, everybody back in place. Action!"

In a flash, the need to get money overcame any hesitation for Keisha. She resigned herself to having to do something she didn't enjoy. She began licking and sucking Trevi's pussy with angry aggression, immersing her face so that it was enveloped. She really didn't know what to do, but it must have been working because Trevi was really moaning loudly.

"Keep going, Keisha," Trevi said, under her breath. "You are doing so good that I'm going to give you a pretty good apartment."

"Good shit," Ray said to Steven. "That's some good shit."

"I don't want a pretty good apartment, I want a great apartment," Keisha said. She bent over and picked up the glass dildo. "This is going to make you give me that apartment."

Keisha gave the dildo to Trevi, who licked it, and then she handed it back to Keisha. Keisha licked the dildo and then put it inside Trevi.

"You like this?" Keisha asked.

"Yeah, move it more," Trevi responded. Keisha began thrusting the dildo back and forth, slowly at first, and then with more speed.

"More," Trevi said. "Go faster, Keisha. Go faster!"

Keisha kept thrusting and thrusting, faster and faster, hoping that she didn't hurt Trevi. But Trevi wasn't known as the orgasm queen for nothing. Trevi began to writhe and moan to every motion Keisha made, and all of a sudden, Keisha was getting more into it.

"Grab my tits," Trevi demanded, and Keisha complied. She kept probing with her left hand and grabbing her breasts with her right.

"I'm cumming!" Trevi screamed.

"Get in close with the cum shot," Ray instructed the cameraman. Keisha was now driving the dildo into Trevi as far as she could. Trevi's lips began to quiver, and she twisted and turned on the black couch.

"Jesus! Jesus!" Trevi screamed. "Oh my God!"

She arched her back and suddenly, her pussy began squirting liquid all over Keisha's hand.

"Fuck!" Keisha said, somewhat disgusted.

"Cut!" Ray yelled. "That's it for this scene. Good job, girls! All right, set up the next scene. I want to get it ready and going in the next ten minutes."

"Damn, girl," Trevi said to Keisha, "that was some great shit. You sure you haven't done this before?"

Marisa came on the set and handed Keisha and Trevi a box of baby wipes. "So, Keisha, how was your first girl-girl scene?"

"Well," Keisha said, wiping off her hand. "I now know that I'm not a lesbian in my private time. Trevi, you're beautiful, and I can appreciate your beauty, but I'm not a pussy licker."

"I don't know about that, darling," Trevi said. "You did a damn good job for not being a lesbian."

"Yeah, I know. I'm wiping off the results," Keisha said.

"Oops," Trevi laughed. "I forgot to tell you I was a squirter."

"You damn near soaked her," Marisa laughed.

Marty walked on the set.

"Ray wants you guys on the bedroom set. Put your dresses back on, and get over there right now."

"Wait, we're not getting a break?" Keisha asked.

Marisa started laughing.

"Honey, this is porn," Marisa said. "We don't get breaks. You fuck and then you go home. Right now, you fuck."

Chapter 18

Anger ventilated often hurries toward forgiveness; and concealed often hardens into revenge.

—Edward G. Bulwer-Lytton

Keisha and Trevi walked into the bedroom set, which looked—not surprisingly—like every other bedroom set in porn. Cheap wood paneling and a cheap bed made it look like the motel room from hell. Don Juan was taking off his shirt, while Bruce Thumper and Long Island Dong were off-set talking to Ray and Steven.

"Goddamn, this room smells like ass," Don Juan said. "Can't they fucking clean this muthafucka up once in a while?"

"Nigga, it's probably your ass," Marty said, laughing. "You've fucked on this set more times than I can remember."

"Nah, it's not my ass," Don Juan said, laughing, "because my ass smells like peaches and cream."

"That's why a nigga can't smell his own shit," Marty said. "Get your clothes off. I've got to talk to Ray."

Marty walked off-set, where he interrupted Steven talking to Bruce and Long Island Dong.

"I need a good reaction from Keisha, so I want you to give it to her long and hard," Steven said. "I mean, I want it rough. Slap her ass, and make that muthafuckin' pussy flap by the time you're done. That'll make some good video."

"Now, you know I go deep," Bruce said. "Do you want me to do some anal?"

"No, no anal," Steven said. "I want to save that for the next video. But she's going to take a dick deeper than she's ever taken one."

"Too bad we can't do a double pen on her," Long Island Dong said. "She's a pretty young thing."

"You may not be able to do the DP, but you can do pretty much anything else," Ray said. "Enough talk. Let's get to shooting."

They all began walking to the set.

"All right, everybody, this is the orgy scene. We're going to get this going and then break for lunch. Keisha, you're lucky. Everybody else will be here well into the night. But we have some new girls coming later on, so you'll be done."

"Thanks, because I'm already tired," Keisha said.

The whole crew laughed in unison.

"You'd better get used to it," Ray said. "Porn is about fucking and fucking for a long time. Besides, these muthafuckas"—he pointed to Don Juan, Bruce, and Long Island—"are the ones that have to do all of the work. You just have to sit back and enjoy it."

"Yeah, right," Trevi said.

"Okay, let's get ready to go, everybody," Ray said, retreating to the side. Steven passed him, walking on the set.

"Keisha, come here." Marisa was touching up her makeup, but she broke away to talk to Steven.

"Yeah?" she said.

"How are things? Are you okay?"

"Yeah, I'm cool."

"Is it what you expected?"

"I don't think you could ever expect something like this," she said.

"Look, this is your first time," Steven said. "But it will get easier as you get used to it."

Keisha stopped and looked at Steven closely. "Really? How do you know this?"

Steven stammered, "I mean, everything pretty much gets easier the more you do it."

"That is a principle I would greatly challenge," Keisha said, walking to the set for her scene and away from Steven.

"Trevi and Keisha, you've decided to come to see the new apartment, and you find Don Juan there by himself. You guys are going to get on the bed and get started. Then the doorbell is going to ring, and you're going to let in Bruce and Long Island. They are the people who live here. And then you'll go back on the bed and fuck again. Give me some great angles, and I want every hole filled. We're doing this both for the hardcore and hotels, so the camera angles will be from both. Anybody need anything?"

"Yeah, tell Bruce to lube his shit, because the last time, he almost bust me wide open," Trevi said.

"I got you, baby," Bruce said.

"There's some more lube in the nightstand drawers if you need it," Marty said.

"All right, let's get started," Ray bellowed. "Everybody, take your places."

He walked back to his monitor.

"Ready—action!"

Keisha and Trevi walked into the bedroom, where Don Juan was lying on the bed, completely naked.

"Oh, baby, what are you doing naked on the bed?" Trevi asked as they stood in the doorway.

"I just finished working on the pipes and I thought I'd take a quick nap."

"Speaking of pipes," Keisha said, sitting on the edge of the bed, "I'd like to see more of your pipes."

"Baby, is it okay?" Don Juan asked.

"It's not only okay," Trevi said, taking off her dress, "but I want to get some of your pipe too."

Don Juan lifted up and kissed Trevi deeply, then kissed Keisha. His breath was minty, very, very minty. It was minty like he'd just eaten a whole forest of mint.

Don Juan leaned back and Trevi began sucking his dick. Keisha was supposed to suck on his balls but instead started sucking on his chest.

"Ooh, baby, that's some good shit," Don Juan said. "Keep sucking that dick, girl. That's right, deep-throat that bitch."

Keisha kept licking Don Juan's chest, tasting all the oil he'd spread on himself.

"Keisha, suck on his balls while Trevi keeps sucking his cock," Ray instructed. The cameraman was literally straddling all three of them. "I want some really good sucking action down there. After a while, I want you two to play tag-team with his dick."

Keisha began putting Don Juan's balls in her mouth, while Trevi kept sucking his dick.

"Gag on that dick, bitch," he said, as Trevi tried to deep-throat it. Keisha lifted up from Don Juan's balls and began to lick the shaft of Don Juan's dick.

"Hold it right there," Ray instructed. "Phil, do your thing."

Phil took more pictures, particularly of Keisha and Trevi kissing Don Juan's dick.

"All right, give me more sucking, and then we're going to bring Bruce and Dong in, and we'll start the fucking. Okay, action!"

Keisha was almost totally exhausted as she kept sucking Don Juan's dick. His dick could have been a cucumber, or a Popsicle, but it didn't represent anything sexual to her anymore. It was just an inanimate thing attached to a person. The short night of sleep and the acting had all conspired to make her feel like a rag doll. She could feel her will lessening, and she was becoming more compliant. In other words, she wasn't thinking anymore, she was simply acting.

"That's it, Keisha, really suck that muthafucka!" Ray shouted. He turned to Marty. "Get Bruce and Dong ready at the door."

"Two bitches on my dick," Don Juan said, reading his lines. "Now that's what I'm talking about."

"Bruce and Dong, knock on the door," Ray said.

Bruce knocked on the door, and Keisha, Trevi, and Don Juan all stopped.

"Who is that?" Trevi asked.

"Goddamn it, that's Chet and Marvin," Don Juan said, standing up. "I told them that I needed some help with the job, and they said they'd come right over."

"Just let them go away," Keisha said.

"Or let them join us," Trevi said, rising and walking from the bedroom set to the living room set. She opened the door and stood in front of Bruce and Dong completely naked.

"Hello, Chet. Hello, Marvin. Come on in," she said nonchalantly. Bruce and Dong walked into the apartment, wide-eyed.

"Damn, girl, does Chuck know that you're here naked?" Bruce got in back of Trevi, while Dong rubbed her breasts.

"Not only does he know that I'm naked, he's in the bedroom."

Trevi took both of their hands and led them into the bedroom, where Keisha was sucking Don Juan's dick.

"I know you said that you needed help, but I didn't know that you wanted this type of help," Dong said, smiling.

"Come on in, take off your clothes, and join in the fun," Don Juan said.

Bruce and Dong took off their clothes in one fell swoop, and now five people were on the bed. Keisha kept sucking off Don Juan, while Trevi laid down on the bed. Dong began eating out Trevi, while she started sucking Bruce's dick.

"That's perfect, you guys," Ray shouted. "Keep it up. Make it look like this is one long, choreographed scene. I don't want to stop for any reason."

"Oww!" Keisha said, lifting up from Don Juan's dick. The cameraman had stepped on her leg while trying to film Dong licking Trevi's pussy. "Watch your damn self."

"Just get back on his dick and do your job," he responded.

Keisha started sucking his dick again.

"Damn, Angie, you can suck a mean dick," Bruce said, reading his line. "Chuck, you are one lucky man."

"You damn right," Don Juan said. "That's why I married her."

"Let's switch off," Keisha said. "I want to suck Bruce's big dick!"

The five unraveled, and Trevi slid down Don Juan's body so that they were in the sixty-nine position. Keisha got on her knees and took Bruce's dick in her left hand, and Dong's dick in her right. She sucked on one and then jacked off the other. And then she'd switch.

"Your dicks taste so good," Keisha said, taking a breath between sucking.

"Girl, you know exactly what to do."

Keisha put her mouth back on Bruce's dick, and he put his hand on her head, forcing her to gag. She pulled back.

"Don't fucking do that again," she said angrily.

"You know you like it," Bruce said, smiling.

"No, I don't. And if you fucking do that again, I'll reduce your dick from ten inches to three."

"Damn, girl, you're fucking hardcore," Dong said, laughing. "I like that."

"All right, enough chitchat out there," Ray scolded. "Let's get to the fucking. Trevi, I want you to fuck Don Juan. Keisha, I want you to get fucked by Bruce while you suck Dong's dick. And then we'll switch it off. Let's get into position. If anyone needs any lube, start lubing right now, because I don't want it happening on camera."

"I've got a question," Keisha said.

"What?" Ray said, walking back to his monitor.

"Do we have condoms?"

Ray looked at Steven and then back at Keisha.

"There's no need," he answered. "This is a no-condom shoot because everybody's been tested. So you don't have anything to worry about."

"Yeah, but—"

"Yeah, but nothing. Let's get ready to shoot. Keisha, get back into position."

Keisha hadn't known that this would be a no-condom shoot, and if she'd known at the beginning of the day, she probably wouldn't have agreed to participate. But now, after having done so much, she suddenly felt that she didn't have the will to either protest or walk away. It was a job that needed to be done. So Keisha got into position, bending over with her hands on the bed. Bruce was in back of her, ready to enter her, and Dong was in front of her, with his limp dick a few inches from her face. Trevi was in the cowgirl position, as Don Juan held his dick, stroking it to keep it hard.

"On my call, get ready for action," Ray said. "Phil, have you taken enough photos?"

Phil went in and out of the scene, and Bruce mugged for the camera, giving his best fuck face for the camera.

"Yeah, I'm done."

"All right, then, let's go, y'all. Action!"

At the word *action,* Bruce started beating his dick against Keisha's ass, and she took Dong's dick into her mouth. Trevi sat on Don Juan's dick and began writhing.

"Oh, baby, give it to me," Trevi said.

It would have been comical to Keisha, all the fake moaning and groaning, but she was too busy sucking a dick and worrying about Bruce to take notice. Plus, she had her lines to deliver. She turned her head toward Bruce and delivered them.

"What the fuck are you waiting for? Give it to me

and give it to me hard," she demanded. Bruce took his dick, twirled it in a circle, and then entered Keisha.

"Jesus," Keisha said under her breath. She stuck out her left hand and tried to put it on Bruce's abdomen so she could make sure he didn't go deep. But he started slow and then started building speed, thrusting deeper and deeper inside her.

"Aww, aww, aww," Keisha said. It wasn't so much a moan as a visceral reaction to being fucked.

"Keep your mouth on that dick, Keisha," Ray instructed. "You're doing great."

Keisha kept trying to get a rhythm, where she'd sway back and forth with Bruce's thrusting.

"Goddamn, this bitch's pussy is tight as a muthafucka," Bruce said to Dong.

"And she can suck a mean dick," Dong responded.

Dong reached over and started rubbing Trevi's breast and French kissing her. Keisha was now gagging on Dong's dick, and the pounding from Bruce was beginning to hurt.

"Oh God," she yelled. "Oh God!"

"Yeah!" Bruce said, taking his hands and slapping Keisha's ass. His hand left a red mark.

"I need some more dialogue from you, Keisha," Ray said.

"Fuck me! Fuck me!" Keisha said. "Fuck me harder, dammit!" That was something she'd never really say during sex, but she couldn't think of anything else. Her mind was blank, and she was simply a vessel in this whole undertaking. For her, it was like being really high on weed, where everything around her became disconnected from her as a person. They just became objects. Bruce and his dick, Dong and his dick, Trevi and her pussy, Don Juan and his dick, her own pussy and mouth, were simply objects connecting together. But strangely, something unexpected began to happen. She began feeling sexual pleasure, almost as an involuntary reflex.

After about five minutes of action, Keisha and Trevi switched. Keisha lay on her back, while Don Juan got on top of her. Long Island Dong mounted Trevi, while she sucked Bruce's dick. Of course, before they could do anything, Phil needed to take more pictures, so Don Juan was inside of Keisha, but not moving. As uncomfortable as that was, at least Keisha could rest while on her back.

"Hurry up with those fucking pictures," Ray screamed at Phil.

"Okay, okay!" Phil took three up-close photos of Keisha's makeup-smeared face and was done. "We're a go," he said.

"Let's give it our all, everyone. We're getting close to the end of this scene, and I'm sure that the crew is ready for lunch," Ray said.

"Yeah," the crew said in unison.

"Give me some good fucking, y'all. Action."

Don Juan started moving slowly inside Keisha's pussy. How he'd stayed hard during the photos was a mystery to her. "I'm going to show you how I give it to my wife," he said to Keisha.

"Bring it, baby," Keisha said. "I want the best apartment you guys have."

"Oh, you'll get that," Don Juan said, huffing and puffing as he stroked Keisha, "and a little bit more."

"Oooh, papi, give me more," Keisha cooed.

Right next to Keisha, Trevi was trying her best to keep Long Island Dong hard, but he just couldn't keep it up. He kept fucking her for a few minutes, and then he lost his erection. So she eventually had to turn around and stroke him until he was hard again.

"Remind me to not use Long Island Dong again," Steven whispered to Ray. "He's fucking up the scene."

"Why the fuck doesn't he use Viagra?" Ray asked, looking at the monitor at the scene unfolding about five feet away.

"Pride," Steven answered. "The motherfucka is one of those old porn men that believe that if you have to take a pill to get hard, then you should get out of the industry."

"Well, he should get out, then, because his dick has been as limp as a wet piece of lettuce for most of this scene."

Everyone was fucking and the scene looked hot behind the monitor. The monitor was sort of a magic filter for Ray. If he looked at the sex scene directly, it looked like a raw, unsexual group of people having intercourse. But when he looked through the monitor, it looked sexy, hardcore, and as though everyone was at the height of orgasmic pleasure. His job was to create and perpetuate that fiction.

"That's enough fucking, everybody," Ray said, leaving the monitor and walking to the middle of the bedroom set. Everyone was sweaty and tired.

"It's time for the money shot. Trevi, I want you to take it from Dong and Bruce in the face, and Keisha, I want you to take Don Juan's load in the mouth. Okay, let's—"

"I won't do it," Keisha whispered.

Ray turned around. "What did you say?"

"I said that I'm not going to take a cum shot in the mouth. I'm not going to do it. You can have him shoot his cum on my ass, but I'm not going to have any man's cum in my mouth or face."

Ray stared at Keisha and then walked right next to her so that only she could hear him.

"If you don't fucking take Don Juan's dick in your mouth and not only take his cum shot in your mouth, but smile while you swallow it, I'll fucking make sure that you don't get paid a muthafucking dime from this shoot. You'll walk off this set one pissed-off muthafucka, and no one will care."

Ray stood up and looked down at Keisha. "Now, do I make myself clear?"

Everyone was staring at Keisha, waiting for her reaction. She raised her head and looked Ray directly in the eye.

"I will not take a fucking cum shot in the mouth," she said, strongly and defiantly.

Ray again stared at her and then silently walked away. He looked at the monitor, and all the actors kept looking at Keisha. They weren't used to someone standing up for themselves. Finally, Ray spoke.

"Don Juan, cum on Keisha's belly," Ray shouted angrily. "All right, action!"

Don Juan started fucking Keisha, stroking her faster and faster, as though they'd been fucking for hours.

"Yes, that's it," Keisha said. "Give it to me, Daddy!"

Trevi was getting fucked by Long Island Dong and was sucking Bruce's dick. Finally, it was time for the money shot, and Long Island Dong took his dick out and walked so that he was side by side with Bruce. Trevi took both dicks in her hands and pressed them together, sucking them both at the same time. She then kept jerking off Bruce.

"I'm going to fucking—cum!" he yelled, and

then he came on her face, white jizz getting on her cheek, eye, and hair. As soon as he came, she deep-throated his dick, as though she wanted to suck all of the cum out of his dick. Next was Dong, who came on the other side of Trevi's face. And she did the same deep-throating.

Phil rushed in to take shots of her face, letting the cum drip off her chin and eyelash. He walked back off the set, and remarked to a crew member, "That's some good shit. We'll be able to put that cum shot on the Web site and sell thousands of subscriptions."

Now it was Keisha's turn.

"Shit, girl, your pussy feels so good," Don Juan said, his face scrunched into an orgasmic mishmash.

"Cum for me, papi. Give me your load."

Don Juan moved once and then twice more inside Keisha.

"Awwww fuck!" he yelled, pulling out as he came on Keisha's belly and tits. Phil again ran over to take as-it-happened pictures of the cum shot.

"That's it, y'all. Let's take a break for lunch," Ray said.

Immediately, the crew struck and walked out for lunch. Marisa threw the guys towels, and Trevi picked up the baby wipes and began wiping the cum from her face.

"I hate when it gets in my hair," she said, trying to wipe it out of strands of hair.

Keisha was quiet. She waited patiently for Trevi to give her the box of baby wipes.

"So, how did you like it?" Don Juan asked her, as he wiped off his dick.

"I can't even think," she said, her expression not changing. "But I'm out."

Trevi handed Keisha the box of baby wipes and

looked at her with compassion. "Then welcome to porn, where thinking is not only not allowed, but heartily discouraged."

Keisha took a baby wipe and slowly wiped the cum off her belly and tits. She was now a porn actress, whether she liked it or not.

Chapter 19

Let's not forget that the little emotions are the great captains of our lives and we obey them without realizing it.

—Vincent van Gogh

Keisha slowly walked into the dressing room, the sensation in her body numb to any emotion or thought. She was just there. Trevi was already in the dressing room, busy laughing with Marisa and Allison, while the rest of the crew was eating lunch. Trevi still had two more scenes to do.

"How are you feeling, Keisha?" Trevi asked.

"I don't know," she responded, taking her clothes off of the rack. She slowly began to dress, putting on her jeans first.

"That's exactly how I felt when I finished my first scenes," Trevi said.

"Don't worry. You'll get used to it," Marisa said. "Every actress does. What you have to develop is a method of coping."

"A method of coping?" Keisha asked wearily. "What the hell is that?"

"Little things," she said. "What you did out there was not intercourse, but penetration."

"Penetration? What's the difference?"

"It's subtle," Trevi said. "Intercourse is what I have with my boyfriend, or in my personal life. That comes with feelings and emotions. What I do on the set is have a man penetrate me, and that's completely different. Penetration is a job. I may cum with both, but there's a big difference. Once you understand those differences, it'll make your job a lot easier."

Keisha stopped. "Don't you feel used, whether or not you figure out a way to not make it personal?"

Allison started laughing.

"What?" Keisha asked. "Did I say something funny?"

"Yeah, you did," Allison said. "You asked if people felt used. Girl, what the hell did you think this was? This is porn! Of course a person feels used, because that's the point of porn. We use each other as much as possible. And when you don't have any more use, you're done. Come on, Keisha, you're smarter than that. You knew what you were getting into, and you got what you expected."

She didn't say another word to anyone until Steven walked into the room.

"Keisha, I just wanted to say that you were great out there," he said, smiling. "You were nervous, but you overcame that. You were a real professional, and you should be proud of yourself. Now in the next scenes—"

"I'm done," she said. "There are no next scenes."

"Wait, you have two more scenes to do," he said, staring at her intently.

"Where's my money?" Keisha said, putting on her top.

"I've got it right here," Steven said, pulling out a

white envelope. "It was money well deserved. I think we're going to sell tons of videos. I want to use you for another video as soon—"

"Just give me my money," she said, grabbing the envelope and her bag. She didn't appear to be angry or agitated, she just wanted to get out of there.

"Do you need a ride home?" Steven asked, as Keisha walked out of the dressing room.

"No, I got it, thanks," she said, without turning around. As she was walking to the door, she passed the cast and crew, who were eating their lunch. Don Juan stopped her.

"I just wanted to say that I had a great time working with you," he said politely. "Maybe we could get together later?"

"Uh, I don't know about that," she said, trying to leave.

"Well, think about it. And, I'd love to work with you again."

"We'll see."

Keisha walked out of the Stage and into the parking lot, then down the sidewalk. As she left, Don Juan looked at Steven.

"Think she'll make it?" Don Juan asked.

"What the fuck do I care?" Steven responded, picking up a soda. He opened it and continued to watch Keisha leave.

"I'll use her as long as I can and then find a new girl," he said, sipping on the soda. "This is L.A., where there are thousands of girls wanting to get fucked for money."

"Just call me when you find them, and I'll be there to fuck them," said Don Juan, laughing.

There were no limos to take her back home, and it was at least an hour bus ride back to Inglewood.

But she had five thousand dollars in her pocket, so it was time to splurge for a cab. She flagged one down and collapsed in the backseat.

"Inglewood," she ordered to the cabbie.

"That's a sixty-dollar fare," he said.

"Did I stutter?" she asked. "Take me to fucking Inglewood."

The cabbie turned around, hit his meter, and started driving to Inglewood. Keisha stared out of the taxi window, seeing nothing.

When Keisha arrived at Patra's apartment, Patra was out. Keisha dumped her duffle bag, purse, and white envelope full of Steven's money on the couch, then dragged herself to the bathroom. She turned on the shower and let the steam rise before she got in. As the water hit her, she took her loofah and started scrubbing. As she scrubbed, tears ran down her face as she scrubbed harder and harder, trying to scrub away the smell of porn, the feelings of porn, and the emotions of porn.

"Keisha, are you okay? I've been knocking on the door for at least five minutes."

"Yeah, I'm okay," she said. "I'll be out in just a minute."

Keisha turned off the shower and stood there for a second, trying to catch her breath and her thoughts. She toweled herself off and put on her robe. Patra was sitting on the couch when Keisha walked into the living room.

"Damn, girl. You had to be in that shower for at least thirty minutes," Patra said as she munched on a cookie.

"How long have you been here?"

"At least forty-five minutes," she said. "So how was the shoot?"

"Fine," Keisha said, averting her eyes.

"Wait a second," Patra said, sitting up. "You just spent about six hours getting fucked on camera, and all you can say is fine? What was it like? Who did you fuck?"

Keisha stood there expressionless, half listening to Patra's questions. "Look, if you don't mind, I don't feel like talking about it. I barely had time to sleep last night, and that shit was hella fucking tiring. I'll tell you about it later."

"Cool," Patra said, backing off. "No problem. I'll go in my room and let you get some sleep."

Patra rose and started to leave.

"By the way, I'll be up and out of here next week," Keisha said. "I found an apartment near UCLA, and they said I can move in next Saturday. School starts tomorrow, and I need to get my mind set up for that."

"Congrats," Patra said. "You know that you can stay a little longer if you want to. When I said that I wanted my space, I didn't mean that you had to leave right away."

"Nah, you've been great," Keisha said. "But I've got to move on."

"Well, it's been great having you." Patra smiled.

"And I appreciate everything you've done to help me. I needed a place to stay, and you came through."

Patra walked over and hugged Keisha. "Get some rest, girl." She then walked into her bedroom, leaving Keisha alone. Keisha lay down on the couch and rested her head on her pillow. She didn't wake up for eight hours.

"So how are the cuts coming, Mario?" Steven asked, standing over his video editor. He was eating a sandwich. Steven wanted to get Keisha's video out and in the stores in two weeks—it was going to be a quick turnaround—and then check the results to see if it was selling.

"They're coming well," Mario said. "Your girl Keisha is raw, but she's pretty hot." Mario was in front of a computer, where he watched a loop of Keisha and Bruce having sex.

"I want you to loop that so the scene lasts about ten minutes," Steven said. "She is really taking it from Bruce, and Bruce is no joke."

"No, he isn't," Mario said, tapping on the keys. "I can stretch it out to about seven minutes without the average viewer knowing that it's looping. I've got a lot of face reaction shots, and then I've got a lot of pussy and dick shots. So we're good to go."

Mario clicked his mouse over a frame on the computer, and a loop of Keisha's face was put on the screen. She was bent down on her knees so that her face was on the ground. Her mouth was open, and she was breathing heavily.

"Ain't it great that with sex, you don't know if it is pain or pleasure if you just look at the face?" Steven laughed.

"I honestly can't tell," Mario said, smiling. "But I'll take her natural moans, add some stock ones, and the viewer will think that Bruce's dick is made of fucking gold."

"Do it," Steven said. "I want to get this thing turned around by the end of the week, and in packages by the next. It'll be in stores by the end of the month, and finally, *Pimp* Video will be in the stores."

"Keisha's a winner, Steven," Mario said, again cutting and pasting on the computer. "She's going to move videos. I hope you have her locked up for more movies."

"No problem," Steven said, finishing his sandwich.

"Strippers strip and then they go into porn. It's a natural progression and there ain't a damn thing they can do about it. I talked to my friend over at Gonzo Video, and he told me that if I can get a bitch—and he meant a really good bitch—then we could make millions. Then other bitches just like her will be lining up to be like her. Keisha is my really good bitch. And I'll keep paying her just enough so that she can't do a damn thing else."

"Yeah, where can you get the money in a day that you can get in porn?" Mario asked, laughing. "Working at the post office? I don't think so."

"Exactly," Steven said, turning to leave. "I always wanted to be a pimp, and I guess that's why I named my business that."

"Better to be the pimp than the bitch," Mario said, as Steven left.

"True dat," Steven said. "True dat."

Chapter 20

It was three in the morning when Keisha woke up. UCLA awaited her, but right now, all she wanted was a simple buzz. She lit a joint and thought about the evening. She had thoughts, all kinds of thoughts, running through her head, but she couldn't deal with them herself. She could hear Patra sleeping in the bedroom, so she was out. There was one other person she could talk to, but could she bring herself to call?

She picked up her cell phone and dialed.

"Who is this?" the voice on the line answered.

"It's Keisha."

"Keisha, what are you doing?"

"Donovan, I need to talk to someone who knows me," Keisha said. "I've had a different day and I need to make sense of it. But can I ask you to do one thing?"

"What's that?"

"Don't judge me."

"Well, you know, that tells me you did something you know I won't like, and, therefore, it's probably not going to be possible to not judge you. I can listen to you, though."

Keisha paused. "Okay, then just listen. I did a porn video today, and I feel like shit."

"Okay," he responded.

" 'Okay' is all you can say? Just, 'okay'?"

"Come on now, Keisha, you were dancing at a titty bar. Do you really think that getting into porn is that big of a leap?"

"I knew you'd judge me," she said, about to hang up.

"Wait," he said. "I didn't judge you. I simply made an observation. Look, I dealt drugs for years, so how in the hell can I judge you? But there are some things I know. If you sell weed, you're going to end up selling some crack, and then you're going to jail. And if you dance at a titty bar, you're going to find yourself doing some type of porn or magazine. So that's what I was talking about. So why do you feel like shit?"

"Because I wasn't in control. It was the first time I've had sex where I didn't feel in control."

"So how come you didn't just get up and leave?"

"Because I needed the money," she said. "I needed the money for school and for an apartment of my own."

"There were other ways to get that money, so you made a choice."

"But what happens if I need the money *now*? I start school today."

"Oh yeah," he said. "UCLA. Look, why don't you just put it out of your mind and never do it again?"

"But I can't forget it," she said. "I can't get the sounds and the sights out of my brain, and I can't believe that someone is going to buy a video, seeing me have sex. I can't take that back, and that's what is making me feel like shit."

"Then we're in the same situation," he said.

"What do you mean?"

"Every time I look out the window," he said, "I see the results of my work. And it haunts me. Crackheads, constantly looking for that next hit, keep coming up to me, looking for drugs. You know how it makes me feel to know that I started many of them on their path of destruction? But I got up one day and said that I had to make a change. And that's the same thing you have to do."

"Why did you change?"

"I don't know exactly," he said. "I was lying in my bed one night, after having just sold about a thousand dollars' worth of crack, but I wasn't happy. I had a dealer on my ass, threatening to kill me. And you know where all of my boys are right now."

"Yeah, dead, in jail, or on their way to both."

"And then I lost you over some stupid shit. So I just started thinking. Why the fuck am I doing this shit? What is the point? I'm hustling, and my community hates me. My family hates me. And it's not like I'm fucking making enough money to get out of my mother's house. So I kept thinking, and realized that I was busy feeling sorry for myself, instead of putting myself in control. So I started taking steps."

"Going to church?"

"Naw, that came later. The first step I took was to write out who I was right then and there, and what I really wanted to be. And most important, I made sure to understand that I was who I was, and I could also determine who I was going to be. But wishing on that shit wasn't going to make that happen. So let me ask you a question. Are you a stripper and into porn?"

"Yes."

"Is that what you want to be tomorrow?" he asked.

"No."

"Then take steps. Take steps for yourself and don't worry about what others think."

Keisha was silent for a second.

"You there?" Donovan asked.

"Yes, I'm here."

"You okay?"

"Yeah. I just wanted to say—"

Donovan stopped her. "Don't worry about it. Just get to where you want to go, and then call me when you get there. We'll have some really good stories to tell."

"That's a promise," Keisha said.

Keisha hung up the phone and walked over to the desk. She took out a pad of paper and started writing down who she was, and what she wanted to be. Despite the fact that she'd gotten into UCLA, she didn't really know why she wanted to go there. She just knew that her mentor had told her that she needed to go there, and she wanted to be just like her. But what did she want out of life? Who was she really? That's what Keisha needed to find out, explore, and then come to grips with. It would be only then that she'd be strong enough to succeed.

"Keisha," Patra said, shaking a sleeping Keisha. "Keisha, get up. Don't you have to go to school today?"

"Oh shit," Keisha said sleepily. "Fuck, what time is it?"

"It's eight o'clock in the morning," she said.

"Shit," Keisha said, rising. "I have my first class at nine o'clock. I gotta get going!"

Keisha walked into the bathroom and turned on the shower.

"Just get showered and I'll run you to class," Patra yelled from the living room.

"Thanks!" Keisha said, as she scrubbed away. She rinsed off and then turned off the water. "Patra, do me a favor and pull out my black jeans and put them on the couch."

Keisha dried off and then ran into the living room. Patra sat in a chair and watched as Keisha put on her clothes.

"Do you need me to pick you up?" Patra asked.

"No, I'm going directly from my apartment to the club," Keisha said, pulling on a T-shirt. "For some reason, Sean scheduled me for today. It's like I've been up for seventy-two hours straight. But today I should be cool. All I have to do is pay for my registration, get my classes, go to the bank, and then drop off my deposit at my apartment."

Keisha put on the rest of her clothes and they ran out of Patra's apartment. As Patra got ready to start the car, she suddenly stopped and looked at Keisha.

"I just thought of something," she said, smiling.

"What?"

"Well, the cliché is that strippers are only stripping because they are working their way through college."

"Okay."

"Well, you really are working your way through college," Patra said. "I just think that's funny."

Keisha smiled. "I'm glad that I can break the stereotype."

Patra started up the car. "Yeah, you're the Rosa Parks of strippers."

As Patra drove through Los Angeles, Keisha thought about the changes she was going to make, and the problems she had to face.

Head-on, she thought. *I'm going to face everything head-on.*

Patra got off the 405 Freeway and turned onto Wilshire.

"Excited?"

"Yeah," Keisha said. "It took me a long time to get here, and I can't believe that I'm actually here."

Finally, Patra reached the campus. "Here we are," she said.

"Thanks," Keisha said, gathering her bag and opening the door.

"Hey," Patra said. "Do your best. I wish I was going to school along with you."

"You know, it's never too late," Keisha said, smiling. "You can always go back to school."

"Nah," Patra said, turning back to the steering wheel. "Some folks are cut out to go to school and others are cut out for stripping. You're a student. And I'm a stripper. And nothing is going to change that fact. Go get to class."

Keisha slammed the door closed, and Patra drove away slowly. Keisha turned and looked out at the campus. Unlike during the summer, it seemed like every space on campus was filled with students. And other than herself, she didn't see any other black people around. *This is going to be interesting,* she thought.

"Keisha!"

The voice sounded vaguely familiar, but as Keisha searched for it, she couldn't find it.

"Keisha!" the voice yelled out. And then she saw him. It was Donovan, sitting on the steps of the student union.

Keisha walked over to Donovan, who was dressed

casually in jeans and a Lakers jersey. He didn't look much different than the other students, except that he had a do-rag on his head.

"What the hell are you doing here?" she asked. She gave him a hug, something she hadn't done in months, because she was genuinely glad to see him.

"I thought about what you were talking about last night, and I thought you needed a little support. Look, I'm not here to embarrass you or anything like that. I just want to say that I'm rooting for you."

"Thanks." Keisha said.

"All right, I've got to get out of here. Give me a call sometime."

"I just might do that."

Donovan started walking off campus, then turned around, looking at Keisha. "See ya later, alligator."

Keisha smiled. It's what they'd said to each other as sixth-graders, and it was enough for them to go together from that point on.

"In a while, crocodile."

Donovan turned and began running off campus. Keisha watched him until he disappeared. She then turned back toward the campus.

"Okay," she muttered to herself. "Let's go do this shit."

Chapter 21

*Sometimes you have to get to know someone
really well to realize you're really strangers.*
                              —Mary Tyler Moore

"Can I help you?" Blackie said, stopping the older
woman from entering. The Chi Chi Room was bursting with people, even with it being a Monday. From
what he heard, there'd been a big drug deal between
the Bloods and the Mexican gangs, and now all of the
black gangsters were coming to the Chi Chi Room
to celebrate.

"I don't know. Can you?" she asked. She looked
vaguely familiar to Blackie, even though he knew he
hadn't met her before.

"Who are you looking for?"

"My daughter," she said. "I'm waiting for Keisha
Montez."

Blackie smiled and looked closely at the woman.
"And your name is?"

"Veronica Montez."

"Wait here."

Blackie walked back into the club. Patra was on
the stage, and the men were going wild.

"Bitch, shake that goddamn ass!"

She put her ass on the pole and then began making it pop, which seemed to put the pervert pit into a frenzy. Blackie ignored all that and walked up the stairs to Sean's office. Sean was sitting behind the desk. On the television was a porno, and he was staring intently at it.

"Yeah? What?"

"I got somebody at the front door who's waiting for Keisha."

"Whatever, man," he said, not taking his eyes off the television. "Tell him that the dancers are not allowed to talk to the customers. The last shit I need is some muthafuckin' police officer saying that we're pimping out the girls."

"I don't think you understand," Blackie said. "This ain't a dude. It's Keisha's mother."

"Keisha's Veronica?" Sean asked, finally turning from the television. "Veronica?"

"You know her?" Blackie asked.

Sean got up from the desk and breezed past Blackie. "Do I know her? Yeah, you could say that. She used to babysit me between going onstage. She was my dad's favorite dancer. And—"

Sean stopped and turned to Blackie. "I lost my virginity to her. And it was goooood! I hated when she just up and quit one day. No explanation. Just gone!"

They both sprang down the stairs, with Sean making it to the front door first.

"Veronica," he said. "It's been a long time."

"Yeah, but I didn't come here for you," she said. "I came here for Keisha. Where is she?"

"No hello? No hug?" Sean said, smiling. "I mean, we have history."

"History?" Veronica said, smiling wryly. "If we

have history, then I don't remember it, because it wasn't memorable."

Sean's smile slowly left his face. "She ain't here. If you want to wait for her, then it's going to cost you ten dollars. Ain't nobody getting a free ride. You should know that, Veronica, even if your memory is slipping in your old age."

Veronica reached into her bra and took out a twenty-dollar bill. She handed the bill to Blackie, who then gave her change.

"Get the fuck out of my way," she said to Sean.

"You're buying your own drinks," Sean said, as she walked by. "I'll make sure of that shit."

Veronica sat down at the bar and took a look around. The place hadn't changed much since she'd danced at the Chi Chi Room before Keisha was born. In fact, Keisha didn't even know she'd danced there. But she'd know tonight.

"Is that you, Veronica?" Debra was going on after Patra and had seen Veronica as she walked past.

Veronica turned.

"Debra?" she asked, slowly recognizing a face from her past.

Debra walked slowly to the bar, not knowing where she stood with Veronica. It hadn't been a good relationship the last time she'd seen her.

"Yeah, it's me." She sat down at the bar and pulled out a cigarette. She offered one to Veronica, who took it.

"What are you still doing here dancing?" Veronica asked, lighting her cigarette, then lighting Debra's.

"You need to put those cigarettes out," Blackie yelled.

"Fuck you," Debra said, turning back to the bar. "Yeah, I'm still here, but I'm pretty sure that I'm in my last days. Shit's starting to get loose, I'm getting old, and niggas are getting younger. That's when it's time to get the fuck off the stage."

"Don't I know that," Veronica said. "You moved my black ass off the stage when my shit got flabby."

"See, that's how these muthafuckas work. They split us apart," Debra said, puffing on her cigarette. "I tried to tell you before you left that I had nothing to do with pushing you off the stage. That was Sean. Sean took over for his old man and said that he was moving me to the weekends, and you were cool with it. I didn't know you weren't until you went off on me and then left. I owed you. I was a dumb fucking eighteen-year-old, and you took me under your wing. I never forgot that."

"Ah, I don't fault you," Veronica said, taking a final draft on her cigarette. "Bitches get the shaft from these muthafuckas. Look at them."

She pointed to the men who were going wild over Patra, who was about to finish her set.

"They don't give a shit about us. Sean doesn't give a shit about us. And nobody in the business gives a shit about us. We're the ones who have to stick together. But we never do."

Debra finished her cigarette, pressed it into the bar, and then flicked it to the floor. "What are you doing here?"

"I'm here to see my daughter," she answered.

"Is she new here?" Debra asked, getting up from her chair.

"No, she's been working here for over a year."

"A year?" she asked. "What's her name?"

"Keisha. Her name is Keisha."

Debra stared at Veronica. "Dammit, I thought she looked familiar, but I didn't connect the dots."

* * *

Keisha's first day at UCLA had been pretty un-eventful. Each class had lasted about thirty minutes, with the professors giving an overview of what the class was about, and they went over the schedule. Keisha was taking four classes: English, Spanish, Intro. Calculus, and Intro. Women's Studies. She had to get her shit together ASAP because UCLA was on the quarter schedule, and that meant tests came fast.

"I know that some of you were the smartest kids in your high school, and you probably skated all the way through your senior year," Mr. Sanchez said to his Spanish class. "But everyone at this school is smart. The defining factor will be who works the hard-est. If you don't work hard, you will find yourself falling behind and then eventually dismissed from school. If you work hard, you'll pass your classes. If you're conscientious, then you're going to excel. It is up to you as to which person you're going to be. I don't take roll, and I don't care if you come on time. It's all up to you."

Keisha listened and took what he said to heart. This was day one of her new life, and she was going to take advantage of it.

Fuck, she thought, looking at her watch. It was the end of the day, and she still needed to set up a bank account and pay her apartment deposit.

She ran down Westwood Boulevard into the bank and sat down at New Accounts. The bank was nearly empty, so when Keisha picked up the clipboard to sign in, no one was ahead of her.

"Keisha Montez," yelled the bank officer.

Keisha got up and sat down at the new accounts desk.

"Hello, Keisha, I'm Janet Dixon. How may I help you?"

"I'd like to deposit a check and open up a checking account," Keisha said, reaching into her purse. The check had somehow gotten smashed in its envelope, and instead of taking it out, Keisha simply handed everything to her.

"That's fine," Janet said. "Here, just fill out this application and we should be done in less than five minutes." Janet handed Keisha a form and a pen, and as Keisha filled it out, Janet took out the check from the envelope.

"Are you a student at UCLA?" she asked Keisha.

"Yes, I am," Keisha said proudly.

"That's great. What year are you?"

"I'm a freshman."

"Excited?"

"Yeah, I guess. Mostly trying to get things done." Keisha signed the bottom of the form and handed it back to Janet. Janet picked up Keisha's check and handed it back to her.

"Now if you could endorse the back of the check, we can then get your account opened."

Keisha scribbled her signature on the back of the check and handed it to Janet.

"Great," Janet said, looking at the check. She opened her desk and put the check in the drawer, then began inputting numbers into the computer.

"Now you know, your checking account is free as long as you keep a one hundred–dollar balance," Janet said, continuing to fill out the computer form.

Janet handed a statement to Keisha.

"Here you go," she said, as Keisha studied her statement.

"Wait, I think there's been a mistake," Keisha said, continuing to look at the statement. "I should be depositing five thousand, and not twenty-five hundred."

"No, I think I got it right," Janet said, opening the drawer again and pulling out the check. "Yes, this is correct." She handed the check to Keisha.

"Twenty-five hundred?" she said incredulously. "I was supposed to get five thousand!"

"Did you have two checks?" Janet asked, trying to be helpful.

Keisha went back to her purse and checked the envelope. It was empty. Keisha was angry now. There was no way she'd gone through what she'd done for only twenty-five hundred dollars. That just barely paid for her quarter at UCLA. It didn't do a damn thing for her apartment.

She stood up angrily. "Just go ahead and put in that deposit."

"You'll get an ATM card in the mail," Janet said. "Good luck at UCLA."

Keisha didn't hear a word as she left the bank. All she saw was red.

How was she going to tell Patra that she needed to stay at her house until she got things straightened out? And how was she going to confront Steven?

Clear the brain, she thought. *Clear the brain. I need to keep to the plan, just like I wrote it out.*

She called a cab. It was a twenty-dollar ride to the Chi Chi Room, but she wanted to get to the club early so she could study a bit before going onstage.

"Do you need a ride back?" the cab driver asked as he drove into the Chi Chi Room parking lot.

"No, I'm straight," she said, handing him a twenty. "Keep the change."

The line was growing in front of the club, so Keisha decided to go in the back way. The back door opened directly to the parking lot.

"Open up," she yelled. "It's me."

Debra opened the door and let Keisha in. Keisha put her bag on the counter and sat down.

"There's a whole bunch of niggas out there tonight," she said. "How are they paying?"

"Pretty damn good," Debra said. "School's back in, so we're starting to get college boys in. I think they've got some financial aid money coming in. Speaking of school, didn't you start today?"

"Yeah, I did."

"So how was it?"

"It was great," Keisha said, smiling. "I really think I'm about to go on a journey, and I just can't wait."

Debra looked at Keisha longingly, as though she saw in Keisha her own youth, and yet she knew she had news she had to deliver.

"Keisha, there's someone here to see you," Debra started.

"Who?" Keisha asked as she started taking out her bikini.

"It's—"

The door to the dressing room suddenly burst open.

"I think I'll wait—" Veronica stopped mid-sentence.

"Veronica?" Keisha said. "What are you doing here?"

"We need to talk," she said.

The two stared at each other, not knowing what to say.

"I think I'll leave you two alone," Debra said, gathering her things. "Good to see you again, Veronica."

"Same here," Veronica said, never taking her eyes off Keisha.

Debra left the dressing room, and Keisha put down her bag.

" 'Again'? You two know each other?" Keisha asked.

"Yes."

Keisha walked to the closet and took down a hanger with her clothes. "How?"

"How what?"

"How the fuck do you know Debra?"

"We used to work together."

"Wait a second," Keisha said, looking at her mother. "You used to give me shit about working here, and you used to dance?"

Keisha slipped into her pants and started putting on her shoes.

"What the fuck are you doing here in the first place?" Keisha asked, waving her hand dismissively. "If you're coming here because you want money, then you're shit out of fucking luck. I ain't giving you a nickel. You stole my muthafuckin' money, and I hope your boyfriend fucking got shot for it."

"If I wanted money," Veronica said, beginning to shout, but getting her control back, "then I would come in here and tell you I needed money. I messed up and I can't take that back. It is what it is. But there's an emergency."

"Then deal with the emergency," Keisha said, putting on the rest of her bikini, "and leave me the fuck alone. I'm not in your life, remember?"

"Do you think I would be here if I could handle this?"

"Yes, you would," Keisha said, walking toward Veronica. "You would bring your ass here because you're selfish. You'd bring your ass here because you don't have a bone in your body that isn't trying to exploit me." Keisha was right in her mother's face now. "So this is what I want you to do. I want you to turn your ass right around and get out of my fucking dressing room. I've got work to do."

"Your dressing room?" Veronica said with an ironic laugh. "I built this dressing room."

"What do you mean you built this dressing room?" Keisha said slowly. Suddenly, it dawned on her. "So you used to dance at this—how did you used to put it—nasty-ass club?" Keisha was now incensed. "You had the nerve to judge me?"

For the first time, Veronica was on her back heels. "I wasn't judging you," she said unconvincingly.

"To hell you fucking didn't," Keisha yelled. "You fucking judged me from the day I got here, and the fucking trip is that you drove me to stripping. Who else was walking around the house yelling that I wasn't shit? Who else was walking around the house saying that I would never amount to shit? Who else used her daughter in a way to make her feel small and fucking worthless?"

Right then, Patra walked into the dressing room from the stage.

"Hey, girl," she said, not realizing the tension in the room. She turned to Veronica. "Who are you?"

"She," Keisha interrupted, "is no one. She's about to leave."

Veronica sucked on her teeth and began making her way to the door.

"Everyone has a chance at redemption, Keisha. Even me."

Keisha walked up to her and got nose to nose.

"I hope you burn in hell," she said with a sneer. "Now get out. I've got work to do."

Veronica turned and left.

"Who was that?" Patra asked again.

"That," Keisha said, checking her makeup again, "was my mother."

Without another word, Keisha walked past Patra and toward the stage. The men started howling and Keisha knew it was going to be a long night.

Chapter 22

Ideals are like stars: You will not succeed in touching them with your hands, but like the sea-faring man on the desert of waters, you choose them as your guides, and following them you reach your destiny.

—Carl Schurz

"Where's Steven?" Marty asked. Ray and Marty shared a second-floor office at *Pimp,* with Marty doing a lot of the go-fer work for both Steven and Ray.

"I don't know, muthafucka," Ray responded. "What do I look like? Radar? Get off your ass and see."

"Fuck you, nigga," Marty said. He got up and walked out of the office and looked down onto the first floor. The door to the warehouse was open, and Marty could see movement.

"Steven!" Marty yelled. "Steven!"

Steven walked out of the warehouse and looked up. "What?"

"Keisha is on the phone. She wants to talk to you! Do you want me to tell her to call back, or do you want to talk to her?"

"Yeah, I want to talk to her. Send her to my cell."

Steven walked back into the warehouse and Marty went back into the office. He picked up the phone and clicked the call over.

"Hello, Keisha. How are you doing?" Steven asked pleasantly.

"Not very fucking good," Keisha said.

"What do you mean?"

"I'm not doing very fucking good because I didn't get all of my fucking money. You said that I was going to get five thousand dollars and not fucking twenty-five hundred. Where's the rest of my money?"

"Hold on one second," Steven said, putting his hand on the phone. He picked up boxes of *Pimp*'s first video, *Inside Keisha!* and checked it for defects. The warehouse was filled with thousands of boxes, and five workers were loading them onto trucks. "Make sure that these get into stores by the morning. I want reports by the end of the week."

He took his hand off the phone. "I'm sorry about that, Keisha. What were you saying?"

Keisha was lying on her couch, tired from her first week of school, and weary of dealing with Steven again. Patra had been cool about letting her stay at her apartment, and the money from the Chi Chi Room meant that she probably could get an apartment by the end of the month. But she wanted her money.

"You promised me five thousand for the shoot and the check was made out for twenty-five hundred. Where's my money?"

"I'm sorry to hear about that," Steven said. "I don't remember promising five thousand."

"You know what the fuck you promised, Steven, so don't go fucking senile on me now."

"Look, Keisha, I want you to be happy and I want you to make a ton of money," Steven said cheerfully. "Hey, if you make money, then I make money. Isn't that right?"

"Yeah."

"Right. And I want you to be happy, because if

I'm happy, then you're happy. But the job required you to do four scenes, and you only did two. So that's why you got a check for half."

"I want my money, Steven."

"Keisha, I've got an idea," Steven said. "I know how you can earn your money back. If you do two more scenes next weekend, then I can add them to the Web site for subscribers. I'll pay you twenty-five hundred dollars for the scenes, and we'll be all square."

Keisha pulled the phone from her ear for a second. She put it back and thought for a second about what Donovan had told her.

"It was a one-time shot, Steven," Keisha said. "I'm not doing it anymore."

"Come on, Keisha, was the experience bad?"

"It doesn't matter. I'm just not doing it anymore."

"Look, maybe you didn't understand, but in your release, you also said that *Pimp* Video has an option, and you are obligated to do a sequel to your first video. So you're going to do another video with us, or you're going to be in breach of contract. And don't forget, Keisha, I'm a fucking lawyer. You'll be working at the Chi Chi Room until you are Debra's age."

"Sue me then, muthafucka," Keisha said. "Because I'm not fucking again for you."

"Suit yourself," Steven said, surprised at Keisha's feistiness. "But understand that every decision has a consequence. Some people get fucked and others are the people who do the fucking. I do the fucking, and if you cross me, you're going to understand that real well."

"I'm not scared of you, or anybody else. Shove that money up your ass."

Keisha hung up the phone and lay back down on

the couch. She picked up Paula Giddings's book and tried to finish it. She needed a dose of black women's history.

Steven hung up the phone and walked up to his office. "Marty, call Joseph Silva and tell him that I need him to come in today."

"He's already scheduled to come in at one o'clock," Marty said. "You have him coming in with the promotional campaign from Keisha's video."

"Dammit, that's right," Steven said. "I'm fucking losing my mind."

Steven turned to leave and then stopped.

"Ray, where did you say Keisha was going to school?"

"I think she's going to UCLA."

"Oh yeah?"

"Yeah, why?"

"Nothing much," Steven said, walking to the door. "But I think I may have found another way to sell out her DVDs."

"How are you finding UCLA?" Mary asked. Keisha had dutifully fulfilled her promise to meet with Mary and as usual, her office was a mess.

"So far so good," Keisha said, sipping on a Jamba Juice. "The classes have been pretty easy, and the teachers pretty cool. I'm hoping that I'm not getting lulled into a false sense of confidence."

"No, I think you're pretty organized and focused," Mary said. "I think you'll be fine. Did you read Giddings's book?"

"Actually, I did," Keisha said, taking the book out of her backpack. "I've done my own reading of black women, but I've got to say that I never understood the depth of our history."

"Most women don't," Mary said, standing up and putting the book back on her shelf. "Gender roles tend to be put in the background when you talk about history. In some ways, it's just like race. With race, we tend to look at white as being the norm, and anything else, such as black or brown, as being the extraordinary. Those groups get little months or weeks for their history but are looked at as mere blips on the whole of American history. The same thing happens with gender. Men in history are assumed as the norm, and only a few women, and even fewer black women, are noticed. So women like yourself grow up as girls without history."

"I think we have history, but it's all bad history," Keisha said. "I just found out that my mother stripped at the same club as I strip. I think if I'd known that, then I might have made different choices."

"Why do you say that?"

"Because I don't like how my mother turned out," Keisha answered. "If I'd have known the path she took, then I would have said that that wasn't where I wanted to go."

"I don't think you can blame your mother for that," Mary said. "You have a brain. You made the decision, so take responsibility for it. By the way, have you made a decision about whether or not you're going to keep stripping?"

"You're a feminist, aren't you?"

"Yes, why?"

"Because I probably can figure out what you think about stripping. You said that I wasn't the first girl to come in here as a stripper, but I bet you still have some views."

"Of course I have views. Do you want to hear them?"

"Sure, hit me with them," Keisha said, lounging back in her chair.

"Okay, since you asked," Mary said, leaning back herself, "I think that when you get on that stage and take off your clothes, you are becoming an object, and not particularly a human sexual object. You're being exploited."

"Now see, that's where you're wrong. I'm exploiting all of the men," Keisha said. "It's their sorry asses that come into the Chi Chi Room wanting to see me. They know that they can't get me, but the suckers keep spending money in the fantasy that I will come to them. So they may see me as an object, but I'm doing the exploiting."

"Oh, really?" Mary said with a wry smile creeping onto her face. "That sounds like some quote-unquote postfeminist thought. Do you know what I mean when I say that?"

"No, I don't."

"A lot of postfeminists like to say that their bodies are their own commodities and if they want to exploit them, then it's okay. If you want a perfect example of that, then take a look at Madonna."

"I agree with that," Keisha said. "I exploit my own self."

"And that makes it better? Being exploited is being exploited. There's no difference in whether you're doing it, or someone else is doing it."

"Okay, but then let me ask you a question," Keisha said.

"Shoot."

"Isn't everyone exploited? I mean, you have an education and the university is exploiting you, isn't it?"

"You got me there," Mary said. "I am being exploited as a wage slave."

"Aha! So you can admit that there's not a big difference between you and me," Keisha said triumphantly.

"No, I didn't say that. There is a difference. When you have to use your sexuality rather than your brain to exploit, you are being stripped of your humanity, as I said earlier. When you use your intelligence, it is not to the detriment of either yourself or the people who pay you for your knowledge. And that's a big difference."

Mary got up and picked up a book, opened it, and found a page. "I remember a quote about exploitation that still rings true. It's by the poet W. H. Auden. There it is. He says that 'Almost all of our relationships begin and most of them continue as forms of mutual exploitation, a mental or physical barter, to be terminated when one or both parties run out of goods.' So now I ask you, Keisha. You're a smart woman, and you're going to get smarter. What is going to run out faster, your youthful, sexual body, or your brain?"

Keisha thought for a full minute, letting Mary's words wash over her. She'd always been conflicted by the feelings she'd had about stripping, versus the money she got. There was a resentment over the men in the pervert pit, and yet she thought herself superior because she had been exploiting them. Now that argument had been undercut, and she knew she had to get out, and get out now.

"Thank you, Mary," she said, tears welling in her eyes because things were now clear. "I needed to hear that."

"I did nothing," Mary said, standing up. "You asked the questions and you came up with your own answers. Now it is up to you to make the decisions."

On her way home, Keisha thought about all of the

decisions she'd made and all of the decisions the women in her life had made. Her mother, stripping at the Chi Chi Room and then chasing after every boyfriend who promised her love; Debra, hanging on to a fading beauty and sexuality because that was all she had; and Patra, young like Keisha, but doomed to follow in Debra's path. In each one of them, she saw a little bit of herself.

As Keisha took her keys out and prepared to walk into Patra's apartment, she heard Patra clearly and loudly yelling, "Ooh, baby, fuck me just like that!"

This wasn't the first time, and it wasn't something that had particularly bothered her in the past. She'd normally go through a routine of turning up the television and staring straight ahead as the john left the apartment in a huff. Patra would typically go into the kitchen and make something to eat, just like nothing unusual had happened.

"Cum for me, baby. I want to feel you cum inside of me!"

Keisha turned on the television, but still she could hear the telltale sounds of a man finally cumming. Then there was silence.

Patra opened the bedroom door and went into the bathroom, where she turned on the water. She went back into the bedroom, and Keisha could hear a little bit of talk between her and her john. Finally, after what seemed like an eternity, the two left the bedroom and began making their way to the living room.

"So you gonna call me?" Patra asked in the hallway.

"Yeah, I think I will," the male voice said. There was something about that voice that struck Keisha as being familiar. And when the man walked into the living room, she knew why.

"Ray?" Keisha asked, as Patra and Ray walked in. "What the fuck are you doing here?"

Ray smiled. "I didn't know you guys lived together. Damn, that's some freaky-ass shit."

Patra walked into the kitchen, pouring herself a glass of soda. "Ray came by the club yesterday and asked if he could spend some time with me. I thought I might have some time available, for a price."

Ray walked over to Keisha and sat down. He had a leering sneer on his face, as though he was a house cat that had eaten the pet canary.

"And that was a great time, well-spent," he said, leaning close to Keisha. "The next time, I might want to spend some time with you, Keisha."

"Get the fuck away from me," Keisha said, standing up and moving to the computer desk. "I wouldn't fuck you for any money."

Ray laughed. "Now, you know you have a price, just like every ho, or you wouldn't be shakin' your ass at the Chi Chi Room or getting fucked on camera. By the way, your video is selling like gangbusters. If you want a copy, I can probably sell you one."

Ray laughed even harder at his joke.

"Get the fuck out."

"Okay, okay, I'm going," Ray said, walking to the door. "Patra, it was great getting to know you, and for five hundred, I think I might know you some more next month. Keisha, it's been good."

Ray then walked out the door.

"What are you doing fucking Ray?" Keisha asked angrily.

"What do you care about who I fuck?"

"I just thought you wouldn't fuck somebody like Ray, that's all."

"Girl, I'd fuck you for five hundred dollars." Patra

laughed. "It's all about the money, darling. All about the money."

"You're better than that, Patra," Keisha said.

"Excuse me?" Patra put down her Coke and stared at Keisha.

"You heard me. You're better than this, all of this. You shouldn't be fucking the Rays of the world. You should be doing something that makes you feel good, that makes you feel like you have worth."

"Whoa, whoa, whoa, just a second," Patra said. "Who said that I don't like to do this? I like fucking, and more important, I like fucking for money. Don't put your shit on me."

"My shit? What is my shit?"

"Come on, Keisha, we both know that you don't like your body and you don't like sex."

"That's some bullshit," Keisha exclaimed. "I do like sex."

"No, you don't," Patra said. "You haven't liked sex from the day you walked into the Chi Chi Room and you know it. All you talked about is how you hated the men in that club."

"But that doesn't mean I don't like sex. It just means that I don't like those men."

"Yeah, but let me ask you this. How many men have you fucked, and I'm not talking about the porno, in the past three months you've lived with me?"

Keisha stopped.

"That's right," Patra continued. "Zero. Nada. No one. If you gained pleasure from sex, you would have at least fucked one person."

"Look, I've just been focused on—"

"Keisha, face it. You've got a problem, and you haven't addressed it. Hey, that's on you. But don't come around here feeling bad about who I am and what I do. Because if I remember correctly, you're staying in my house, something I've paid for. You're working at the Chi Chi Room, the same as I do. And you've done porn, something I haven't had to do. If a stripper is a stripper is a stripper, then you are the same as me. And don't forget it."

Patra walked out of the living room and back to her bedroom.

Keisha sat there, stunned.

Well, she thought, *hasn't this been a fucking life-changing day?*

Chapter 23

Nothing is more difficult, and therefore more precious, than to be able to decide.
                                    —Napoleon Bonaparte

"I want out, Sean, and I don't want to hear any bullshit. I want out and I want out on my own terms," Keisha said. She'd come to the Chi Chi Room early, right before she had class, because she wanted to get this out of the way.

"Whoa, baby, why are you doing this to me?" Sean asked, twitching as he looked at Keisha. "Haven't I treated you nicely? Haven't I been good to you? You've made money hand over fist."

"Hey, I give you dap for letting me strip but now I think I have to move on. It's nothing personal, but I can't go back onstage anymore."

Sean looked around the empty club and then focused back on Keisha. "Look, if you're going to leave, don't leave me in the lurch. If you just up and quit, then I'm not going to have a headliner for this next week. Give me at least a week and go out with a bang. After that, you can cut with no hard feelings."

Keisha thought for a second. Sean was the very

epitome of the sleazy strip club owner, but he'd never been harsh or bad to her, except when he'd tried to screw her out of two hundred and fifty dollars for the *Pimp* shoot. But he'd been cool for the most part.

"I'll do this," Keisha said. "I'll work next Saturday. After that, I'm done. That should give you enough time to find another girl to take my place. Why don't you just use Patra as a headliner?"

Sean took a cigarette out of his pocket and lit it. "Patra's on a short rope with me. And I know that you're her roommate, so I don't need to tell you that this is strictly between you and me. But I think she's been hoeing on the side with some of the customers. If that's true, then I've got to let her go. I can't risk losing my license because she wants to make some money on the side. Plus, they'll put my ass in jail for pimping, and I don't do jail. That's for the niggas who come here. I do money. And I'll always protect my money."

Keisha wondered if she should give Patra the heads-up about Sean's plans. She decided not to say anything until she was gone.

"So we good?" Keisha asked, sticking out her hand.

"We good," Sean said, shaking her hand. "Too bad, because we were just about to blow up. From what I heard, and you know I haven't seen it yet, but your video is the hottest seller on the market right now."

"Yeah, I heard that from somebody," Keisha said evasively. "I'm not going to pick it up, though."

"Why not? It's your work."

"Yeah, but I'm not proud of all my work."

"All right, but I can tell you right now that you're going to hear about it. Negroes have been phoning the club all week, asking if you're going to be dancing. So expect it."

Keisha left the Chi Chi Room and took the bus to campus. Classes had been going well, and she'd found the pace to be fast but manageable.

When she got off the bus, she made her way to Belinda's office. She had sent Keisha an e-mail that said it was urgent that she come see her that day. So as Keisha walked up the Murphy Hall steps, she wondered what Belinda wanted to talk to her about.

"I asked you to come in today," Belinda said, closing the door behind Keisha, "because I have some great news. Remember—I told you that I would work on your case, didn't I?"

"Yeah," Keisha said, intrigued. "What happened?"

"Well," Belinda said, opening up a file, "I was able to find a special scholarship that had been forgotten and not even applied for. It is a scholarship donated by an alumna named Felecia Hall. Felecia went to UCLA back in the '70s and made it big with IBM. She sent money to the university under the stipulation that it go to a needy female from the South Central area of Los Angeles. That would be you. It is a renewable scholarship whose only requirements are that you maintain a 3.0 grade-point average and keep high moral standards."

"So let me get this straight. I'm getting a scholarship?"

"No, you *have* a scholarship," Belinda said, beaming. "Congratulations!"

Keisha suddenly felt as though she were floating above Belinda, as she was in a state of euphoria that she'd never felt. There was a sense of relief, as though all of the tension she'd been carrying had suddenly left her shoulders.

"I—I don't have words," she stammered. "The only thing I can say is thank you. Thank you very much."

Keisha stood up and hugged Belinda.

"Now stop this before I start crying," Belinda said.

They both sat down, with Keisha smiling like a kid at Christmas.

"Now, the scholarship pays for your room and board, so do you want to move into the dorms?" Belinda asked.

"Yes, I do. I've been trying to save my money to get an apartment, but something always messed me up. So yes, I want to move in as soon as possible."

Belinda picked up some papers and handed them to Keisha. "Take these papers home and get them back to me as soon as possible. After you get them back to me, it should take about a week for the checks to be cut, and then we'll pay for your dorm for the year. In the meantime, you should get ready to move."

Belinda looked in another drawer and pulled out even more papers.

"Fill out these housing papers and indicate if you want to have a roommate. If I'm correct, you can get a single with this scholarship, but you might like—"

"I think I'm done with the roommate thing, thank you very much," Keisha said, smiling. "I'd rather meet new friends on campus and then come home to my own space."

"I am with you on that," Belinda said. "Okay, that seems to be all. Just get this back to me and then do well in your studies, and you should be fine."

"Thank you very much, Belinda," Keisha said, standing to leave. "I can never pay you back."

"Now that's where you're wrong. You can pay me back by graduating. I pulled a lot of strings, Keisha, and I'm counting on you not to blow it."

"I won't blow it and I won't let you down."

Keisha walked to her next class, knowing that her perseverance had paid off. Donovan had been right.

If you make good choices, then good results would come.

I've got to call him, Keisha thought, *and thank him.*

"All right, is everyone here?" Steven asked. Ray, Marty, Rosario, and Joseph Silva, Steven's head of promotions, were all sitting down waiting for the meeting to start. Steven had been exceedingly excited over the past few days, and no one knew why. The magazine had been going well, and *Inside Keisha!* had been flowing out of the warehouse, but Steven had been jumping around like he had a secret to tell and couldn't hold it in. But all the principals were there, so they knew it was about to jump off now.

"I wanted to give all of you an idea of where we are at *Pimp,*" Steven started. "Marty, could you please hand me that packet over there?"

Marty walked to the desk, picked up a brown manila envelope, and handed it to Steven.

"This," Steven said, waving the envelope in the air, "is from the Magazine Association of America." He opened the package and pulled out a certificate. "It says that *Pimp* magazine is the leading adult black magazine in terms of sales for 2006. I want everyone to give themselves a hand! You guys made this possible!"

There was sporadic applause, but nothing very enthusiastic. In most of their minds, *Pimp* was simply a place to go to work, see some naked women, and then pick up a check. If *Pimp* made money, cool. If it lost money, cool. It didn't matter to them either way. But Steven liked to think of *Pimp* as being one big family. So they played along with the facade.

"But this isn't the real reason that I have you gathered. I wanted to bring you here because of *Inside Keisha!* The video has been a blockbuster in our normal retail stores, and it looks like we might have a breakout star with Keisha. So I don't want to limit ourselves to just the brown-bag and trenchcoat crowd. I want *Pimp* videos to be as mainstream as a risqué music video on BET. I want people to feel good about buying a *Pimp* video, and I think *Inside Keisha!* is the video to do it. But we have a small problem that needs to be fixed. And for that, let me yield the floor to our head of promotions and advertising, Joseph Silva. Joseph?"

Joseph was a small, dapper man who looked like he should be selling insurance rather than adult videos. But he did sell adult videos, and he was good at it.

"As many of you know, our initial strategy was to take a girl that had some sex appeal, a local following, and then propel her to adult video stardom, so that *Pimp* Video would have an identity. In other words, we were looking for our own Jenna Jameson. We needed someone who we could not only promote to the pervs, but also to the suburbs. And I think we found our girl with Keisha Montez." When Joseph talked, he spoke in a very matter-of-fact manner, as though he were talking about widgets rather than adult actors.

"*Inside Keisha!* has been flying off the shelves, but Keisha herself has presented us with a problem. Steven has informed me that she has threatened to quit the business. Ladies and gentlemen, we can't allow that to happen. So we have to move to Plan B."

Joseph shuffled through an oversize black presentation case and pulled out a poster.

"This is what our Plan B centers on," he said, pointing to the poster. It had Keisha on all fours, obviously being penetrated from behind. The facial expression either read passion or pain, depending on your point of view. "The poster reads, 'UCLA's Keisha Montez stars in *Inside Keisha!*' "

"Why are we putting UCLA on the poster?" Ray asked.

"We're doing that for a number of reasons. One, through marketing surveys, we know that the men who buy our videos like to believe that the women in the movie are just turning eighteen, or who are college students. That's a great hook. And we're doing it for another reason. We need to smoke our Keisha out. The reason she doesn't want to do any more videos is that she thinks it will mess up her reputation. Well, we're going to create her reputation. Beginning next week, we're going to plaster the campus with thousands of these posters. And then we're going to do as many press conferences as possible. *Los Angeles Times,* the *Daily News,* and the student newspaper, the *Daily Bruin* will all hear from us. Keisha is going to be a star, no matter what she says."

"That is insane," Ray said, smiling. "But I like it!"

"By the time we're through with her, Keisha Montez will beg us to do films. She won't have any other options because whatever she does, she'll always be known as a porn star. The question is whether or not she'll be *our* porn star."

"Is this man a genius or what?" Steven asked, giggling. "I have a problem and Joseph solves it. Guys, if you ever own a business, find a guy who graduated from Harvard business school and hire him. Joseph is that guy for me."

Steven clapped his hands together. "Okay, do we have any questions?"

"Who is in charge of putting up the posters?" Marty asked.

"I want you and Ray to put them up at midnight next Sunday. When the students get to campus Monday morning, they're going to be surprised that one of their own is moonlighting. I want them plastered everywhere."

"I've got an idea," Ray said, excitedly. "Why limit this to just UCLA? We could go to all of the campuses and put the posters there. I could hire some guerrilla marketers and we could have her face everywhere."

"Good idea, but that is the secondary strategy," Steven said. "I want to put the squeeze on Keisha gradually, like a boa constrictor. We'll expand our poster strategy each week so that it's unescapeable."

Steven stopped and rested his arm on a chair.

"Look, guys, Keisha is a pretty girl and I think she could make us a lot of money, but I want to be clear that this isn't really about that. I could go out and find another girl just like her in about five minutes. But Keisha is trying to fuck me, and no one fucks with Steven Cox. I need to make sure that she understands that and that any other girl who comes to *Pimp* understands the example I set with Keisha. When I tell a girl to fuck, I want her to fuck. When I tell a girl to suck, I want her to suck. I invest money—my money—and I don't want any fucking wishy-washy bitches flaking out on me. And to ensure that, Keisha is going to pay the price. So everyone, let's get at it."

Everyone stood up. "I can't wait to see the look on that bitch's face when she walks on campus to see this damn poster! That's going to be priceless," Marty said.

"I may sit in the bushes with a camera just to see her face." Ray giggled.

"Nah, that's not going to be what's great," Steven said, as he made his move to leave. "What is going to be great is watching her come back into this office, begging to do another video. I'm going to crush her, and that's going to be a moment to see."

Chapter 24

No problem can withstand the assault of sustained thinking.

—Voltaire

Andre and his mother sat in her living room. Andre had just finished smoking a joint, and his mother was drinking a glass of Wild Turkey. In other words, this was a normal Saturday night at the Montez house, with Andre getting high and his mother getting drunk. But this wasn't a normal Saturday night. Andre had some things on his mind, and for once, he had something to say.

"So you went out there and didn't tell her?" Andre asked. "Goddamn it, Momma, you only had one thing you had to do, and you couldn't do it."

Veronica put down her glass of bourbon and looked at Andre as though she couldn't believe what she'd heard. Andre sounded like he was challenging her, and that she couldn't stand.

"She didn't want to fucking hear me. Do you understand?" Veronica said, agitated that she had to explain herself. "She didn't want to hear anything that I had to say. So get off my fucking ass."

"Her father is back in town, dying, and you couldn't get those words out of your mouth? I don't understand. I simply don't understand," Andre said.

"What the fuck don't you understand? She doesn't like me and she didn't want to listen. Don't blame me," Veronica said. "Blame your sister. She's the hardheaded one. I don't want to hear it. Fuck her. I wish I'd had an abortion like I was going to back then."

Veronica walked into the kitchen, opening and slamming shut cabinet doors.

"Where are my fucking cigarettes?" Veronica yelled. "Andre!"

Veronica stormed back into the living room.

"Where the fuck are my cigarettes?" she shouted, holding an empty carton in her hands. She then threw it at Andre. He didn't flinch. "I'm tired of your lazy ass sitting in here, eating my shit, and smoking my cigarettes."

Andre sat in the dining room chair and stared at his mother. "You know, I've stuck by you throughout the years mainly because I was too damn lazy and too fucking scared to do what Keisha did, which was to get on up from this house. For years, you've told me that Keisha wasn't shit and how everyone was against you. But now I know that was some bullshit. You're the fucking problem. You're the one who told Keisha that she wasn't shit, because you were shit. And now I sit here, high as a muthafucka, trying to numb myself to the life you set up for me."

Andre stood up and got in his mother's face for the first time in his life. Normally he would have just retreated to his room rather than confront anyone. But something in him had changed.

"The only thing you had to do was to tell her that her father, someone she hadn't seen since she was little, is dying, and you couldn't even do that. Stop talking about Keisha. She's braver than you and me combined. You're not shit and I'm not shit, but at least I can be honest and say it. You're still delusional."

Veronica turned her back and walked over to the empty Wild Turkey bottle and threw it at Andre, but it missed by a mile. It ended up breaking a mirror, shattering glass all over the floor. Andre stood up and looked his mother in the eye.

"Funny, isn't it, but that was just like your life," he said with a smirk. "Everything you do is destructive and full of bad luck. I'm going in my room. Tomorrow I'm going down to the club to tell your daughter what you couldn't seem to. And then I'm going to make plans to get the fuck out of this place."

He picked up the empty cigarette carton from the floor and casually tossed it back to his mother.

"And from now on," he said, walking toward his room, "buy your own damn cigarettes."

"My name is Jack, Jack Bing, and my manager told me that you're looking to buy a car. Do you know exactly what you're looking for?" Jack asked. "We have some really nice ones over here."

With her new scholarship in the bag, Keisha could use her money for something other than getting a new apartment. And the first thing she'd thought about was getting off the bus and into a car. Having a car in L.A. was a necessity, and she finally could have the freedom she wanted. So she made her way to Wilshire Automotive, where she made the acquaintance of Mr. Jack Bing, car salesman.

"I want something simple," she said. "Show me a used Jeep Liberty."

"Good choice," Jack said, "because we're actually running a special on 2003 Libertys. I have three to choose from. Follow me."

They walked to the center of the car lot, where there were three Libertys.

"This is what we call our patriotic trio," Jack said, pointing to the three cars. They were red, white, and blue, respectively. "Do you know which one you'd like? They're all the same price."

"I want the red one," she said, opening its door and getting inside. "But I want it at fifteen hundred off."

"Whoa," Jack said, as though Keisha had asked for a million dollars. "I don't know if I can give you fifteen hundred dollars off. Maybe we can talk about another—"

"I don't want another car," she said. "I want this car. And I want it for fifteen hundred off, and I want that fifteen hundred to come off the student discount. If I can't get that, then I'll walk."

Jack squinted at Keisha as though he was trying to figure her out. And as he calculated his commission versus her resolve, it became very clear.

"Let's go draw up the paperwork," he said.

As Keisha pulled out of the Wilshire Automotive parking lot in her new Jeep, she smiled to herself. She had accomplished a lot in the past few months. She'd gotten out of her mother's house, school was right on track, and she was getting out of the skin biz. She'd fallen into the trap a lot of girls in her neighborhood had, but she had also pulled herself out. And after finishing her last week at the Chi Chi Room, she could leave all that behind, she thought.

She arrived back at the apartment, parked the car,

and hoped Patra didn't have a john in there when she opened the door. She was excited about finally moving out, but sad that Sean was trying to move Patra out.

When she opened the door to the apartment, Patra was sitting on the couch, smoking a joint. She didn't look up when Keisha walked in.

"Hey, girl, how are you?" Keisha asked, walking past Patra and into the kitchen. She opened the refrigerator and pulled out a can of soda.

"Not too good," she responded, still looking straight ahead.

"What happened?"

"This," Patra said, reaching over and picking up a plastic tube and tossing it to Keisha, "is what happened." Keisha picked up the tube and looked at it closely.

"According to that, I'm pregnant," she said, still looking away from Keisha.

"Pregnant? How did you get pregnant? Didn't you use protection?"

"Of course I used protection! What do you think I am, stupid?"

"No, I wasn't saying that," Keisha said, walking back into the living room. "I just thought—oh, I don't know what I thought. What are you going to do?"

"What do you think I'm going to do? I'm going to take care of it."

"You're going to have an abortion?"

"Goddamn, Keisha, yes, I'm going to have an abortion. I've had one before, so I know what to do."

"Hey, if you need anyone to be with you when you go, I'll—"

"Thanks, but no thanks. I think I'll handle this myself. I've set up an appointment for next Monday. I promised myself that I'd never do this again, but

I'll be damned if I have a baby by a father I don't know."

Patra got off the couch and walked into her room. She closed the door, but Keisha could hear the muffled sounds of crying.

This was not the time to tell her about Sean's plans, and she wasn't going to tell her about her own plans. It was simply a time for Patra to be alone.

Keisha started on her homework but instead decided to call Donovan.

"Keisha," he said. "Hey, babe, how are things? How did school go?"

"Fine, things are going fine. Hey, what are you doing now?"

"Nothing, what's up?"

"I wanted to show you my new car."

"What? You rollin' now?" he exclaimed.

"Yeah, wanna see it?"

"Sure, come on by."

"I'll be there in a few minutes."

"Bet."

Keisha hung up the phone, went into the bathroom to freshen up, and then surprised herself by putting on some perfume.

Perfume for Donovan? she thought. *I haven't done that since we were going together.*

Keisha left the bathroom and thought about telling Patra that she was leaving, but decided against it. She left the apartment, got in her car, and began making her way to Donovan's.

When she turned down her old block, she looked to see if her mother's car was in the driveway. It was about dusk, and she didn't want her mother to see her.

Keisha hopped out of the Liberty and walked to Donovan's door. She took a deep breath and then knocked. She hadn't done that in more than six months. She heard some shuffling of feet, and then the dead-bolt locks turning.

"Hello, beautiful," Donovan said, opening the door.

"Hello yourself," she responded. He was wearing a white linen shirt and light green drawstring pants. He looked cute. "Damn, is that your car?" He left the doorway, walked out to the car, and checked it out. "This is sweet," he said. "Now you know that if you need some rims, I can pull some strings."

"Wait a second," Keisha said. "I thought you were out of the game."

Donovan smiled and looked down at the ground. "I didn't say that I would do the getting, I just said that I could pull some strings. I'm still on the right track."

A breeze blew through the block and seemed to drop the temperature ten degrees in five minutes. The palm trees rustled and suddenly, in a place where the seasons all seem to run into each other, it felt like fall.

"You want to come in?" Donovan asked. "It's getting too damn cold out here."

"Sure," Keisha said. They walked into the house and something seemed different. Where were all of the knickknacks? His mother used to have tons of glass baubles and doilies around. All they did was collect dust and get on Donovan's nerves. Now the house looked clean and even modern.

"My mother decided to buy another house but let me rent this one from her," Donovan said. "And before you ask, yes, I can pay her rent."

"I didn't say you couldn't," Keisha said. "I was just tripping that she moved. I thought your mother was going to die in this house."

"So did she, but then she got her pension and said

'to hell with it, I'm moving to Riverside.' So I got to keep the house."

Keisha casually strolled around the house. Things were definitely different. Donovan went into the kitchen and Keisha could hear the refrigerator open.

"Are you thirsty?" he asked. "I've got apple juice, and red Kool-Aid. Which one do you want?"

"I'll take some apple juice," she said.

Donovan brought two glasses to the living room. "You like what I did to the place?"

Keisha took the glass of juice from Donovan. "It's nice," she said. "If you had told me that you had a place to yourself, I would have expected a living room filled with black-light posters. But this is tastefully done."

"Been watching Home and Garden Television." Donovan laughed.

Keisha sat down on the corner of a chair. "So where are you working now?"

"Oh, I got a job at Western Construction," he said, crunching a piece of ice in his mouth. "It wasn't easy getting a job with my, uh, résumé. But they gave me a chance and I've been coming in early every day. They're going to have to pry me off this job."

"That sounds great," she said. "What are you doing down there?"

"A little bit of everything," he said. "Want some more?"

"No, thank you."

Donovan took the two glasses and walked back into the kitchen.

"I'm trying to figure out which skill I want to do, and then train for it so that I can join the union. If I can join the union, then I will make the big bucks. I think I want to do carpentry, and that's why I'm taking a class in it at Trade Tech."

"Okay, this is a bit much to take," Keisha said incredulously. "What happened to the Donovan I once knew? The one slinging rocks on the corner? The one who used to get up at one P.M. because he had spent most of the night at the club? What got into you?"

"I told you. I just got tired of the decisions I was making. It was that simple. Once you do that, then you move forward. Speaking of that, are you still at the club?"

"I put in my notice. This is my last week and then I'm done."

"Cool."

"But that's not the news I wanted to tell you. I have even bigger news," Keisha said. "I just got a full-ride scholarship to UCLA."

"You serious?" Donovan said, grinning. "I mean, you are shitting me! A full ride?"

"Yes, a full ride," Keisha said excitedly. "And I have to give you credit. You helped me figure things out."

"What do you mean, me?"

"I mean, you talked to me at my lowest time, and for that I thank you."

Donovan stood in front of Keisha, looking at her. "I don't know what I did, but if it helped, I'm glad."

"Well, you did and I thank you," she said.

Keisha stood up to leave. "I've got to go. I've got some reading to do and a couple of papers to write. This is going to be a huge week for me."

She walked to the door and Donovan opened it.

"It was nice seeing you, Keisha," he said, looking into her eyes.

"It was great seeing you, too," she said, giving him a hug. She'd intended the hug to be a friendly hug, but for some reason, all the emotions and feelings she'd had about Donovan suddenly came flooding back.

She pulled back from Donovan and looked in his face. Then she slowly and gently cradled his face and began kissing him softly. He began kissing her back, with the hunger of a man who'd changed and wanted to prove that he'd changed. But suddenly he stopped.

"We don't have to do this," he said softly. "We can take it slowly if you want."

"I do want this," she responded. "And I want it now."

Chapter 25

*Let your love be like the misty rains, coming
softly, but flooding the river.*
                                        —Malagasy proverb

The two began kissing and making their way to
Donovan's bedroom. Keisha fell backward on the
bed and Donovan stood over her, as though looking
at his prize. Slowly, he began unbuttoning his linen
shirt and exposed his ripped six-pack abs. *Whatever
conversion Donovan has done,* Keisha thought, *he's
still doing his one thousand crunches a night.*

Everything was quiet, and Keisha couldn't hear
anything except her own beating heart.

Donovan then leaned down and began kissing
Keisha on the neck. Keisha began feeling a sensation that she had never had. She hadn't had it with
Donovan before, when he was slinging on the block
and she was aimless, and she certainly hadn't felt it
when she was on the porn shoot. For the first time,
she felt comfortable with who she was. She didn't
feel like something was happening to her. She felt in
tune with Donovan, and that felt good.

"Oooh, that feels so good," Keisha cooed, and

Donovan slowly rubbed her side and kissed her neck. She took her hand and felt the muscles in his back. As she rubbed his back, she started nibbling on Donovan's ear.

"I love you," Donovan said, raising up and looking straight into her eyes. "I really do."

Keisha didn't want to say that, not now. But she did want him.

"Just kiss me," she said, putting her hands around Donovan's neck and pulling him toward her.

They began kissing passionately, with Donovan beginning to unbutton her top. She began pulling down his pants, and he began pulling down hers.

"You are still beautiful," he said. He began to slowly kiss her on her chest, and she began to arch her back, loving each succulent kiss. Keisha reached behind her and unclasped her bra. Donovan instantly began kissing her breasts, sucking on her areolas and flicking them with his tongue.

"Don't stop," she whispered. Keisha leaned her head back and just let the pleasure roll over her as she felt herself getting wet.

"Don't worry, I won't," he said, smiling. "I'm going to kiss you here." He kissed her on her stomach. "And here, and here." He kept going until he reached her belly button, where he licked it over and over.

At that point, Donovan began pulling down Keisha's panties, rubbing her ass, slowly and firmly. And then he came back up to her face, and they began kissing passionately. Keisha nibbled on Donovan's ear and then turned him on his back.

"Now it's my turn," she said. Keisha ran her hand over Donovan's chest, letting her index fingers trace the creases of his muscles. She slowly began kissing his chest and then moving back to his neck. As she kissed him on his neck, her right hand slid under his boxers and began to rub his dick lightly with her fingertips. She grabbed it firmly and began to stroke it slowly. He was rock-hard, and his hips slowly gyrated to her rhythm. She then took her little finger and began to probe his balls, tickling them as she continued to stroke and kiss him up and down his torso.

"God, that feels so damn good," he moaned. Keisha ran her fingers over the tip of his dick, and then she began pulling off his boxers. His dick stood erect, and Keisha started licking Donovan's balls, slowly, with long, full licks.

"Do you like that?" she asked earthily. Donovan said nothing, and she took his silence as a yes. She then kissed the length of his shaft, finally taking it into her mouth. Before, Keisha hadn't liked giving head to Donovan. It had made her feel vulnerable and uncomfortable. But now she felt safe, and for the first time, she was enjoying giving pleasure. She moved her head up and down, sucking and licking with her tongue.

"Jesus," Donovan muttered. "Keep going, don't stop."

Keisha moved faster and faster on Donovan's dick until he put his hand on her head, stopping her.

"Am I doing something wrong?" she asked, wiping her mouth.

"Not a thing," he said, raising up. "But now it's my turn to pleasure you. Turn over on your stomach."

Keisha scooted to the top of the bed and placed her face on the pillow. Donovan slid down to Keisha's feet and started kissing her calves. He then moved to the insides of her thighs.

Keisha's hands began to dig into the pillow, as the pleasure began rushing over her again. Then Donovan put his hands under Keisha's thighs and lifted them. He began licking Keisha's pussy, darting his tongue in and out.

"Aww, aww, aww," Keisha whispered. This was something new for Donovan. Back in the old days, he'd decried any brother who ate pussy as being a punk. And now, there he was.

And then he stopped. Keisha stayed on her stomach, her breathing slow and steady. Without a word, Donovan walked to his drawer and pulled out a condom. He put it on and came back to Keisha. She turned over to look at him. His dick stood erect, and his body was silhouetted by the dying sunlight filtering through the window shades.

"I want you like I've never wanted another man before," she said, looking directly into his eyes.

"I want you too," he said. He lowered himself and entered her. Her hands found the small of his back, and as Donovan began thrusting slowly, she let herself relax and feel his fullness. He moved slowly, letting her feel his length as he probed all around her pussy. She felt her pussy grab his dick and control it, willing it to spots where Keisha felt the most pleasure. Donovan lifted her upper body so he could see Keisha react to him.

Keisha's mouth was open as Donovan began thrusting faster and faster.

"Shit, shit," she uttered. "Oooh, shit!"

Donovan would go deep and then pull out slowly. And then he moved his pelvis so that he circled her pussy, over and over. He was hitting her clit steadily and she could feel her mind going blank. There was nothing but the sound of her voice and his gutteral noises, and both were making her even more aroused.

Like a domino effect, Donovan's movements moved

her closer and closer to orgasm. And when Donovan moved his body so that his dick was hitting her G-spot, it was too much. It felt like her nipples were going to burst, and her ass kept clenching and un-clenching.

"I'm cumming," she said, almost matter-of-factly, but nothing was matter-of-fact. Donovan kept doing the same thing, hitting her clit just right, and then it happened.

When Keisha came, she had a high-pitched scream that came from deep within her. When she finished, she could feel Donovan become harder than ever. He started thrusting faster and faster, and Keisha could do nothing but hold on.

"Cum for me, baby!" she screamed.

"Gawd!" Donovan yelled. As Donovan came, his ass tightened up and Keisha could feel Donovan spasm inside her, with three final violent thrusts to complete his orgasm. And for thirty seconds, Donovan lay on top of her, still inside her. It was as though he didn't want to lose that feeling of intimacy. Finally he pulled out and lay beside her.

"Does this change everything?" he asked softly.

"I don't know," she said, putting her hand on his chest. "We'll just have to see."

Keisha had fallen asleep on Donovan's chest. She was awakened by the early-morning rays peeking through the window shades. Donovan was already up, and she could smell coffee brewing. She turned over and looked at the digital clock. It read six o'clock in the morning.

"You can go back to sleep if you want," Donovan said, dressed in his work clothes. "But I've got to get to the construction site by seven, or I'll break my never-late record."

He walked over to the chair and picked up a yellow construction hat and then sat on the edge of the bed. He looked at Keisha longingly.

"But I would break that record just to sleep next to you all day," he said, smiling.

Keisha smiled and ran her fingers along Donovan's arm.

"That's sweet, but go to work," she said. "I've got to get up and go to school. After that, I'm going to get ready to do my last performances anyway."

"Why don't you just quit the club?" Donovan asked, standing up to go. "I can give you the money to make up for these final days."

"Thank you, baby, but the days of anyone taking care of me are over," she said, sitting up. "I'm doing this because despite what anyone thinks of Sean, he did give me a chance to accomplish my goal, which was to make enough to go to UCLA. I've done it, and it's partly due to him. So I'm not going to leave him in the lurch."

She slipped out of the bed and put her panties back on. "And the other reason is that I want to go on that stage and feel what it's like to be out there for the last time. I want to identify all of the places where I felt embarrassed and ashamed. I want to hear the men yelling the most vile things to me so I'll never go back to it. I need to know that all of that is behind me. I'm closing chapters and I need to close this one with authority."

Keisha kept picking up various pieces of her clothing, finding a bra here and a sock there. She looked adorable to Donovan, so he walked to her and gave her a kiss.

"Then do your thang. But I've got to go," he said. "There's orange juice in the refrigerator and enough stuff for breakfast. Just lock the door behind you and we'll talk later."

He began walking out the door and then turned back around and kissed her again.

As she heard Donovan drive away, Keisha began thinking about what last night meant. Did she want to have a relationship with Donovan?

That's something I'll have to think about, she thought.

She poured herself a cup of coffee, sat on the living room couch, and stared through the curtains at her mother's house across the street. Most people would have a sense of nostalgia looking at their childhood home, but Keisha's was one of dread. There was nothing positive about her old home, and it represented a past she was trying to put behind her. But something still drew her to it. Just like closing the chapter with the Chi Chi Room, she yearned to do the same thing with her mother and brother.

Then the front door of her old house opened, and Andre sat on the front steps, looking like Doughboy from *Boyz n the Hood.* He had on white socks and house shoes, black shorts, and an oversize old-school Magic Johnson Lakers jersey. It was nearly seven o'clock, and he was dressed for another day of doing nothing, Keisha thought.

Keisha finished her coffee and went back into Donovan's bedroom, grabbing her clothes and putting them on. She had class at nine, and she wanted to get back to Patra's so she could shower. But as she got to the front door, she saw that Andre was still sitting on the stoop, and he didn't look like he was moving.

I've got to get out of here, she thought, eyeing her

car and Andre. But she didn't want Andre to see her. So she stood at the door and, like waiting for a telephone to ring, waited for Andre to go back into the house.

After thirty minutes, Andre finally stood up and went inside. Without a second to spare, Keisha opened the front door and walked outside, rapidly trying to open the door to her car before Andre came back outside. But it was too late. Andre came back out and saw Keisha as she got into her car.

"Keisha!" he yelled. He started walking across the street, and Keisha kept trying to put her keys into the car's ignition. But she kept missing.

"Keisha, wait!" Andre yelled again. "Roll down the window. I have something to tell you."

Now he was at her car door and Keisha felt trapped. All she could do was lower the window a bit. "What do you want?" she asked.

Andre already had bloodshot eyes from smoking weed. Keisha wanted to keep things short and sweet, but Andre had something to say.

"What are you doing here?" he asked curiously. Then he looked at Donovan's house. "Oh, you back with Donovan?"

"I said, what do you want? If you ain't got shit to say, then get off my door and let me go."

"Wait, I just wanted to tell you that you were right," he said. "Momma is full of shit."

Keisha looked at him with a frown. "I needed you to tell me that?" she asked sarcastically.

"No, you didn't. But I needed to tell you that," he said. "But that's not exactly why I came over here. Daddy's back in town."

Keisha shot him a look. "How long has he been back?"

"For about a week," he said. "But there's something else."

"What?"

"He's in the hospital and he's got terminal cancer. He wants to see you before he dies."

Keisha put her head on the steering wheel. This was the last thing she'd expected to hear. Her father had left one evening when she was a baby and she hadn't seen him since. At first she'd been angry, really angry, about him leaving. But then she'd started looking at her mother and found herself resenting how her mother had treated him. So she considered herself without real parents. But now that he was back in town, she needed to see him—today.

"Where is he?" she asked, holding the wheel tightly.

"Over at Cedars-Sinai in West L.A. If I were you, I'd go there now if you want to see him before he dies. He's in pretty bad shape and I don't think he has much time. That's what Momma was supposed to tell you when she saw you, but like always, she failed."

"Yeah, of course." Keisha started up her car. "Thanks for telling me."

"No problem," Andre said. "Hey, I'm going to move out and straighten out my life. It's going to be hard and I don't know how it's going to end up. But I want to say I'm sorry for believing Momma. You were the one with the fucking brains, not her. Now I need to get some brains."

Keisha looked at her brother. Yes, he was still smoking weed, but he sounded sincere, and not full of shit, as he usually was. *What the fuck is going on around here?* Keisha thought. *Everyone is getting their shit together.*

"Don't worry, you've got brains," Keisha said. "You've just got to use them." Keisha turned on the ignition and started to drive away. She stopped and turned around. Andre was making his way back to the house.

"If you need anything, just holla," she yelled after him. He stopped and smiled. She drove off to the hospital.

Chapter 26

I can forgive, but I cannot forget, is only an-
other way of saying, I will not forgive. Forgive-
ness ought to be like a cancelled note—torn in
two, and burned up, so that it never can be
shown against one.

—Henry Ward Beecher

Keisha pulled into Cedars-Sinai's parking lot, trying to gather her thoughts. She hadn't seen her father in all these years, and to see him in this condition? It was too much to comprehend. She slowly walked through the hospital doors and went to the admissions desk.

"Hello," she started. "I'm looking for Felice Montez."

"Just one second," the nurse said. She tapped on the computer and pulled up his record. "He's on the fifth floor."

"Thank you," she said, beginning to walk to the elevator.

"Wait a second," the nurse said. She began riffling through her drawer. "You need to sign in and then put this on."

The nurse handed Keisha a clipboard and a wristband. Keisha signed the clipboard and put on the wristband.

"Thanks," she said.

The doors to the elevator closed and even though three others were sharing it, she didn't notice them. As the floors flew by, she became more and more anxious. Finally the doors opened and she walked to another nurse.

"Which room is Felice Montez in?" she asked.

"In 512," the nurse said, going back to her work.

Keisha turned the corner and slowly walked to Room 512. As she got closer, she could see through the room's window that a nurse was standing over her father. She stood at the door's entrance for about ten seconds, before her father noticed her.

"Keisha," he said in a low, raspy breath. Felice Montez, who'd once weighed 225 pounds at six-feet-two, was now an emaciated man.

He doesn't weigh more than 150 pounds, she thought.

"Yes, Daddy, it's me," she said. The nurse finished adjusting a tube on Felice's throat and then turned to go.

"Please keep your visit to about five minutes," the nurse whispered. "He's not too strong and he's going in and out of consciousness."

"Thank you," Keisha replied. The nurse left and Keisha slowly walked to her father's bedside. A tube was inserted in his trachea, and he was having trouble breathing. But his eyes were bright.

"Not the way I wanted to see my favorite daughter, but it'll have to do," he said, with a little humor. "Come give me a hug."

"Nope," she said, looking into his eyes. "I won't hug you until you tell me why you left."

Felice slowly turned his head away from Keisha, trying to avoid her eyes. "Oh, Keisha, do we have to go into this now?"

"Yes, we do," she said defiantly. "You owe me an explanation and I'm not going to wonder for the rest of my life why you did what you did."

"Okay, so you want the truth," he said, turning back to her.

"Yes, I want the truth."

He took a deep, raspy breath. "Your mother and I decided that I would go to Las Vegas to get a job, work at it for six months, and then bring you guys out. I desperately wanted to get you and Andre out of South Central. I could see what it was going to do to both of you. You were doing great in school but Andre was drifting. I thought if I could get you guys out, then you would have a better future."

"But why didn't you bring us out? What happened?"

"Things happened," he said. "The more I was away from your mother, the more I remembered how unhappy I was with her. We just grew apart, and the more we were apart, the more we couldn't get together."

"How come you didn't just call us and tell us that?" Keisha asked.

"I tried, but your mother stopped me at every point. I wanted you guys to come to live with me, but she wouldn't hear of it. She wanted to punish me, and she did. I'm just sorry that you guys got caught in the middle." He looked at Keisha with teary eyes. "Will you forgive me?"

Keisha stood there, torn. The anger of not having a father for all those years welled up within. And yet she was looking at her father, a father who was going to die at any second. So she lied, kissing him on the cheek. "Yes, I forgive you." For about thirty seconds, he held her in his arms. She was his little girl again.

"Yes," she said, "I forgive you."

"I don't have much time," he said. "Smoking all those menthols finally caught up with me. I've got throat cancer and they've pumped me up with so much medicine, I can barely keep up with where I am half the time. But I'm glad you came, because I have something for you. Go over to that bag."

He pointed to a black briefcase at the side of his bed. Keisha picked up the bag and brought it to him.

"Open it and look for an envelope that says *Keisha*," he said. She peeked into the briefcase, riffled through some papers, and found a yellow envelope.

"They say that I may only have a week left to live," he said. "But I don't want you crying about that. I've lived a very full life and I'm at peace. However, I have something I need you to do for me when I die. And the instructions are in that envelope. Don't open it until you've heard that I've passed. Can you do that for me?"

"Yes," she said quietly. "I can do that."

"Now tell me what you're doing with yourself. You look great," he said. Felice was fading fast and he looked like he could go to sleep at any time.

"I'm a student at UCLA and I've just gotten a full scholarship," she said quickly.

"A student at UCLA," he said with a smile. "Well, if you aren't a chip off the old block. I wanted to go there and you're going. That is so beautiful . . ."

Felice started fading and then went to sleep. Keisha pulled the covers up so he was comfortable and then kissed him. As she left the room, the nurse was coming back in.

"How long does he have?" she asked the nurse.

"It's really day to day," the nurse replied. "If I were you, I would start preparing."

"Thanks."

Keisha reached into her pocket and took out a pen.

"Could you do me a favor?" she asked, writing down her phone number on a piece of paper. "I'm his daughter. If something happens, could you please contact me as soon as possible? I'll have my phone on, so you can't miss me."

The nurse took the paper. "I'll make sure to give this to the head nurse and she'll put this in the computer so that if there's any change in his condition, you'll be contacted."

"Thank you very much," Keisha said.

Even though her father was dying, Keisha left Cedars-Sinai feeling better than she had walking in. The great mystery about why her father had left so unexpectedly had been solved. And now she was at peace with her father, and she thought that he was at peace with her.

When she arrived back at Patra's apartment, she found Patra in a better mood than the night before. Keisha decided to not bring up the pregnancy and just let Patra deal with her own business.

"So where were you last night?" Patra said, smiling at Keisha as she came into the apartment. "I noticed that you didn't come home."

"I hooked up with an old friend," she said.

"Was it good?"

Keisha laughed. "I didn't come home, did I?"

"Girl, that doesn't mean shit." Patra laughed. "I've spent the night with plenty of Negroes simply for the nice meal and not the Negro. So I ask again, was the dick good?"

"Damn good," Keisha said, smiling. "And the only thing about good sex is that it makes you want more good sex."

"Well, go on, then," Patra said. "I must have been

wrong about you. You do like a little nooky from time to time."

"Yep, but it has to be the right nooky," Keisha said. "All nooky ain't good nooky."

"Sure it is," Patra said.

Keisha sat down on the couch and put her dad's envelope in her duffle bag.

"So what are you feeling about your last day at the Chi Chi Room? All of the girls are talking about it and who's going to take your weekends."

"So you heard, eh? I bet every bitch in there has done all they could to get my Saturdays," Keisha said.

"You know it!" Patra said. "Even old-ass Debra is trying to get it. I tried to tell her that she didn't have a chance in hell to take your spot, but she's straight tripping. Why are you leaving?"

"I found out that I was going to get a full ride to UCLA. So I'll be moving out on Sunday."

"Damn, all this happened and you didn't tell me?"

"It's been a whirlwind couple of days. Sorry about that." Keisha walked into the kitchen and poured herself a soda. "Bought a new car, too."

"Goddamn, girl, you really were on a mission."

"So who do you think is going to get it?" Keisha asked curiously, coming back into the living room.

"Me."

"You?"

"Yeah, why you so surprised?"

"It's not that I'm surprised," Keisha said. "I just never thought you'd go for it."

"With the money that comes on Saturday, you think I'd pass that shit up?" Patra laughed. "Hell, I can't understand why you're passing that shit up. I told Sean the other day that I want it and he said that he'd think about it."

Keisha hesitated. She wondered if she should tell her that Sean was trying to get her out, but then she thought again. With the pregnancy and everything, the last thing she needed to hear was that Sean was going to get rid of her. So she kept quiet.

"Work your thang, girl. Work your thang," Keisha said.

"I will," she said. "It's what I do."

"Where are the posters?" Steven asked. "Are they stacked in the warehouse?"

"Yeah," Marty yelled. He was in the warehouse moving boxes around, and since the new issue of *Pimp* magazine was about to go to print, there was a lot of organizing to do.

"Bring one to me upstairs," Steven instructed. Three black women were sitting in front of him, each with massive breasts and a massive behind spilling out of a string bikini. Ray was setting up a camera.

"Ladies, we at *Pimp* magazine and *Pimp* Video are looking to find the finest black women in the country. And if you think you have the stuff, we'll put you in our magazine. If we get a lot of positive feedback from your magazine shoot, then we'll move on to video."

"How much do we get for the shoot and how much do we get for the video?" one woman asked.

"We pay five hundred for the shoot, and one thousand for the video," Steven said as Marty walked into the room. He handed Steven a poster of *Inside Keisha!* Steven held it like a trophy before the women.

"And if you are really successful, we can make you a star," he said proudly. "Now go over there and take off your clothes. Ray needs to take pictures of you."

The three women walked over to Ray and began undressing.

"Come with me," Steven told Marty. They both left the office and walked down to the warehouse. "I want all of this taken care of by tonight. On Sunday, you guys are to meet us at midnight."

"How many people are we going to use?" Marty asked.

"We need to have at least ten people ready to help out. This operation is going to be lightning-quick, and I don't want any fuck-ups."

"We'll be ready."

Chapter 27

All changes, even the most longed for, have their melancholy; for what we leave behind us is a part of ourselves; we must die to one life before we can enter another.

—Anatole France

"Surprise!"

It was Saturday, and Keisha had entered the dressing room from the back, like always. But this time, all of the strippers had gathered, waiting for her.

"I told you that we bitches have to stick together," Debra said, smiling. There was a cake with GOOD LUCK, KEISHA written on it, and a banner wishing the same. Keisha smiled as she looked around the room.

"Well, I didn't know all you bitches cared in the first place." Keisha laughed. "But thank you."

"Somebody light the candle so Keisha can say some words and make a wish," Patra said.

"This ain't no damn birthday," Debra said, smiling. "Keisha, you want to say something?"

Keisha had been unprepared to talk to anyone this evening. In fact, she'd only thought she'd do her gig and then leave forever. But now, feelings started coming to her that she didn't even know she had.

Who knew that she would suddenly hope that Debra would find a new way to make a living when she couldn't strip anymore? Who knew that she'd hope that Patra would stop stripping and escorting? She even wished Sean well, and hoped that he could fulfill his dreams. But what to say?

"I've learned something about myself at the Chi Chi Room," she started, looking directly into the faces of all of the women. "I learned that in reality, I am worth something, and it's not the dollar bills that the old men in the pervert pit throw onstage. I've learned that shaking my ass is not the whole part of me. And I've learned that each one of you can make it, and that I want you to make it."

She walked over to Debra.

"This woman showed me what it takes to survive in this game, and I'll always be grateful." She then walked over to Patra.

"And when I needed a lifeline, this woman provided it. And I always will thank her for it."

She walked back to the middle of the room.

"In a few minutes, I'm going to go out there and shake my ass, pick up my money, and go home. There's no glamour and there's no glory in what I'm doing. But each of you can keep your dignity as you do it. Do it for yourself and no one else. And you'll walk off the stage with your head held high."

Everyone was quiet. Finally Patra spoke up.

"Damn, bitch, we just wanted a 'thank you very much,' and now you got me tearing up!" Everyone laughed and began eating cake.

"How many sets are you doing tonight?" Debra asked, handing Keisha a piece of cake.

"One big one. That's all. After that, I'm out of here."

With a bang, the door to the dressing room opened. Only one person blasted into a room like that, so when it was Sean, no one was surprised.

"Shit, what the fuck is all of this?" he asked, looking around. "And how come no one has offered me any cake?"

"Get your own damn cake," Debra shot back. "You're a grown man."

"And you a grown woman, so get me some shit, or you ain't working here," Sean said, shifting from side to side as usual. Debra cut him a glare but went and got him a piece of cake. Sean leaned over to Keisha and whispered into her ear.

"I need to see you upstairs."

"What for?" she asked.

"Can't talk down here," he said. Debra brought him a tiny piece of cake and he stared at it like he was insulted. "Just get up there in five minutes."

He turned to leave. "Don't you bitches eat too much. I don't want fat, flabby asses on the stage tonight."

"Fuck you," someone said.

"Yeah, and you'll get fucked if you don't stay in shape."

And with a huff, Sean left the dressing room.

"What the fuck did that nigga want?" Debra asked.

"He wants me to meet him in his office."

"Watch that fool," Patra said, finishing her cake. "Ain't nothing good ever happened at one of his meetings."

"Don't worry," Keisha said, putting down her plate. "That fool ain't got nothing I want."

Keisha walked to the door and turned around.

"Thanks, girls," she said. "I've got to go see about something. I hope y'all watch me onstage. I'm going to do some moves that I'll give away for free. I won't need them anymore."

"You never know!" someone shouted.

"Yep, I know," Keisha said, smiling. She turned and walked out of the dressing room into the club. The Chi Chi Room was already packed with men. The first stripper had gone onstage, but these men were here to see Keisha one last time. Her name had been on the marquee all week, and Sean had done all he could to promote this.

"What's up, Blackie?" she shouted as she made her way to the stairs.

"Good luck, Keisha."

Keisha walked up the stairs and into Sean's office. To her surprise, Steven, Ray, and Marty were sitting down.

"Why are you Negroes here?" she asked. This wasn't what she'd expected.

"We're here to wish you good luck on your last night." Steven smiled. "At least I could get a hug."

"You're a snake, and I don't hug snakes," Keisha said. "Sean, what did you want?"

"I think this is more about Steven than me," Sean said. "Come in and sit down."

Keisha looked at all of them. "No, I don't have to come in. I can walk and never have a damn thing to do with any of you. So if you have anything to say, you'd better say it now or get the fuck out of my life."

Steven looked at Ray and Marty. Then he looked back at Keisha.

"You've always been to the point with me, Keisha, and I like that. So I'm not going to bullshit you. We want you back doing more videos at *Pimp*."

Keisha frowned. "This is going to be a short conversation, I see. I told you that I'm done with that shit. You got your one video, so find some other girl for your shit."

"We like you, and I think you need to know that it's not so easy to just walk away from us," Steven retorted. "I put thousands into your video, and I don't intend to waste my investment. So as I told you before, if you don't play ball with us, we're going to have to ratchet it up a level. And that could have negative repercussions for you."

Keisha walked over to Steven and looked him directly in the eye. "You don't scare me like you could all those girls downstairs. You fuck with me and I'll ruin you. But I won't stop. I'll not only ruin you, but crush you into the ground. You better remember that."

"This bitch has lost her mind," Marty said, laughing.

"No, this bitch has her mind straight," she said, pointing to herself. "All you muthafuckas better understand that."

Steven stood up and smiled. "Okay, have it your way. Ray, Marty, let's get out of here. We don't want to ruin Keisha's last night. Good luck, Keisha. I wish you well."

"And I wish that you go to hell," she responded.

And with those words, Keisha left Sean's office and went downstairs. Sean looked at Steven.

"I've listened to you all these years, and we've played ball. And I don't attach myself to any of these hoes. But I'm giving you a warning. Don't fuck with Keisha. She's different."

Steven walked over to Sean and smiled.

"As long as you live, don't you ever tell me what I can or can't do," Steven said. "It ain't good for your health."

Keisha made it back to the dressing room, where everyone had already left. Patra had finished her gig, and there was nothing left but for Keisha to go onstage.

"So what did he want?" Patra asked.

"Oh, he didn't want anything," Keisha said, taking off her clothes. Patra tossed Keisha her bikini and Keisha began putting it on. "But Steven, Ray, and Marty were all there. Steven is still pissed that I'm not going to do any more videos for them. He threatened me, but I ain't afraid of them."

"Screw them," Patra said. "Let's get ready to go. I'll glitter you up."

Patra dipped a brush into some glitter and began brushing Keisha all over. Debra opened the door.

"Don't you look pretty," she said. "Are you ready?"

"Let's get this going," Keisha replied.

Keisha started walking out but was stopped by Debra.

"Take a look at this," she instructed. Keisha saw that the strippers had formed a traditional honor guard for her.

"I'm touched," she said. "But let's get this going."

Keisha stood at the doorway of the dressing room, ready to go onstage for the last time. Patra and Debra flanked her, and the rest of the girls lined up as an honor guard. Sean stood on the stage with a microphone.

"Gentlemen, the Chi Chi Room has had some beautiful women dance on this stage, but one of the best has been Keisha Montez."

The pervert pit erupted in shouts, whistles, and catcalls.

Sean smiled. "Tonight we have the sad occasion to say goodbye to Keisha. But I want everyone here to give her one last standing ovation as she comes to the stage. So without further ado, Keisha Montez!"

The honor guard of strippers began clapping and Keisha slowly made her way to the stage. She was dressed in a black string bikini and, as usual, she was spilling out of it. She'd worn her special glass high heels for this night, and when she got to the stage, Sean handed her the microphone.

"I just want to say that I've enjoyed dancing for you guys, and let's do this one more time," she said.

With that, she handed the microphone back to Sean, who leapt off the stage. The DJ then cued up 50 Cent's song "P.I.M.P."

How ironic, Keisha thought as she began gyrating on the stage to the sound of the beat.

Tonight, Keisha was going to give the pervert pit a show. She walked to each side of the stage, letting them see her full body. She then made her way to the golden pole in the middle, where she took her hands and rubbed it up and down.

Then she wrapped her legs around the pole and slid so that she was upside-down. It was then that she undid her bikini top. Her breasts, always perfect, stood at attention for everyone.

"Oh my God," a man yelled. "You are fucking fine!"

Keisha blew a kiss to the man, and the dollar bills came flying.

She slid off the pole and then went to the edge of the pit. She pulled on her bikini bottom so that her ass was accentuated to the men behind her.

"Show it, baby!"

Keisha got on the ground and began crawling like a stalking cat, her ass high in the air. Then she got on her back and slowly began taking off her bikini bottom. The men started cheering like they'd never seen a woman before.

"Ooww!" they yelled at her. The money flew at her like a green snowstorm.

Keisha twisted on the floor and then started to hump it, and each man watching imagined that he was the floor.

The music was almost over and Keisha decided to give each man one more look at her body. She stood up next to the pole and, with one hand on it, she did a full turn.

For the first time in her life, she realized that she had options beyond this stage. She could use her brain to take her where she wanted to go, and she could use sex for love on her terms. No, these men no longer gave her validation, but she wanted them to know what they were missing.

And just like that, it was all over. She picked up her bikini and began collecting the money. She leapt off the stage and ran to the dressing room with the groping hands of the men behind her.

"So how do you feel?" Patra asked.

"Like a liberated woman," Keisha responded. "I feel like a woman who is about to travel to a different universe, leaving this one behind. And that feels good, damn good."

Chapter 28

The world is round and the place which may seem like the end may also be only the beginning.

—Ivy Baker Priest

Keisha got up early on Sunday and began packing her things. It wasn't going to take a lot to move, but she still wanted to get things all set so that she could move into her dorm room early on Monday morning. But before she did all that, she wanted to do something nice for Patra.

"Get up," she yelled outside Patra's door. Patra came to the door and sleepily walked past Keisha.

"Thanks for getting me up," Patra said sarcastically. "God help me if I'd wanted to sleep in on a Sunday morning."

"You're not sleeping in this Sunday," Keisha said cheerfully. "I'm taking you to breakfast."

Patra stumbled around the kitchen, looking for a coffee filter.

"That's sweet, but you don't have to do that," she said, finding the filter in a drawer. She put it into the coffeemaker, opened a coffee can, and scooped in some coffee.

"Nonsense," Keisha said. "You let me stay here for all this time, and this is the least I could do."

Patra watched the coffee brew for a second and then turned to Keisha. "You know, you're right. It is the least you can do."

They both laughed. Keisha went into the bathroom and shouted out to Patra. "Where do you want to go eat? I was thinking about heading over to either Aunt Kizzy's or Dulan's. Which one do you want to go to?"

"Let's go to Dulan's," Patra said. "I feel like getting an omelet."

"Then Dulan's it is," Keisha said. "And by the way, thanks for setting up everything last night."

Patra sipped on her coffee. "No problem. Might as well send you off like a star since you're escaping to a place none of us can even dream of."

Keisha looked at herself in the bathroom mirror and suddenly felt a bit guilty. She did have a bright future ahead of her. She walked out of the bathroom and sat down on the living room couch.

"Patra, I have something to tell you, and it's going to be difficult," Keisha said. Patra was still standing in the kitchen sipping her coffee. She started walking into the living room.

"What?"

"Look, I wasn't going to say anything, because I didn't want to hurt your feelings," Keisha started. "But when I told Sean that I was quitting, I asked him if he'd put you on the weekend. He said—"

"I already know," Patra said. "Don't trip. I figured it out when he took this new girl up to his office. I kept asking him about headlining and he kept telling me he was going to make a decision later. Always later. So I'm going to handle it."

"I'm sorry, Patra," Keisha said.

"I'm not," she responded. "I may go downtown and see if one of those clubs want a black girl. If not, then I may get out of this shit altogether. I may do some movies."

Keisha walked into the kitchen and poured herself a cup of coffee. "Are you sure about that? Do you really want to do movies?"

"Do you know what I did before I got into stripping?" Patra asked. Keisha walked back into the living room and sat down.

"No, what?"

"I was a preschool teacher," Patra said, smiling. "I took some classes at El Camino and got my teacher certification, and I was happy keeping those little brats in line. But I'm naturally sexual, Keisha, and I like having as much sex as I can. And that doesn't work when you're working with kids. They put you in jail for that. So this is the industry that I chose. I hate the bullshit around it, but I enjoy dancing, the attention, and the sex. I've just got to make it work for me."

"As long as you're happy, that's all that matters," Keisha said. "Enough of that shit. Let's get dressed. I'm ready for grub."

Keisha and Patra got ready and then drove to Dulan's, which was packed, as usual. Patra got her omelet and Keisha ate her meatloaf and stuffing.

"The one thing I'm not going to miss about working at the Chi Chi Room is watching my weight," Keisha said, taking a bite of stuffing. "Even though Sean said that he liked his women thick, I never felt that I could eat what I wanted."

"You ain't getting heavy no matter what you eat," Patra said. "You don't have that type of metabolism. Now me, on the other hand . . ."

Patra started laughing as she finished her omelet.

"I'm going to miss you, Keisha," she said unexpectedly. "I hadn't thought that I would miss having a roommate, but I think I'll miss having you around, even though you were asleep most of the time."

"I'll miss you too," Keisha said.

"Here's"—Patra held up her glass of orange juice—"to us. Friends for life."

"I'll drink to that," Keisha said, toasting Patra.

Breakfast with Patra had been fun. She'd gained a friend, even though she was going in a different direction. When they'd gotten back from Dulan's, Patra had left to get her hair done, leaving Keisha to box up the rest of her stuff. She'd planned to pack things up and then see her father again, but a phone call interrupted her plans.

"Did you miss me?" Donovan asked, speaking on the phone.

"Yes," Keisha cooed. When she heard his voice, goose bumps actually came up on her arm. "Did you miss me is the real question."

"You know I did," he said. "Are you done at the club?"

"Yes."

"That's good. That's really good," he said. "Why don't you come on over?"

"I don't know," Keisha said, continuing to put her things into boxes. "I've got to get this stuff done. I'm moving into the dorms early tomorrow morning, and then I have class all day. Plus, I've got a Spanish test that's going to be a killer. So I can't mess around today."

"Ah, so you're just going to do me and then leave me?" he said mischievously. "I feel so used."

"Yeah, I bet you do," Keisha said. "Nah, I've got to pass. But why don't you come to my dorm room later this week? I've got a single, so I don't have to worry about any roommate."

"Think they'll let a roughneck like myself on campus?"

"They don't have a—"

Keisha's phone beeped. "Hold on," she told Donovan.

"Hello," the voice said on the other line. "May I speak to Keisha Montez?"

"Speaking."

"Ms. Montez, this is Cedars-Sinai, and I have news about your father."

"Yes?"

"I regret to inform you that your father has died."

Keisha grew numb. She didn't feel like crying, but she felt like she'd been cheated. Cheated from knowing her father.

"Is there a way to see my father before he is taken away?"

"Yes, if you come down now, you can see him."

"Thank you very much."

Keisha hung up, forgetting that Donovan was on the other line. He called back.

"Hey, was that some other Negro on the line?" he said kiddingly.

"No, I'm sorry. The hospital just called and said that my father just died."

"Damn, I'm sorry, Keisha," Donovan said. "I didn't even know that he was back in town."

"I found out when I ran into Andre."

"What are you going to do? Do you want me to come over?"

Keisha started looking for her bag. "I'm going to go to Cedars-Sinai to see him for the last time."

"I'll meet you there," Donovan said.

"You don't have to do that."

"Forget that," Donovan said. "You don't need to go through this by yourself."

"Thank you, Donovan."

Keisha got into her car and drove as fast as she could to the hospital. She parked her car and ran to the hospital elevator. She got to the fifth floor and walked to the nurse.

"I'm looking for Felice Montez."

"He's still in the room, but they are about to move him. Are you a relative?"

"Yes," she said, walking to the room.

The nurses were dressing Felice and were almost ready to take him to the morgue.

"Hello," one of the nurses said. "Are you his daughter?"

"Yes," she said.

"He wanted you to have this," the nurse said, handing her his briefcase.

"Thank you very much," Keisha said.

The nurses started moving her father out of the room, and out of the corner of Keisha's eye, she saw the elevator open. Cascading out were her mother and Andre.

"Wait a second," Veronica said angrily. "He had some papers that I need."

The nurse kept moving Felice into the elevator, leaving the three Montezes in the hallway.

"You couldn't even take a second and look at him?" Keisha said to Veronica. "All you care about is some fucking papers?"

"He left me," Veronica said disdainfully. "So fuck him."

"Momma," Andre interjected, "not now."

She didn't listen to him. She started walking to

his room and when she found it empty, she looked for a nurse.

"Where is all of his stuff? Where are his things?"

"The only thing he had was a briefcase, which he wanted us to give to his daughter," the nurse said, annoyed that she had to deal with a belligerent woman. Veronica turned to Keisha.

"So that briefcase is his? Give it to me."

At that moment, Donovan walked off the elevator.

"He gave it to me, so it's mine," she said. "We're not even having this discussion."

"Momma, let Keisha have the briefcase. We need to go," Andre said.

"Shut up, Andre," Veronica said. "Look, Keisha, I'm not going to play with you. Give me the damn briefcase right now."

"No."

Donovan tried to get in the middle of this impending disaster. The nurses started staring, and one got on the phone to call security.

"Why don't you guys talk later about all of this?" he asked helpfully.

"No, this is going to end right now," Keisha said. "I don't know what's in this briefcase. And honestly, I don't care. But you've tried to take everything you could from us—our self-esteem, our dignity—and you ultimately took away our daddy. But you're not taking this."

Veronica took a step toward Keisha, but Keisha didn't flinch.

"Take another step and that will be the last step you ever take," Keisha said. "And I mean it."

Andre took Veronica by the arm, and Donovan took Keisha by the arm. The elevator opened and a security guard walked out.

The nurses pointed, but Keisha and Donovan were already on their way to the elevator.

"There's nothing to see," she said. "We're going."

The elevator doors closed, and Donovan looked at Keisha. "Are you okay?" he asked.

"No, but that's not unusual," she said sadly. "Funny, but it's not because my father has just died. Yeah, I'm sad about that, but for some reason, I don't think my brain has even contemplated that he's back in my life, much less having died. It's almost like someone else's father has died, and not my own. It's going to hit me later, but not now. But really, what disturbs me is that my mother is just so greedy and selfish. I can't stand her."

"What the hell is in that briefcase?" he asked curiously. "And why did your mother want it so bad?"

"Who knows," she answered as the elevator opened on the first floor. "I think she just wanted it because she wants everything she can get her hands on. But there may not be anything but bubble gum in this case. I just know that she ain't getting it."

They walked outside to the parking lot.

"I'm over there." Donovan pointed. "You want me to come over and help you pack?"

"No, I've got it," said Keisha, holding the briefcase. "I can handle it. Thanks for coming through, though. I appreciate it."

"Not a problem. You sure you'll be cool?"

"I'm fine."

Donovan reached over and gave her a tender kiss. "See you later this week?"

"Of course. You've got to christen my dorm room." Keisha laughed.

"It'll be a pleasure."

Chapter 29

Calamities are of two kinds: misfortune to ourselves, and good fortune to others.
                                        —Ambrose Bierce

"Everybody over here," Steven yelled, with his hands in his pockets. It could get cold in Los Angeles during September. Not midwestern cold, but cold enough to bundle up.

"Wait a second," Marty said, picking up a bundle of posters. "I need to put these in the car."

It was three o'clock Monday morning, and there were about ten people at the warehouse. They knew what they had to do, but Steven wanted to give them just one more bit of instruction. He wasn't going to dirty his hands by actually going to UCLA, but he needed his surrogates to get the maximum impact.

Marty walked over to the group. Everyone was ready.

"You've got about two hours to post the flyers everywhere," Steven said. "I don't want anyone getting arrested, do you hear me? Not one of you mutha-fuckas better get caught. But if you do, you don't know me. Everybody understand?"

"Yes!" they all shouted.

"Okay, then get the fuck out of here," Steven said, retreating into the office.

"You heard the man," Marty said. "Let's go."

The group all got into their cars and began to drive toward UCLA. The campus wasn't too far away, but what was going to be tricky was getting on campus without the campus police seeing them. For that, they'd come up with a plan. Five groups of two would spread out at different places on campus and then drive off once they put up every poster.

"*Inside Keisha!* is going to be the biggest thing to hit this campus since they won a national championship," Marty said, smiling.

Ray was in another car, with Steven having given him private instructions to make sure Marty didn't fuck it up.

The five cars all stopped and parked, and everyone began picking up posters, tape, and staple guns. They had over five hundred posters.

"I want these posters on every pole on campus," Marty whispered to everyone. "If you can't find a pole, then tape them down on the sidewalk so that everyone can see them as they walk. And then put them on the buildings. We have about an hour to do this before the light comes up, so don't fuck around."

The five groups began spreading out and taping *Inside Keisha!* posters to everything they could find. Marty was taping them to windows, poles, and even on the vending machines.

Every so often, they would see the lights of a campus policeman, but surprisingly, they never ran into an officer who was walking a beat. After about forty-five minutes, all the posters were up. It looked like the campus had been spammed.

As they made their way back to their cars, everyone was excited, including Marty. Steven had given him a job, and he'd pulled it off.

"Great job, everyone," he said. "Here's your money."

He paid everyone fifty dollars, and the group began walking to their individual cars. Marty and Ray got into Marty's car and started back toward *Pimp*.

"Do you feel a little bit for Keisha?" Ray asked, looking at the sunrise over the horizon. It was pretty, and he couldn't help feeling a sense of regret over changing Keisha's life forever. "I mean, we didn't have to do this. Steven could just have gotten another girl and moved on. But he wanted to teach her a lesson. I just feel a little bit sleazy about this."

Marty looked at Ray with his mouth wide open. "College boy is feeling a bit sleazy?" he said, laughing. "Maybe you didn't notice, but we're in the sleaze business. We make money off of sleaze. Didn't you tell me way back that you do what you have to do? Or was it that you go where you have to go? That's just what you did, cat. You went where you had to go."

Ray didn't look at Marty because he knew he was dead right. As they pulled into *Pimp,* Marty nearly ran to the door, wanting to tell Steven that he'd done good. Steven was in his office, lying on his couch, watching television.

"So how did it go?" he asked, lifting his head to look at Marty and Ray.

"Without a hitch," Marty answered. "No one even knew we were on campus. We didn't see a single cop, and we got the campus plastered in less than an hour. She'll be the number-one topic on the minds of students in about an hour."

"Great," Steven said, laying his head back down on the couch. "Step two is to call Keisha in about an hour. I want to hear what she has to say."

"I can't wait." Marty giggled. "That will teach that bitch to fuck with us."

When Keisha got home from the hospital, she kept packing her boxes until she was done. It was as though keeping busy would take her mind off her father passing, and it did. She'd put the briefcase on the floor, right next to the envelope her father had given her earlier, but she couldn't bring herself to open either one.

Patra had come in after getting her hair done, but Keisha could barely remember the conversation. She had so many mixed emotions that she was having trouble dealing with them. She had been about to move into the dorm and get her education, but then her father had died. She was done with the Chi Chi Room, but she still had a porno circulating that she hoped no one would ever see. Her friend Patra had been so kind, but she was now facing an abortion and being out of work. And then there was Donovan. What did she want to do with him?

As she wrapped her hair for the night, she decided to focus on what was right in front of her face and nothing else.

Tomorrow things will be different, she thought.

It was six in the morning when her cell phone rang. She instinctively reached for it, thinking that it was Donovan.

"Hello?" she said.

"Keisha!" Steven yelled cheerfully. "How are you doing, baby?"

"What the fuck are you doing, Steven?" Keisha asked. She almost hung up, but something told her not to.

"I was just calling to let you know that I've been

working overtime to make you into a star. I know
that you wanted to leave us behind, but I don't think
that's going to be possible."

"What do you mean?"

"What do I mean?" he asked, laughing. "Hmm.
Well, I mean that when you get to UCLA today,
there are going to be some things that you just may
be interested in. If they do interest you, give me a
call. I look forward to hearing from ya! Ciao, baby."

Keisha hung up the phone and thought to herself,
*What the fuck is Steven doing and why is he still
fucking with me?* She didn't want to fuck for *Pimp*
anymore, so what? *Get another girl,* she thought.

That muthafucka is dangerous, she thought, *lying
awake in her bed.* She picked up her phone again.

"Donovan."

"Yes," he said. "Keisha?"

"Yeah," she said. "Do you have to go to work
today?"

"Yeah, I was about to leave. What's up?"

"I just got a call this morning from Steven Cox,
the guy who runs *Pimp*."

"You did? Why? How do you know this guy?"

"He ran the video I did and he's pissed that I told
him I wasn't going to appear in any more videos."

"So what did he say?" Donovan asked.

"He was vague. He said that when I got to UCLA,
there were going to be some things that interest me.
I don't know what he's talking about, but I'm a little
scared."

"This is what I'll do," Donovan said, picking up
his keys. "I've got to get to the construction site at
seven, but I'll tell the foreman that I might have to
leave early. I have a perfect record, so it shouldn't be
any problem. If you get to school and there's something wrong, you call me."

"Thanks, I appreciate it," she said.

"Get some rest and don't worry about it," he told her.

"I will."

Keisha hung up the phone and still couldn't sleep. Patra wouldn't be up until noon, so she couldn't talk to her. And the dorms didn't open until eight, so all she could do was watch television and try to get back to sleep. She watched it with one eye, trying to let the talking heads on the news lull her to sleep. But when they went to the local segment of the news, she found herself wide awake.

"So we go to UCLA," the anchor said, "where Jean Van Zandt is covering a strange occurrence on campus. Jean?"

"Yes, Bob," Jean said. Jean was standing in the main quad, where hundreds of students were just beginning to walk on campus. "The big story is a poster that has been plastered all over campus. It's an X-rated poster about an X-rated movie called *Inside Keisha!* According to this poster, Keisha is a student at UCLA."

Keisha sat ramrod straight. *This can't be happening,* she thought. But it was.

"We've tried to identify if this is a hoax, or if there really is a UCLA student named Keisha in this movie, but we haven't been able to get a response from school officials. Right now, the campus police are going around trying to take down all of these posters, and, Bob, there are thousands."

"Jean, have the students seen these posters, and what are their reactions?" Bob asked.

"Let me ask one of them right now," Jean said, collaring a student with a poster. "Hello, my name is Jean Van Zandt with KFOX. What's your name?"

"Roland," the student said. He was a thin kid with a shock of blond hair.

"Roland, what do you think about these posters?" Jean asked, putting the microphone right in his face.

"Well, I didn't think I'd see something like this on campus, but I think it's cool," he said.

"You think it's cool that someone on your campus is apparently starring in an X-rated movie?"

"Yeah," he said. "I mean, who knows if this is real or not, but if we did have a student in a porno, it wouldn't bother me at all."

"Thank you very much, Roland."

"Bob, that's the word from UCLA. We'll keep an eye out for the reaction from campus officials. Live from UCLA, I'm Jean Van Zandt."

Keisha stood up and began pacing back and forth. *Jesus,* she thought. *Jesus. So this is what that muthafucka had in store for me.* The more Keisha thought about the humiliation, the more she felt like she really wanted to hurt someone, badly. She hopped into the shower and then got dressed as fast as she could.

It was no time to deal with moving—she could do that later. She needed to get to UCLA as fast as she could. She didn't know what she was going to do when she got there, but she knew that she had to deal with this. The genie was out of the bottle in the one place she didn't want it to be.

"Patra, I'll come back by to get my shit," she said, sticking her head into her room. Patra mumbled something sleepily, but Keisha didn't wait to hear it. She was on her way to school.

Chapter 30

It is better to be bold than too circumspect, because fortune is of a sex which likes not a tardy wooer and repulses all who are not ardent.

—Machiavelli

Donovan arrived at the construction site at his usual time and began to work. Joe, his foreman on the job, was in the bungalow they were building, so he didn't have a chance to ask him about getting off early. So he got to work, worrying about Keisha and what was supposed to be happening at school. What was this Steven guy up to?

"Donovan, come here!" the foreman yelled. Donovan ran over to the bungalow.

"Sit down, Donovan," Joe said. He had a serious look on his face. Donovan didn't have a clue what was coming next. The television buzzed in the background.

"Before I start, I just want to say that you've been doing great work here," he said, looking away from Donovan—never a good sign. "And you've done something I never thought would happen when we brought you on board. You've never missed a day and you've always given a great effort."

Donovan was listening to his foreman, but suddenly he was focusing more and more on the television, and what it was saying.

". . . The big story is a poster that has been plastered all over campus. It's an X-rated poster about an X-rated movie called *Inside Keisha!* According to this poster, Keisha is a student at UCLA . . ." the television said.

Donovan was stunned. He failed to hear what his boss was telling him.

"Donovan, are you with me?" Joe said. Donovan snapped back to the present.

"I'm sorry, what did you say?" Donovan asked.

"I said that you are now a member of the union," the foreman said with a smile. "Congratulations!"

"You're shitting me," Donovan said. "I'm in the union?"

"Congrats," the foreman said, extending his rough hand. Donovan took it and shook it vigorously.

"Damn, damn," Donovan said over and over. "I'll never let you down."

"Oh, I know you won't," Joe said. "Now get your ass back to work."

"Joe, can I ask for one favor?" Donovan asked uncomfortably.

"Sure, what?"

"I came here today on time because I didn't want to mess up. But I need to help my girlfriend with something very, very important. Could I leave now and make it up later this week?"

"I don't know about that," Joe said, looking at his worksheet. "You would leave us short today."

"Joe, I swear that I'll never leave early again in my life, but I really need to go."

Joe looked intently at Donovan.

"Get out of here," Joe said, smiling. He opened

the door. "This is your one and only day off, but I guess since you're in the union, we can let it slide."

"Thanks, Joe," Donovan said, running out of the bungalow. "I'll be back at seven tomorrow."

Donovan got into his car and headed to UCLA. He didn't know where he could find Keisha, because she wasn't answering her cell phone. But he knew there'd be a crowd of television cameras, and if he found those, then he'd eventually find Keisha.

As Keisha drove to a UCLA parking lot, she felt as though every eye was on her, when in reality, it seemed like no eyes were on her. But it was different when she got on campus. She could see all of the news stations camped out in the main quad, and she figured that they'd do their damnedest to stop every black woman they saw in order to ferret out whether this *Inside Keisha!* star was real or imaginary.

So Keisha decided to take the back route to Murphy Hall. She needed to get some advice—and fast—about what to do. And the person to give that advice was Belinda. As she scurried through Murphy Hall, no one looked at her face.

"May I speak to Belinda, please?" Keisha asked. She was out of breath trying to hurry to Belinda's office without running.

"She has a student, so you'll have to wait," the receptionist said. Keisha wasn't waiting. She breezed past the receptionist.

"Hey, you can't go in there!" the receptionist screamed. Keisha didn't stop. She got to Belinda's door and opened it. Belinda was talking to a student, and they both looked up at Keisha as though she were an alien.

"Keisha, I'm with a student," Belinda said, slightly annoyed. "You're going to have to wait."

"I can't wait," she answered. "I need to talk to you now."

"I've got to go anyway," the student said. "I'll talk to you later, Belinda." The student got up and left, and Keisha closed the door and sat down.

"So how can I help you?" Belinda asked.

Keisha looked at her queerly. "Have you seen what is going on outside? They're all looking for me!"

Belinda leaned back in her chair and looked at Keisha. "Yes, I know what's going on, but so what? The school is not going to release any information about you, so they'll cover the story for a little bit, but after something more interesting comes up, they'll be gone. So relax and stay low, and things will work out."

Keisha leaned forward and started pounding her fist on the desk. "You don't understand these people. The people who did this are not going to stop. They are going to release my name and then try to embarrass me."

Belinda stood up and walked over to Keisha. "Keisha, what is a smart girl like yourself doing in a porno movie?"

"I needed some quick money," she said. "I thought I could do this one thing, get away with no one knowing who I was, and then come to school and start over. But when I told this guy that I wasn't going to do another movie, he did this. He's not used to getting told no. Now this is going to jeopardize my scholarship, and going to this school."

Belinda sat back in her chair and looked out at the campus. She could just about see the boom mikes and the reporters talking in front of their cameras.

She had to think of a good strategy to get this young woman out of her bind. There was only one solution she could think of, but it was probably the hardest one.

"Keisha," she began, "you have to understand your problem before you can come to the best solution. You have a unique problem, at least as unique as I've seen over the years. But I think there is a solution."

"What is it?"

"The only thing this porno guy has over you is the fact that he can embarrass you. And he can continue to exploit you by making you hide. Do you want to hide from this all of your life, or do you want to look it in the eye and deal with it?"

Keisha sat silent for a second. She stood up and looked out the window. "I'm going to face it."

Belinda stood up and put her arm around Keisha. "Well, if you're going to face it, then you're going to face it with support from me and Mary."

"What about my scholarship?" Keisha asked. "Doesn't it say something about high morals, or something like that?"

"Yes, it says that," Belinda said. "But there's nothing in there that says people can't make mistakes and keep their morals. Don't worry about the scholarship. It took me a hell of a lot to get it for you and I'm not going to allow someone to take it away from you. I've got your back."

"Thanks," Keisha said. "Call Mary and let her know what I'm about to do, please."

Belinda got on the phone and dialed Mary. "Hey, Mary, this is Belinda. Keisha is about to address the situation. Can you meet us in my office? Good, we'll see you in fifteen minutes."

Belinda hung up the phone. "Done."

"Thanks," Keisha said.

"Ready to do this?" Belinda asked.

"When Mary gets here."

Mary left her office as soon as she got the call from Belinda. She'd seen the posters on her way to campus and she'd seen the cameras. This was definitely a first for her. And as she walked across campus to meet Belinda and Keisha, she tried to figure out a plan. But in less than five minutes, she was in Belinda's office, facing Keisha. She really didn't know what to say. "I never knew that it would come to this, but we can get you through it."

"Thanks," Keisha said. "I said that I wanted to be a women's studies major. Well, we'll be talking about this moment for the rest of our lives."

"That," Belinda said with a wry laugh, "is an understatement. But we're going to make this story a one-day story. No one will even remember this tomorrow. Are you girls ready to go?"

"Yep," Keisha said. "Excuse my French, but in the words of South Central, let's go fuck these muthafuckas up."

"Well, okay," Mary said, smiling.

"Have you seen this shit?" Steven yelled to everyone in the office. "We are getting coverage hand over fist. KFOX has us on the air. I saw the posters on KABC. And I bet that we get coverage on the *Today* show tomorrow!"

Steven was so excited, and he got even more amped when he took a long sip of his coffee. The caffeine put him into another dimension. He was literally bouncing off the walls.

"What adult video company has wall-to-wall coverage? *Pimp* does. That's who. This was fucking brilliant. I'm almost at the point of saying 'fuck Keisha,' this shit can just sell more DVDs."

Ray watched this from the corner, looking at Steven exalt in his grand strategy, and noticed how much his movements reminded him of what he watched on the History Channel. Steven moved just like Hitler. He was full of power, and he thought he was untouchable. It was fascinating to watch, but Ray also knew that it was dangerous. Here was a man who loved crushing people, and if he could crush Keisha, he could easily crush both him and Marty. It was just a matter of time.

"Steven, we've got five girls ready to go and we're set to do more of the *Inside* series in the next month. We got the publicity we wanted for *Pimp* videos. Why don't we let it go? This shit can come back to backfire on you."

"Let it go?" Steven said in a low voice. "Let it go? No, Ray, when someone decides to fuck me, then I'm going to fuck them even harder. And I'm going to fuck Keisha so hard, her unborn kids are going to feel it."

"But damn, why her? What did she do besides not want to do any more videos? And you're a fucking ex-lawyer, not some fucking hit man."

"I put one hundred thousand into her video," Steven said. "We've got more hoes coming to do shit, but Keisha had that 'it' that we needed to really fly. Fuck it, we've already gone over the one hundred thousand video mark, and there's no sign that it's slowing down. She was going to be my Jenna

Jameson, and then she fucking quit. Now she's going to pay."

"How the fuck does she get out of this?" Ray asked. "Do you want her to do another vid? If she does, will you let her off the hook?"

"She doesn't," he said, laughing. "She's going to be trapped by what she did, and I'm going to squeeze her."

"So there's nothing she can do," Ray said.

"When she grovels, then I'll stop," Steven said as he left the office. "Until then, I'm on my way to UCLA. And if you still want to have a job after all of this, then you'd better get off your ass and come with me."

Like ants out of an anthill, Steven, Marty, Ray, and Rosario poured out of the *Pimp* headquarters.

"Rosario, I want you to watch my back if anyone tries to harm me," Steven said, pulling out of the parking lot. "You never know when one of those feminazis will come out of some bushes and try to attack me. It'll be cool to have one of their own sisters fucking them up."

"Why don't you just have Rosario attack someone?" Ray said sarcastically. "I mean, wouldn't that make better copy?"

As Steven cruised to a stop sign, he turned around and looked at Ray. "Why are you suddenly concerned with Keisha? Still trying to get in her pants?"

"I never wanted to get into her pants, and I really don't give a shit about her," Ray said. "But I know that sometimes enough is enough. And I think you are about to go over the line."

"I am the line, Ray, and don't you forget it," Steven said, driving away. "In my business, there's always some kid with fifty thousand of his daddy's money who wants to make a porno because he thinks it would be cool. Usually it's some white-boy college dropout and he'll make more money than I would in ten years. So if I wasn't born a shark, then you are seeing me turn into one. Gotta do it if I want to survive. And you'll do it if you want to survive with me. Am I making myself clear?"

"Clear as day," Ray said softly.

Chapter 31

Courage is not the absence of fear, but rather the judgment that something else is more important than fear.
—Ambrose Redmoon

Like the Three Musketeers, Belinda, Mary, and Keisha walked out of Murphy Hall. It was like they had something to conquer about five hundred yards away, and to do it, each step needed to give them the courage to face their task. Not one of them knew what they were going to say, but they knew that between the three of them, they could figure it out.

As they walked into the quad, they noticed that all of the reporters were lying around, wondering where this mysterious "Keisha" was. So when Keisha finally got to the middle of the quad, no one took notice. No one noticed until they started comparing the face on the *Inside Keisha!* poster to the young black woman in the quad. All of a sudden, everyone began rushing toward Keisha.

Keisha didn't flinch. She walked over to the library steps and walked to the fifth step, just so that she could look down on the photographers, cameras, and reporters. She was going to be in control, and not them.

"Hello everyone, my name is Belinda—"

Belinda was trying to speak, but suddenly Keisha tapped her on the shoulder. She didn't want anyone speaking for her.

"My name is Keisha Montez, and I am the woman on the *Inside Keisha!* poster," she said. The cameras flashed and the reporters began moving toward her. "There really is no story. I'm a freshman here at UCLA and I did this as a way to make money for school. Now it has come back to haunt me. But I'm here to tell you today that it will not haunt me for life."

"You're damn right it's going to haunt you for life," Steven yelled from the back. Steven, Marty, Ray, and Rosario were standing to the side. His voice resounded.

"Who is that?" a reporter asked.

"That is the slime who is trying to embarrass me with these posters," Keisha said calmly. "Turn the cameras on him, please. Let your viewers see who is trying to make me hide."

Steven suddenly looked nervous. It took him a second to gain his composure. "I'm not trying to do anything of the sort. My name is Steven Cox and I'm the president of *Pimp* magazine and *Pimp* Video. We are the leading black-adult company in the country, and all I'm doing is getting the word out."

The reporters suddenly turned from Keisha and moved to Steven. Ray found himself on the outside of the crowd, staring at Keisha.

"*Inside Keisha!* is our first release, and it has been blowing out of the stores. This poster"—Steven held up a poster—"is just our way of letting people know who we are and what we have to offer. We're proud of Keisha and we wanted to let everyone know that she was a part of our *Pimp* family."

"Bullshit," Keisha yelled, walking down the steps toward Steven. The cameras followed her. "Steven is just mad that I made the decision to not do this anymore, and now he wants to embarrass me. That's not going to happen."

"Mr. Cox, did you do this to embarrass Keisha?" a reporter asked. "If not, why would you plaster the campus with these posters?"

"I did it because we are trying to get another demographic for our videos. Today," he said with a smirk, "we were able to accomplish that. And for that, I thank you."

When Belinda heard Steven talk about having put the flyers out, she took out her cell phone and started dialing. Keisha, on the other hand, was simply angry.

"Keisha, do you think that now that you've been identified as a porn actress UCLA will accept you for who you are?" a reporter asked.

"They have no choice," she said. "But I'm not worried. I'd rather be known as a porn actress who got out than a pornographer that stays in."

From the corner of her eye, Belinda could see three campus police drive up and begin walking toward them. She got off the steps and ran toward them, pointing toward Steven and the group. They walked up to Steven, Ray, Marty, and Rosario.

"Excuse me," a police officer said. "Are you responsible for these posters?"

"Yes," Steven said hesitantly.

"Then I'm going to need you to come with us," the officer said, pointing and instructing his colleagues to take them.

"I'm a lawyer, and if you're not arresting me, then I don't have to come with you," Steven said, protesting. The camera suddenly forgot about Keisha and focused on Steven's predicament. The officers weren't listening to Steven and began taking him toward their car.

And as suddenly as it all began, it ended. Keisha had expected to have two hours of questions, but it seemed like all of the networks were telling their reporters that the story had run its course and to come back in. They all reached into their pockets and gave Keisha their cards, and told her that they might want to interview her again. But Keisha didn't believe them.

A small crowd of students had gathered as Keisha and Steven had bantered back and forth, and as the camera crew began dispersing, they began making their way to her.

"Hey, I support you," one said.

"Don't worry about it," one other student said. "Just put it behind you and no one will ever remember it."

Mary came up to Keisha and gave her a hug.

"When a woman looks her fears in the face and confronts them, no one can stop her," she said proudly. "You did something that you regretted, but you didn't let him run over you. That makes me proud of you."

"Thanks," Keisha said, looking at both Belinda and Mary. "But I'm not done. Steven is like a roach and he's going to come back with something else."

"Not if I have something to say about it," said a voice from behind. It was Donovan, and he'd watched everything. He walked over and kissed her.

"This is my boyfriend, Donovan," Keisha said, introducing him to Belinda and Mary.

"Nice to meet you," he said to them. He looked back at Keisha. "I can tell you that you won't have any other trouble with Steven."

Keisha took Donovan to the side. "Donovan, I've got this. Don't go doing anything that you may regret later. Not for this."

Donovan smiled. "Don't worry. I'm much smarter than I used to be, and I'm not going to do anything that I think will get me in trouble. But Steven has got to learn a lesson, and if he doesn't, then he'll always be around here. That's not going to happen."

Donovan kissed her and began walking away. "Don't worry about a thing," he said, trotting off the steps.

"That," she murmured to herself, "is what makes me worried."

"You want to come back to my office?" Belinda asked.

"No, I've got a test to study for," she said. "And I'm going to do well."

"Are we being arrested?" Steven yelled at the officer. "If we're not being arrested, then I want you to let us go."

"Calm down," the officer said. The policemen had taken Steven, Ray, Marty, and Rosario to the UCLA police station, and they had been trying to calm them down. "You're not being arrested."

"Then let us go," Steven said.

"No, not yet. I first need to get some information from you," the officer said, picking up a form. "You are the president of *Pimp* magazine and video?"

"Yes."

"Then we are going to fine you for trespassing on

the UCLA campus," the officer said. "You can't place posters on the campus without permission."

Steven took out his checkbook. "It's a fine that I'll gladly pay. I got my money's worth today."

The officer looked annoyed as he looked at a chart. "According to this chart, we charge you per poster we find."

"How much is it?" Steven asked, picking up a pen.

"One hundred dollars per poster," the officer said, smiling. "And from what my officers are telling me, you're going to have quite a fine."

"Shit," Steven muttered under his breath. He was mentally calculating his fine, and it was big. If the officer got every last one, this fine was going to be close to fifty thousand.

"No need to pay right now," the officer said. "We'll send you a bill."

Steven put his checkbook back into his pocket and took the citation from the officer.

"Let's go," he told Ray, Marty, and Rosario. As they walked out of the police station, they began making their way to Steven's car.

"So did you get what you wanted out of this?" Ray asked.

"You're damn right I did," Steven said, opening the car door. "And I've got even more shit ready."

Everyone got into the car except for Ray. "Count me out," he said.

Steven was already sitting in the driver's seat. "Get in the car, Ray," he said.

Ray closed the door and started walking away. Steven got out of his seat and stood outside the car, watching Ray leave.

"Get back in this goddamn car, Ray!" Steven yelled.

Ray turned around and gave Steven the finger. "Fuck you, Steven," he said, backing up. "Even I have some fucking limits." He turned around and kept walking. Steven got back into the car.

"Does anybody else want to get out and leave?" he said, looking at Marty and Rosario.

"Nope," Marty said. "That nigga was speaking for himself."

"Good, because we've got more shit to do," he said, peeling out of the parking lot.

As Ray walked off the campus, he thought about the dreams he'd once had about going to college. Yes, he'd had a cup of coffee at Cal State Northridge, but too much weed, too many women, and not enough studying had meant that he was out on his ass and in need of a job. So when Steven had gotten canned at his law firm and decided to open up *Pimp* magazine, it seemed like a good way to get paid, get laid, and stay high.

But something had happened to him. Watching Steven try to destroy Keisha for no good reason suddenly struck a chord in him that he hadn't even known he had. All of a sudden, he cared about Keisha as a person.

As Ray sat down at the bus stop, waiting for a bus to take him to his apartment, a brother sat down next to him.

"What?" Ray asked.

"Weren't you with the owner of *Pimp* just a few minutes ago?" he asked.

"Yeah, so what?"

"This is what," he said. The brother pulled out a knife. "My name is Donovan, and I'm a friend of Keisha, the girl you tried to smear back there. If I

hear or see one of you muthafuckas even think about
Keisha, I'm going to stick this muthafucka in your
ass. Do you understand?"

"Yeah, I got ya," Ray said. "But look, man—"

"Ain't no 'look, man,' " Donovan said. "I don't
want to hear a goddamn explanation. Just leave her
the fuck alone. Got it?"

"Got it."

"And tell your boss that I'm coming to get him,"
Donovan said with his face right next to Ray's. Ray
could see that Donovan had a scar on the right side
of his face, and to Ray, it looked like a knife wound.
"You make sure to tell him that. You hear me?"

And just as quickly as he'd come, Donovan left.
Now Ray was conflicted. Who was this guy? And
should he contact Steven to let him know about him?

This is that muthafucka's bed, he thought as he
got on the bus. Let him get out of it. Plus, Rosario
can handle this.

Chapter 32

Opportunities fly by while we sit regretting the chances we have lost, and the happiness that comes to us we heed not, because of the happiness that is gone.

—Jerome K. Jerome

Keisha got to Patra's apartment and sat down. Surprisingly, the Spanish test had gone swimmingly, and the rest of the day was on the up compared to how it had started. Just like Belinda and Mary had said, this was going to be a one-day story and nothing more. So she was bracing herself for the evening news.

When she turned on the television, the early evening news shows were just beginning.

"Early this morning, there was a commotion at UCLA as the campus was plastered with these posters," an announcer said, holding up an *Inside Keisha!* poster. The station blurred the image. "The posters are for an adult video called *Inside Keisha!* and the Keisha in this movie is UCLA freshman Keisha Montez. She stood on the steps of the UCLA library and addressed the cameras."

"My name is Keisha Montez, and I am the woman

on the *Inside Keisha!* poster," Keisha said on the television. As Keisha watched herself, she was proud at how calm she looked. "There really is no story. I'm a freshman here at UCLA and I did this as a way to make money for school. Now it has come back to haunt me. But I'm here to tell you today that it will not haunt me for life."

Patra walked into the apartment as Keisha continued to talk on the television. She put down her purse and started watching the television.

"Girl, I heard about what happened on campus," Patra said. "Fuck! Why was that fool trying to fuck you like that?"

"For revenge," Keisha replied. Patra sat at the end of the couch. Patra watched on the television as the police took Steven away. "He wanted to make an example of me."

"Steven Cox, owner of *Pimp* Video, was taken away by UCLA campus police and later cited for violating the UCLA ordinance on posting flyers and posters. From the UCLA campus, this is Kathy Head reporting for KFOX television."

Keisha turned off the television.

"So this fool plastered the campus with posters?" Patra said. "That was fucked-up."

"You know, at first I was tripping," Keisha said. "But then I started thinking about it. Paris Hilton is fucking on tape and no one even trips. So why should a little black girl from L.A. trip off these fools. So I stopped tripping on that nigga and went out there and confronted the cameras. Fuck him and fuck *Pimp*."

"Look at you," Patra said, laughing. "Superbitch!"

"I'm finally going to get my shit out of here tomorrow," Keisha said, looking at the boxes piled up.

"Don't worry about it," Patra said, laughing. "Your ass will finally leave when people stop fucking with you."

Keisha walked into the kitchen and began making herself a sandwich. "So what did you do today? Do you have to work tonight?"

Patra walked into her room, but Keisha could still hear her talk. "I don't have to work tonight. Sean is letting me have the day off."

She came back into the living room dressed in some shorts. She was getting comfortable for the night.

"And today," she said, lying on the couch, "I went to Planned Parenthood to get things fixed."

Keisha stopped making her sandwich and came back into the living room. Patra was staring at the ceiling.

"You okay?"

"Yeah, I'm okay," Patra said. "I just keep telling myself that I'll never find myself in this position again. I just can't do it anymore."

"I'm sorry," Keisha said.

"Have you ever had an abortion?" she asked Keisha.

"No."

"Make sure you don't unless you really have to," she said.

There was a knock on the door, and Keisha got up to answer it. She looked through the peephole to see who it was, but she couldn't make him out.

"Who is it?" she asked.

"It's Ray," he said. "Let me in."

Keisha turned to Patra. "Were you expecting Ray?"

"No," Patra said.

"What do you want, Ray?"

"Let me in because I need to talk to you," he said.

Keisha frowned and reluctantly opened the door. Ray stood there looking more unsure than Keisha had ever seen him.

"What the fuck do you want?" Keisha asked. "You tried to fuck me at my school and now you have the fucking nerve to come to my house?"

"Keisha, I'm sorry about all that," he said. "Let me come in. I've got something to tell you."

Keisha stepped aside and let him come in.

"Hey, Patra," he said.

"What up," she said, not looking at him.

Keisha closed the door and then took a seat. Ray stood in the middle of the living room, actually shifting his feet in the same way Sean did.

"I first want to apologize for the shit that went down today. It was fucked-up. I knew it was fucked-up. And I should have said something before agreeing to participate in that shit. But you know Steven— when he gets something in his head, his ass becomes fucking stubborn."

"You came over here to tell me that shit?" Keisha said angrily. "That 'oops, I shouldn't have tried to fuck up your life'?"

"It's some poor shit, but that's all I got."

"Ray," Patra said, looking at Ray for the first time since he walked in, "you've been full of shit ever since I met you. So before you start talking, why should Keisha believe a damn thing you've got to say?"

"Maybe you will, or maybe you won't. All I know is that I'm here and I didn't have to come," he told Patra. He turned to Keisha. "After all that shit went down, I told Steven that I wanted out. I couldn't be a part of shit anymore."

Keisha walked over, picked up her sandwich, and took a bite. "I'm happy for you."

"But that ain't it," he said. "I'm out of it now. I'm done. That shit was getting old anyway. But the reason I'm here is that one of your friends paid me a visit when I was leaving UCLA. Do you know a Donovan?"

Keisha perked up. "What about Donovan?"

"He pulled a knife on me and said that I was not to fuck with you again," Ray said.

"That's not true," Keisha said. "Donovan wouldn't do that now. He's changed."

"I don't know the muthafucka, so I have no idea if he's changed or not," Ray said. "All I know is that a couple hours ago, I was staring at a knife, and your friend Donovan was holding it. You need to call your boy, because he made a threat against Steven."

Keisha got up from her chair and picked up her cell phone. "What a fucking day," she muttered. "What a muthafuckin' day. This is not good. This is not good at all."

She dialed Donovan's number, but there was no answer.

"Donovan, this is Keisha. Give me a call as soon as you get this message, and don't do anything stupid. I already know that you threatened Steven. Again, don't do anything stupid."

"What did he say exactly that he was going to do?" she asked Ray.

"I don't know. He just said something about going after my boss."

"Did you tell Steven?"

"Nah."

"Why the fuck not?" Keisha asked angrily. "You don't know Donovan. He's turned his life around, but he is definitely not a person to be fucked with. He can be dangerous if he wants, and it seems like he wants to be now."

"I told you. I'm out of the game now. That's his problem. Plus, why the fuck do you care anyway? Just a few hours ago, he tried to fuck you up with that poster shit."

"Yeah, but I don't want the muthafucka killed," Keisha said. She grabbed her bag.

"Where are you going?" Patra asked. She got up off the couch and put on her shoes.

"I'm going to head over to *Pimp*. If he said that he was going to take care of his boss, then he's probably going to confront Steven. I need to get over there to stop him."

"Then I'll go with you," Patra said.

"Me too," Ray said.

"Throw me your phone," Patra instructed Keisha. "I think we're going to need some backup if things go down and neither one of you can do the job." She started dialing the phone.

"Hey, Blackie, it's Patra. I need you to do me a favor. Meet me down at the *Pimp* headquarters. I'll tell you what this is about when I get there. Don't go in when you get there. I want to talk to you outside. All right, I'll see you there in about thirty minutes."

Patra hung up and they all started to leave.

"You know that Rosario fucked up Blackie awhile back," Ray said. "It wasn't pretty."

"I didn't ask for Blackie for Rosario," she said. "I'm hoping that he can stop Keisha's boyfriend."

Donovan left Ray where he was because he knew he was just a soldier in Steven's organization. To end all this, Donovan needed to go directly to Steven. He didn't know where his organization was located, but he did know one person who probably did know.

"Sean," Donovan said, calling on his phone. "What up, nigga? This is Donovan."

"Hey, what's up, nigga?" Sean said. "Where your ass been?"

"Ah, man, I've got a job at a fucking construction crew. Things have been things."

"What the fuck are you doing on a construction crew?" Sean laughed. "Your ass is working nine to five building houses and shit?"

"Something like that," Donovan said. "Hey, man, got a question for you. Where is *Pimp* magazine located?"

"Uh, *Pimp* magazine is located down on Manchester. Why?" Sean asked.

"I want to talk to the cat who runs it."

"Steven Cox?"

"Yeah, that cat."

"Why, you got some hoes you want to get into the magazine?"

"Nah, nothing like that shit," Donovan said. "But I've got some business to talk to him about. What's his exact address?"

"I don't even know. I just know that it's right down the street from Briarwood. I think it's across the street, and it has his logo on the door. You shouldn't be able to miss it."

"Cool," Donovan said. "All right, man, stay up."

"We got to get together, man," Sean said. "Get with me."

"Later."

Donovan hung up the phone and started driving toward Manchester. When he got there, he didn't know what he was going to do. He just knew that he had to do something about Steven trying to exploit Keisha.

I wanted to leave this shit behind, he thought as he sat in his car. *But then muthafuckas keep bringing me back in.*

Donovan got out of the car and walked to the door of the *Pimp* headquarters. There was a security system in place, and Donovan had to buzz in to get through. He pressed the intercom buzzer and waited for a response.

"Yes," the voice said. "Who are you here for?"

"I'm here for Steven," Donovan said. "Sean at the Chi Chi Room sent me. He thought that I might be able to help him."

"Hold on."

Marty turned from the intercom and walked into Steven's office. Steven was watching the television coverage of the whole Keisha affair.

"I looked good during this shit," Steven told Marty. "You can't buy this type of publicity."

"Well, you did that fine," Marty said. "Hey, there's a guy at the door who says Sean sent him."

"What's his name?" Steven asked, not turning from the television.

"I don't know."

"Let him in and bring him up here," Steven said. "If he knows Sean, then he should be cool."

"Right."

Marty left Steven's office and went back to the intercom.

"I'll buzz you in," he said through the intercom. "When you get in, go up to the second floor and I'll meet you there."

Donovan pulled the door when he heard the buzz. He was in.

Chapter 33

To carry a grudge is like being stung to death by one bee.

—William H. Walton

Keisha, Patra, and Ray arrived at *Pimp* magazine before Blackie got there. They got out of the car, and Keisha got a bit panicky when she saw Donovan's car, but not him in it.

"Fuck," she said, as they walked across the street toward the *Pimp* building. "He must already be in."

They got to the door, and Ray was about to pull out his passkey when Blackie showed up. Blackie didn't know what was going on, but he knew that when people called, it usually meant trouble.

"So what's up, y'all?" Blackie asked. He was dressed in all black, looking even more intimidating than usual. "What's up, Keisha?"

"I don't have time to explain, but I need you to have our back if something goes down," Keisha said.

"You got it. This is Steven's place, right?"

"Yeah."

"Cool. I've got a score to settle."

"You guys want to go in or do you want to fuck around out here?" Ray asked.

"Let's go in," Keisha said.

Ray passed his card over the infrared pad, and the door opened. They all walked through cautiously. The first floor was deserted, but they could hear a commotion upstairs.

"They must be up there," Ray said. He started sprinting up the stairs, with everyone else following him close behind.

They quickly passed the general office, which was empty, and they heard voices coming from Steven's office.

Donovan stopped, crossed himself and muttered to himself, "Jesus forgive me. I'll only do this one last time."

Donovan stormed into Steven's office.

"Muthafucka, I told you that you're going to pay for fucking with my girlfriend," Donovan said, holding his knife to Steven's throat. "And now you're going to learn what it feels like to get hurt."

"Donovan!" Keisha yelled. Donovan was ready to cut Steven, and standing helplessly were Marty and Rosario. Both of them looked like they'd been worked over good.

"Do you know this muthafucka?" Steven asked. "He's fucking crazy!"

"Damn, Rosario," Blackie said, "he fucked you up!"

Rosario said nothing and looked like she was floating in and out of consciousness.

"This fool came in here and started wilding," Marty said excitedly. "He said that he wanted to teach us a lesson and then pulled out a knife."

Keisha slowly walked toward them. "Steven, I

told you to not fuck with me, but you wouldn't listen. You don't fucking know who I know. Donovan is the fucking sane one of my group of friends, and I've seen him cut a man from head to toe. So you better listen to what he has to say."

"I spent five years in juvie for assault with a deadly weapon. The kid decided that he wanted to steal from me, and I had to make an example of him."

"Ask him how much the kid stole," Keisha instructed Steven.

"How much did he steal from you?" Steven asked, trying to stay away from the knife.

"A dollar," Donovan said. "He stole a dollar out of my backpack."

Steven's eyes grew wide. "You spent five years in jail over one dollar?"

"Do you think anybody fucked with me in there?" Donovan asked.

"That's some gangsta shit right there," Ray said. "I warned you that you went too far, Steven, but you didn't listen to me. Now you got a crazy muthafucka on your ass."

Donovan turned to Keisha. "Enough talk. Do you want me to cut him, Keisha? Just say the word and I'll make this muthafucka bleed from now until Tuesday."

Keisha stopped for a second and looked deep into Steven's eyes. "That depends."

"Depends on what?" Steven asked, panic set deep in those eyes. "What the fuck does it depend on?" His voice rose to the point of being a shriek. He was laid bare now, and it was an unusal position for him.

"These are my demands," Keisha said. "I want

you to recall every DVD of *Inside Keisha!* that's in the stores and destroy them. Understand?"

"You must be shitting me," Steven said. "Destroy *Inside Keisha!* Hell, no."

Donovan raised his knife and nicked Steven's ear.

"What the fuck are you doing?" Steven said, holding his ear. A little trickle of blood began running down his fingers, and soon his hand was completely red. "Jesus Christ!"

"Surprised by how much blood there is?" Donovan said. "There are about thirty points on the body that make just as much blood, and I know where twenty-eight of them are. You want me to search for the two others?"

Steven looked at Donovan, then back at Keisha, and then back at Donovan. "All right, I'll get the DVDs back. Then what?"

"Ooh, I like this situation," Keisha said, walking almost next to Steven. "You once told me that there are people who get fucked and there are people who do the fucking. I think I believe that now, Steven. So here's what I'll do. I'll tell Donovan here not to cut you into pieces, and you'll never bring my name across your lips ever. If someone asks you if I ever did a film, you tell them you've never heard my name. You'd better sweat every time someone says a name beginning with the letter *K*. Got it?"

Steven smirked, but he didn't have a choice. "Yeah, I got it."

Donovan slowly lowered his knife and flicked it so that the blade was withdrawn. He put it in his pocket and then patted Steven on his head. "You made a good decision," he said. "You really must be a smart businessman, because if you don't do what she said, I'll be back. And you won't have Keisha's kind heart to save you next time. I'll just do the business. Understand?"

"Yeah, I understand."

Keisha turned back to Patra and Ray. "Guys, I think our work here is done." She then turned back toward Steven.

"Doesn't feel good to get fucked, does it, Steven?" Keisha asked. Everyone began walking out. Steven grabbed a towel and put it to his ear. He walked to the edge of the doorway, watching them leave.

"So that's it, Ray?" he shouted. "You're on their side? Then don't ever show your fucking face to me again."

Ray never turned around, and he walked out of *Pimp* with everyone else.

"Turns out that you didn't need me at all," Blackie said, smiling.

"That's what insurance is all about," Patra said. "You have it around just in case."

"Donovan," Blackie said, "you are one crazy muthafucka. I'll stay on your good side."

"You came through for my girl," he said, "so you're cool by me."

They gave each other a handshake and Blackie rolled to his car. "Thanks, Blackie!" Keisha shouted after him.

Keisha turned to Donovan and began pounding him on his chest.

"Do you know what trouble you could have gotten in?" she cried. "You were about to throw everything away."

"I said I'd changed, but sometimes you have to go for your inner Negro and get medieval on a muthafucka."

She kissed him. "Thanks, but don't do that shit again. Let's get out of here."

Everyone piled into their cars and headed for Patra's apartment. Patra started making drinks and they all started getting a little buzz on.

"So what are you gonna do, Ray?" Keisha asked. "Steven looked pretty damn pissed."

"Yeah, I know," he said. "You actually inspired me. I think I might try to go back to school. I can get a job anywhere and then get my degree."

"Cool," Patra said. "That sounds like a plan."

Donovan poured another drink and looked at Keisha. "Through all of this, I forgot to tell you that I'm now in the union."

"What does that mean?" Patra asked.

"Health benefits and a damn big raise in pay is what it means," Donovan said, laughing.

"Congratulations!" Keisha said. "You deserve it. You never were late for work, and hell, that should get you in the union at the least."

"So, Keisha, how does it feel to get a fresh start?" Patra asked.

"It feels good," she said. "Damn good."

Keisha had finally moved into her dorm room and found herself missing Patra. It seemed like she was much older than the other students in the dorms, as though she'd lived life and they were naive to the re-alities of life.

Her father had requested that he be cremated, and since her mother hadn't taken care of anything—she was still mad about not getting access to his belong-ings—Keisha had taken care of all the arrange-ments. It had been a pretty antiseptic deal, with just a series of papers to sign, and then she was done.

But now it was time to finally open her father's briefcase and the envelope he'd given her. She sat with them in front of her, worried about what she'd find. But she knew she had to open them. First she opened the envelope. What she saw blew her away.

What the hell? she thought as she started pulling things out of the envelope. She turned the envelope over and a seemingly endless supply of one hundred–dollar bills began spilling out, one after the other.

There has to be over ten thousand dollars here, she thought as she stacked the bills into a neat pile. As the final bill fell out of the envelope, there was a note.

> *My dear Keisha,*
> *Please take this money as a way to give yourself the life you've always wanted. Always know that I never stopped thinking about you and never stopped loving you. And although I may not have much, I can at least give you all I have. Remember always that your daddy loved you.*
> *Papi*

Keisha hadn't cried at any time since she'd seen her dad, but now the tears silently flowed down her face. Suddenly she felt a sense of loss, a sense that she'd been cheated out of a love that hadn't been fulfilled.

Now it was time to open the briefcase. She lifted the two latches and opened the case. Inside were various papers that detailed his property and bank accounts. She also found a will.

I've got to sit down with Andre and go over this, she thought.

As she was about to close the case, she noticed something she hadn't seen before. It was a reminder of a happier time. It was a picture of her mother, her father, her brother, and her as a baby smiling at the Santa Monica pier.

Keisha turned over the picture and read the inscription. "Life only has so many good moments. This is one of them."

Keisha took the picture and put it on her nightstand.

I'm going to make sure that I have many good moments, Daddy, she said to herself.

Enjoy the following excerpt from

FRIENDS WITH BENEFITS
by Lawrence Ross

Available now wherever books are sold!

Chapter 1

At first it had been cool, but now it was beginning to piss Jason off. Not because of what it was, but because of what it represented. Every Friday night, no matter how late he got home from the law office, he knew a warm dish of beef Stroganoff was waiting for him. It didn't come from his mother or from a girlfriend. It was a weekly bowl of sympathy made by Mrs. Olga Petroff, an older Russian woman who lived in his apartment building.

"Every man should have a woman cook for him at least one meal a week," Mrs. Petroff had exclaimed two years ago. "That is an old Russian proverb. What woman cooks for you, Jason?" Even after thirty years in this country, her English was still lightly accented with Russian.

This was not a discussion Jason had anticipated having with Mrs. Petroff. In fact, he'd only talked to her that day because he'd run out of milk and he didn't feel like going to the store. He knew she was always home, so he'd knocked on her door in order to save time. But there he was, standing in front of an old woman trying to explain that he was going through a dry spell on the dating scene.

"I don't have a girlfriend right now, in fact I haven't had one for a while, but I'm hoping that changes soon. I'm just sort of, well, waiting for the right woman. So I guess I don't have that woman in my life that cooks for me," he answered.

"Oh, yes you do! Me!" she exclaimed eagerly.

She grabbed Jason by the arm, pulled him into her apartment, and suddenly he was sitting in an impeccably outfitted kitchen. Shiny brass pots hung from the ceiling, fine china was displayed in the cabinets and a fresh cherry pie was cooling on the counter. This was the kitchen of someone who took cooking seriously. Mrs. Petroff bent down and pulled out a green-and-white cookbook that looked like it had been passed directly from Russian czars to her. It had little slips of paper stuffed throughout, as though she'd created addendums to the original recipe. She had.

"In this country, I don't understand. Men and women work, work, work, and don't take care of each other. When you find a woman who will cook for you, you should keep her," she commented, flipping through the cookbook. "Until then, I will cook for you. What is your favorite meal?"

"Well, I like—"

"Do you like beef?"

"Yes, and I like—"

"Until you get a girlfriend, I will make you beef Stroganoff every Friday," she said, pointing to a page in her book. "Beef Stroganoff is the dish of Russian kings, and it will keep you strong. Plus, it will bring you good luck."

"Okay," Jason said, who wanted to back out of her apartment as soon as possible. "Thank you very much, Mrs. Petroff."

"You're going to find a good woman and she's going to make a great man of you," she said as they slowly walked to her front door.

Then, as she opened her door to let him go, Mrs. Petroff suddenly turned around, her face full of concern.

"You're not a homosexual, are you, Jason?" she asked.

"No, ma'am," Jason stuttered, startled that this old woman was now asking if he liked men. Did he project that? he wondered. "I'm just on sort of a dry streak when it comes to women."

"A dry streak?" she said, not really understanding.

"I just haven't had a lot of luck with women lately."

"Oh, don't worry, you'll find one!" she said, pinching his cheeks a little too hard. "But I did want to make sure you weren't a homosexual. I don't have anything against homosexuals, but the Stroganoff wouldn't help you there. It will only bring you luck if you are looking for a woman."

And with that, she started preparing Jason's first batch of beef Stroganoff.

So it came as no surprise when Mrs. Petroff greeted him on this particular Friday with the same question she'd asked for the past two years.

"Have you found that woman yet?"

Jason literally had his key in the door, and Mrs. Petroff had come bursting out of her apartment with the energy of a forty-year-old and not the sixty-year-old she truly was.

"No, Mrs. Petroff, no woman again."

"Don't worry, she'll come. And when she comes,

you'll know it because she'll be the right one." She then handed him his weekly dish of beef Stroganoff.

"Thank you, ma'am."

And there it was. A Jason Richards Friday night punctuated by a steaming dish of beef Stroganoff, handed to him by an elderly woman obsessed with his love life. There had to be a better way.

"What's up, y'all? You have now reached Jason Richards's residence. Please leave a message and I'll holla back at ya when I get the time."

Jason pressed the pound sign on his phone to re-trieve his messages.

"You have no new messages," the computer voice said.

Jason heard those words, and it reminded him about how lonely his life truly had suddenly become.

Not even bill collectors are calling my house, he thought. Is this all worth it? Is the end result worth what I'm giving up?

He wearily sat down in his leather chair and turned on his television. Jason had never gotten used to the silence of being alone, and the television created enough white noise to help cut it. It may be only white noise, but it is noise all the same.

And so he sat there, thinking. He was Jason Richards, a twenty-eight-year-old rising star at the Ketchings & Martin law firm, and targeted for suc-cess from the minute he walked into the office two years ago. Peter Ketchings had even taken him into his office during his first week at the firm to tell him so.

"Jason, we're really happy to have you on board," Peter Ketchings had said. Peter Ketchings was a quiet intimidator. He'd made his money as a trial lawyer against corporations, and continued to make his money by attacking everything from lead paint to restaurants serving too-hot coffee. He didn't lose often, and didn't hire losing lawyers. "Over the past five years, we've been trying to diversify our firm with excellent lawyers from every background, and I think that if you work hard, you can go far here. We're always looking for stars at this firm, and you have the potential to be one. But you have to work hard and be willing to give up a lot to win. I only want winners here at my firm."

"Sir, I thank you for the compliment," Jason said, confident in his skills. He looked Ketchings directly in the eye. "I want you to know from the start that no one outworks me. I can guarantee that. Before you get into the office, I'll be here. And after you leave the office, I'll still be here."

"I wish we could transplant your attitude into some of the lawyers we have," Ketchings said, smiling. He handed Jason a manila folder. "I'm putting you on the Burger World lawsuit. Steven Cox was on it, but I'm taking him off of it. He'll brief you. Good luck, Jason."

Jason had walked out of Ketchings's office determined to prove himself. Jason had graduated at the top of his class in law school, so he knew he was good. But he also had a sneaking suspicion that the firm needed a black lawyer to "color up" the firm, and he'd fit the bill perfectly. If they were manipulating him, that was fine with Jason. But then he was going to manipulate them by advancing as far as he could, as fast as he could. He wanted to be a partner in the firm, and nothing was going to stop him.

"This case is a hellhole," Steven Cox told Jason as

he transferred a box of files to him. "I think they give cases like this to new lawyers just to test them. They take a lot of time and there's little reward at the end."

"How long did you work on the case?" Jason asked, opening some of the folders.

"Six fucking months. And that was six fucking months too damn long."

Steven Cox was the other black lawyer at the firm, although he was so light skinned, Jason doubted that many of the white lawyers even knew he was black. He dressed impeccably, with tailored suits that looked ripped from the pages of *Esquire* magazine. He'd arrived at the firm about a year before Jason, and had represented Ketchings & Martin when Berkeley had invited law firms to recruit their students. Everything about him had impressed Jason, from his dress and the way he carried himself, and his example was a deciding factor in choosing Ketchings & Martin over everyone else. But when Jason got to the firm, it was clear that Steven was struggling to make a mark, and the Burger World case was one of the reasons. Steven looked at the Burger World lawsuit as an albatross around his career, and was happy to get rid of it.

"This shit was cutting into pussy time, if you know what I mean," Steven said, smiling.

"Yeah," Jason said, still shuffling through the papers.

Steven leaned back in his chair and studied Jason.

"You really believe that shit Ketchings and the others talk about, don't you?"

"What do you mean?"

"About being a star at this firm, and shit like that? You actually believe that shit, don't you?"

Jason stopped shuffling through the papers and looked up.

"Yeah, I believe in it. I believe that if I knock out something like this Burger World case, then I can move up. I'm not satisfied with being an associate. I got into law because I want to be a partner. And I don't care what I have to sacrifice to get it."

Steven smirked at Jason as though he'd seen and heard this all before.

"Ah, you're one of those ambitious Negroes I keep hearing about!" Steven laughed. "You're going to work your ass off for eighty hours a week, week after week, month after month, year after year, in order to prove to these white folks that they didn't make a mistake when they hired a black lawyer. I can see it in your eyes."

"I don't know what you're all about Steven, but I know what I want out of being a lawyer," Jason said, annoyed. "I didn't come here to fuck around, but to do the best I can. So I guess I am one of those ambitious Negroes you heard about. So as long as you don't fuck with what I'm trying to do, then we won't have any problems. We understand each other?"

Steven ran his fingers through his hair. He took the final pile of papers and dropped them on Jason's desk.

"Whatever you say, brother," he said sarcastically. "If you turn this bullshit into something, I'll be the first to kiss your ass. Don't hold your breath."

Jason turned away.

"Hey look, cat," Steven said, grinning. "If you want to be Johnnie Cochran up in here, I ain't gonna stop you. I just want to get my check and roll, myself. But the fact is that there are only two brothers in this bitch, you and me, so we should have each other's back. You cool?"

As Jason looked up from his desk, Steven offered his hand. He didn't dislike Steven, but he didn't trust him either. But he was the only other brother at the firm.

"Cool," he said, shaking Steven's hand. "Now tell me about this Burger World lawsuit."

"Do you really want to know?" he asked.

"Yep."

Steven popped open a Red Bull and took a sip.

"Okay, here it is," Steven started. "An Australian guy brings his family to California for a little vacation. It's winter in Australia during our summer, and he figures they could get a little sun and see the sights. You know, take the kids to Disneyland and the whole nine."

"Right."

"So everything's going well. The kids are happy because they've gone to Disneyland and got some Mickey Mouse ears, while the wife's happy because she's walked down Rodeo Drive and shopped in the same place Nicole Kidman shopped. And of course the dad is happy because the kids and the wife are out of his hair."

"Okay, so what's the problem?"

Steven smiles.

"The dad is kicking it poolside, checking out women not his wife, when he gets a text message on his Blackberry. It's from his best friend Ainsley, who's back in Melbourne. He tells our Aussie friend that no matter what he does, he's got to stop at Burger World and get a Burger World big all-beef burger with extra beef. He says that he's never tasted anything like it and it has to be experienced to be appreciated."

"I love those damn things," Jason said. "Had one last night."

"Well, you might not love them after I finish telling you the story," Steven laughed. "The idea sounds good, plus he loves hamburgers, so he takes his family to get one. He goes to the one right next to Graumann's Chinese Theater in Hollywood so he can kill two birds with one stone."

"The kids and the wife could check out Clark Gable's footprints at Graumann, and he could get some grub."

"Exactly," Steven said, taking another sip of his Red Bull. "Right after he finds out that he has the same shoe size as Gary Cooper, he takes the family across the street to Burger World and orders a Burger World big all-beef burger with extra beef. And damned if it doesn't taste good to him. He eats half of it, and then takes the rest to the hotel to finish later. But that's when the problems begin. He's sitting in his hotel room when his head begins swelling to the size of Shaquille O'Neal's."

"Damn," Jason said, enthralled.

"Yeah, and that's what the wife said. I suppose if she had her druthers, she would have picked something else to swell as large as Shaq's beside her husband's head, but I digress."

"So what happens? Did the dude die?"

"Nah, he didn't die. But they take him to the emergency room where the doctor asks the wife whether her husband is allergic to anything. They go over the usual things, medicines, penicillin, all that shit. She's saying no to everything the doctor asks until she remembers that her husband was allergic to one thing."

"And that was?"

"Hold for it," Steven said, giggling. "Kangaroo meat. Isn't that funny? An Australian allergic to kangaroo meat! She remembered that when they were first married, they'd gone on a trip to the Australian outback and stayed at a hotel where kangaroo meat was served. The husband, trying to impress his new wife, ordered it and damn near had the same reaction. But where had the man eaten kangaroo meat in California?"

"At Burger World?"

"Bingo, my ambitious Negro lawyer," Steven said. "It turns out that the Burger World big all-beef burger with extra beef ain't made of beef. So after the swelling goes down, the Aussie comes to us and we file a lawsuit on his behalf."

"How come Burger World didn't just make it go away?" Jason asked, reading a paper from the files. "It says here that we started negotiations for a settlement, but things broke off."

"Yep, I almost got them to settle. But Country Bob Briggs owns Burger World, and he's a stubborn bastard. His lawyers told him they could make the lawsuit go away, but he feels that Burger World hasn't done anything wrong. So we're at loggerheads. And that's why you have the case. Ketchings & Martin wants to win this case badly because they think this isn't a one-off thing. They think folks have been eating kangaroo meat for years."

"So they've given it to a green lawyer looking to make a reputation?" Jason asked.

"Who better?" Steven said. "More experienced lawyers were already handling cases, so they gave it to me. And now I give it to you. Good luck, 'cause you're going to need it."

That had been two years ago. Jason now sat on his couch, exhausted from working eighty hours a week, month after month, just as Steven had predicted. That was the deal with the devil he'd made. But as a result, relationships of all kinds got kicked to the side. Friends, women, family, all came in second place behind his career ambitions as a lawyer. But he now realized that he needed some balance in his life other than torts, beef Stroganoff, and ESPN.

Jason's cell phone rang and he checked the caller ID. It was Steven.

"Jason, it's Steven. Are we still on for G. Garvin's with the girls?"

"Yeah," Jason answered.

"Good, I need my wingman for Carole."

"You're going after Carole?"

"You damn right. I know you've known her for a while, but damn, have you seen that ass? I've got to keep trying to hit it."

"Only you would interpret one hundred straight rejections by the same woman as interest," Jason said.

"That's why I'm me and you're you, baby. I never give up."

"See you in a couple of hours."

"Later."

Jason went into the bedroom and pulled out some clothes. Tonight, Jason and Steven were meeting with two friends, Marcia Cambridge and Carole Brantford at G. Garvin's, the hot new spot in Beverly Hills. But before that, Jason had a call to make.

"Hello, Vanessa, Jason calling. Hey, we met about a month ago and I was wondering if you would like to go out for drinks? I'm free next Saturday, so give me a call at 323-555-4525 and we can hook things up. All right, I'll talk to you later."

Jason met Vanessa at the Conga Room last month. The firm met there to celebrate Peter Ketchings's birthday when Jason saw her sitting at the bar, stirring her drink and looking damn sexy. A milk-chocolate sister and built just how Jason liked his women, Vanessa was about five-foot five, with a large chest and perky ass, not too big, not too small. Her purple blouse was cut low, as was her white skirt. When

Jason approached her, it wasn't without confidence. It's just that damn dry streak that kept getting in his way.

"Can I get a Jack and Coke," Jason asked the bartender. He was now standing right next to her, and she hadn't noticed him. So he pressed. "What's your name?"

Jason held out his hand for her to shake.

She looked up slowly and stared at Jason's face, as though searching for a secret message.

"Vanessa," she said. She shook his hand with only the tips of her fingers touching the tips of his fingers, as though she'd calculated that this was the absolute minimum she had to do in order to interact with him.

"Hello, Vanessa, my name is Jason. Do you come here often?"

Vanessa looked down at her drink and took a sip. The bartender smiled as though amused at what he was seeing.

"Look, Jason—that was your name, right?" she said.

"Yeah."

"I don't think you're my type. So why don't you just try talking to someone else."

Jason was stunned. He hadn't even really started trying and he was already getting rejected.

"Damn, sister, am I that hideous?"

"No, you're actually pretty good-looking, but you have some loose ends that you need to take care of before trying to talk to someone of my caliber." When Vanessa said *caliber,* she ran her hand down the length of her body. Here was a woman who knew she looked good.

"Okay, then enlighten me. Let me know what I need to do to get a woman of your caliber."

"Buy me a drink and I'll tell you," she said, looking into his eyes.

"What are you drinking?"

"Bartender," she said, leaning over the bar. When she did, her low-cut blouse became even lower cut. "Please fix me an apple martini. Put it on Jason's tab."

The bartender fixed the drink and Jason gave him his American Express Platinum.

"Now that's not a bad start," she said, pointing to his Platinum card. She took the martini, licked the edge of the glass, and then took a sip that just crossed her pursed lips.

"You have potential but you're about ten pounds overweight and while that's not fat, it tells me you don't care about your body. Do you work out?" she asked.

"No, I don't. I never thought I needed to." Jason did a mental Special K pinch check of his waist. She was right. He could stand to lose a few pounds.

"Uh-huh. Since you are already in your late twenties, it's probably flab city from here," she said. "That's if you don't start working out. You remind me of the cute skinny kid who hasn't come to terms with not being skinny anymore. You're not fat, but you aren't toned."

Jason began thinking that maybe he didn't really want to know all of this. He took a big gulp of his Jack and Coke and braced for more.

"And then there is your style of clothing."

"What's wrong with my style of clothes?" Jason said, looking at his outfit. "These are new clothes."

"Well that's it, you don't have any style. You're wearing tan chinos and a blue shirt," she said, eyeing him from head to toe. "Boring. I bet you bought those clothes at the Gap or maybe the Men's Ware-

house because they told you it was a great look for
both the office and after work."

Okay, now Jason was beginning to hate her. His
gear *was* from the Men's Warehouse and the salesman had said those exact words to him.

*Now this is a look that works well at both the office
and after work,* the Men's Warehouse salesman had
said while mentally trying to calculate his commission. He was a sixty-year-old white man who would
have sold Jason pink-and-black-checked Sansabelt
slacks from the 1970s if he knew Jason was going to
purchase something worth more than $100.

Why in the world did I follow his advice, Jason
thought at this moment.

"Your attitude and your clothes, everything points
to being an extremely plain and safe young man," she
continued, long after Jason had hoped she'd stop.
"You have no sense of adventure, or spontaneity
about you.

"I bet you've never done an impulsive thing in
your life."

She paused for a second, staring at him. She stared
at him for a good thirty seconds, bringing her face
directly in front of his, almost touching his nose.

"What?" he asked, getting nervous.

She moved her face and sat back in her chair.

"See, if you were daring and dangerous, you
would have taken me by the face, kissed me with the
most passionate kiss you've ever given a woman,
and then told me 'How's that about spontaneity?' "

She got up from the bar and gave him one last
piece of advice. "But you didn't, and so you missed
out, darling. See, you have to understand that I, and
every other woman on this planet, get safe and plain
everywhere else in my life. I don't want it in a lover
or even a boyfriend."

She finished her martini and placed it on the bar. She reached into her purse, pulled out a piece of paper and wrote down her number.

"So what is my final piece of advice to you? Go get you some money, or look like you have some money, and then get yourself some style. You're probably smart as all hell, but women don't look for smart at the start. We look at looks, which of course means that we are as superficial as you guys. Look me up when you've got your stuff together. I'll still be here."

And just like that, she smiled and left, with her number on the bar. And it was at that moment that Jason knew things had to change. Before Vanessa, he would have settled for a Friday night of beef Stroganoff and television. But not tonight, not after that reality check. No, this Friday was going to be different. He was getting dressed to go to G. Garvin's. And he was looking for a woman.

GREAT BOOKS, GREAT SAVINGS!

When You Visit Our Website:
www.kensingtonbooks.com
You Can Save Money Off The Retail Price
Of Any Book You Purchase!

- **All Your Favorite Kensington Authors**
- **New Releases & Timeless Classics**
- **Overnight Shipping Available**
- **eBooks Available For Many Titles**
- **All Major Credit Cards Accepted**

Visit Us Today To Start Saving!
www.kensingtonbooks.com

All Orders Are Subject To Availability.
Shipping and Handling Charges Apply.
Offers and Prices Subject To Change Without Notice